Alba Nuova
A New Dawn

A True-Life Novel

The Story of a 19th Century Italian Immigrant

Claude E. DaCorsi Sr.

Copyright © 2016 by Claude E. DaCorsi, Sr.

All rights reserved. No part of this publication may be reproduced, distributed, or transmitted in any form or by any means, including photocopying, recording, or other electronic or mechanical methods, without the prior written permission of the author.

Printed and bound in Charleston, South Carolina,
United States of America

First Edition

ISBN-13: 978-1534925045
ISBN-10: 153492504X

Published 2016 at Auburn Washington 98002

This story is a true life novel and largely a work of fiction. Certain names, characters, businesses, places, locations, events and incidents as featured in this book are either the products of the author's imagination or used in a fictitious manner. Any resemblance to actual persons, living or dead, or actual events is purely coincidental.

Specific references to places, locations, lineage, vocations, some specific businesses, local church pastors, local church references, historical events and excerpts, family names, family history of the direct relatives of the author and names of individuals as indicated in photos, newspaper clippings, and similar referenced material are factual.

This book is dedicated to my wife Mary

My greatest supporter, critic, and proofreader
My best friend and my companion

You kept me on task for completing this work

You are the love of my life
You are the air that I breathe

Ti Amo Grappoli
(Love You Whole Bunches)

Preface

My paternal great-grandfather, Pasquale DaCorsi immigrated to the United States in 1898 from Naples, Italy. This story details the late nineteenth century immigration as derived from The Statue of Liberty – Ellis Island Foundation®. The passenger records were made available on the Foundation website and include the ship manifest, a picture and description of the steamship, and other detail that provides a look into the immigration journey.

Many details are difficult to obtain, especially those of other relatives, such as Pasquale's sister, who had immigrated to America sometime prior to Pasquale. There are no records for the sister except a poorly handwritten first name by an immigration officer on Pasquale's manifest showing that he was joining his sister in America. Individual records such as his sister's married name and other details are not found in the Foundation records. With only a first name provided, there is no opportunity to search further.

While the immigration record detail is factual, most of the descriptions of the arrival in America and the voyage to the New World are purely fictional. This story provides my interpretation in true-life novel form of the immigration of Pasquale DaCorsi. The places are real. Vocations are true. Relative's names are factual. Other names in this book have been changed for story purposes or are fictional. Any resemblance to real persons, living or dead is purely coincidental. The family traditions, typical to the Italian culture are what I most treasure and remember and are included in my rendition of the immigrant's story. While I did not have the opportunity to meet my great-grandfather, I have visited the mausoleum at the cemetery in my hometown many times to see the vaults that contain the remains of Pasquale, his wife Raphelia, his son Arturo, and his son Eduardo and his wife Maria.

The DaCorsi family tree from before Pasquale's time has been a challenge to uncover. As a child up I did not have the opportunity of the early family history being presented to me. DaCorsi cousins and other relatives have also performed searches, all with little results from earlier than the Pasquale era. Pasquale was born February 15, 1851 in Naples. There are still relatives in Italy and the Dacorsi or DaCorsi name is still known in both Italy and in the United States. Many relatives in Italy are known only through the wonder of Facebook®. My wife Mary and I now have six generations descending from Pasquale with our grandchildren. The latest arrival, Quentin DaCorsi, was born in October 2015. He is our tenth grandchild and sixth grandson. Pasquale is our grandchildren's great-great-great grandfather.

The history of this journey is to share the rich culture and heritage of an Italian family that still to this day is proud to be called Italian-Americans.

Claude E. DaCorsi, Sr.

One

September 30, 1898 the journey begins for Pasquale DaCorsi. After years of pondering the decision to make a new life in America and after many months of preparing for the journey, finally clearing the vast amounts of required paperwork, and obtaining his passport, the day has finally arrived. Pasquale gives one last endearing kiss and a long embracing hug to his wife Raphelia. He warmly hugs and kisses his sons, ten year old Arturo, thirteen year old Eduardo, and fifteen year old Francesco. He tells Francesco that he is now the man of the family. Francesco nods in agreement. The family will depart for America in a few months.

Pasquale was SS Aller passenger ID 603014030176 and number 18 on page N14 of the List or Manifest of Alien Immigrants for the Commissioner of Immigration (The Statue of Liberty, 2010). Passengers listed on the manifest indicated ages from a few months to those in their sixties. The chance to see a relative or friend or to start that new life in America was appealing to the young and old. Many had husbands, children, cousins, and other family members who had ventured sometime earlier. Many would be separated from family members both in

Italy and those already in the United States for many months or longer. Intercontinental travel during this period of history was solely by means of ships.

For years Pasquale had dreamed about America. The tales of America told by elders and the immigrants who had returned to Italy whetted his appetite even more. Italy was a divided region with no prospects of freedom. As a child Pasquale knew of the conflicts being fought. Pasquale longed for the day when Italy would be one. The nineteenth century was a time of revolution. Between 1848 and 1866, three wars of independence took place in Italy.

Italians longing for freedom were destined to immigrate. For centuries Italians had been subjected foreign rule and continuous conflict. Since France's invasion of the territory in the late fifteenth century, the country was in constant war. Napoleon's campaign in Italy in the late 1700's to the early 1800's conquered northern Italy. The unification wars began in 1848 and lasted until 1860. Even beyond that time, through 1870, during the annexation of Rome, conflicts continued.

The Italian General and nationalist Giuseppe Garibaldi was instrumental in defeating Austria in Lombardy 1859. All of northern Italy became united at that time. First, Garibaldi attacked Sicily and then the Kingdom of Naples. His success in these conflicts was overwhelming. The mass desertions of the

Neapolitan forces secured the victory. Following these successes Garibaldi relinquished his command to the King of Sardinia uniting northern Italy and southern Italy under one ruler (Wars of Italian Unification).

Italian unification took place in 1861. The Risorgimento or Rising Again movement created the Kingdom of Italy. This event led to the freedom of Italians who had been under foreign control. The movement was an ideological and literary surge that instilled national awareness in the Italian people (Risorgimento, 2014).

Millions of Italians would immigrate to other countries between 1884 and 1914. More than three hundred thousand Italians would arrive in America in the 1880s. More than six hundred thousand followed in the 1890s. With one flag of unification as a result of Risorgimento, the catalyst to the late nineteenth century departure was established. Although Italy as a land had been unified, the people were not unified. Poverty was extensive. Violence and social disorder resulted in chaotic situations. American prosperity was known as immigrants who had returned to Italy told stories of successes in America. Those stories and the work of recruiters from the United States convinced millions to leave the homeland for that new beginning in America (Immigration -The Great Arrival).

Wiping tears from his eyes after saying goodbye to his family, Pasquale boarded the great 450 foot steamship, SS Aller

(The Statue of Liberty, 2010). Although boarding the vessel brings brief excitement for the soon-to-begin trip to America, a sense of trepidation arises within Pasquale. At the age of 47 he is leaving the homeland and his beloved family. Italy and his way of life will be left behind once he boards the SS Aller. He has doubts but he knows in his heart this is the right decision for his family.

Pasquale's tenseness remains as he steps aboard the ship surrounded by more than twelve hundred fellow passengers seeking the same new beginning. His nervousness is somewhat soothed as he knows his sister Maddalena, who voyaged to America three years earlier, is anxiously anticipating his arrival. His contemplation and excitement to reunite with his sister gives him some relief. He patiently stands in line waiting for the ship officers to give further orders. Pasquale was surprised to see that there were some officers who could speak Italian. Even with his Neapolitan dialect (from the southern part of Italy) he could understand most of what was said by the ship's crew.

The first order of business on the SS Aller is to have each passenger examined by the surgeon physician, an employee of the owners of the ship. That process begins just before seven o'clock in the morning. The commanding officer also inspects each passenger. The examinations and inspections took only a few seconds or so for each passenger or about four hours for all passengers boarding the ship. One of the duties of the commanding officer was to certify that in his belief passengers were not criminals, did not have contagious diseases, and were not by immigration definitions idiots or insane persons.

The attending physician would personally inspect and examine the physical and mental condition of each passenger. Passengers also received a series of stinging vaccinations and a smelly dose of disinfectant. The surgeon physician and the commanding officer verify the manifest data, sign an affidavit that they have inspected each passenger on the manifest list, and certify the passengers had met the criteria for boarding the ship. All documents are recorded and kept in the ship's office of the commanding officer. Upon arrival in New York, the commanding officer will turn the manifest and other related documents over to the United States immigration officers.

The journey from Naples to New York will take about 12 days. The ship remains stationary at the port for about one hour after completing passenger boarding and inspection and while preparations for departure are underway. Shortly before 11:00 a.m., the great steam horn blasts through the air signaling departure. The crowds at the dock wave frantically to their loved ones on the ship. Passengers wave back and blow kisses.

All of the great steamships were identified by the SS designation. The SS referred to the ship as a screw steamer. The single screw thirteen hundred horsepower, two funnel, two masts, and the triple expansion engine of the SS carries about five thousand gross tons of steel. These great ships used an innovative concept with the engine design that increased efficiency. The triple expansion engines would work in a manner where the steam that was generated would expand in three or four cylinders to increase the pressure of the steam. The multiple cylinders efficiency controlled temperatures that lessened the stress on the engine. The fuel economy with the high pressure steam greatly improved steamship travel (Solem, 2004).

As the behemoth begins to slowly move, some of the passengers are startled. The sounds of the screw and the creaking of the ship were unfamiliar to most passengers. Most have not traveled on a large ship. Those sounds had some convinced that the ship would break apart and sink. More experienced passengers began to spread the word that the noise and movement of the ship was normal.

Pasquale shouts out loud, "*Napoli addio*" (goodbye Naples) as the majestic steam horn announcement is once again declared by the ship captain of the SS Aller. Pasquale begins to map the route in his mind as the ship slowly moves from the Port of Naples and into the Tyrrhenian Sea. Pasquale closes his eyes to the vision in his mind of the travel through the Strait of Sicily into the Mediterranean Sea where the real voyage begins, crossing the passage between Spain and Morocco through the Strait of

Gibraltar to enter the North Atlantic Ocean. The goodbye waves and hand blown kisses from friends and family crowding the dock begin to fade. The SS Aller makes one last blast of the horn signaling the final departure.

Before obtaining his ticket for the travel, Pasquale and all other passengers were required to complete a long list of questions as part of the ship's manifest for the record and inspection process. This was a requirement to comply with the 1893 U.S. immigration law. The law stipulated certain information that was required of each passenger. The information was gathered from each passenger and hand recorded by the ship's officers on the manifest documents.

While most of the questions about name, age, sex, marital status, health condition (physical and mental), nationality, occupation, and race seemed routine, other questions about physical abnormalities and causes (being crippled or deformed) were not routine. Other questions were about names of relatives or friends in America, if the immigrant could read and write, last residence, final destination, who paid the passage, and if the immigrant had thirty dollars or less in their possession, the equivalent of approximately eight hundred fifty dollars today.

They were also asked whether they had ever been in the United States previously. Character questions included if they had been in prison or an almshouse, or if they were a polygamist.

Work-related questions asked if they were under contract (express or implied) for labor in the United States. Religious affiliation was recorded. Upon arrival in America, a document known as the Supplement to Manifest of Alien Passengers would be completed. That document detailed information regarding country of origin, province, mother tongue, and subject of what country the immigrant alien was from.

All documents contained sufficient information about the immigrant. Even with the rush to complete paperwork in as little as time possible, mistakes were made. Language barriers, poor handwriting by ship's officers and immigration officers, and perhaps missing details by the immigrant would sometimes delay the processing of immigrants leaving a country and upon entering America. Fortunately, some safeguards had been put in place under the Immigration Act of 1891and was supplemented and revised with the Immigration Act of 1893 that created Boards and Special Inquiry to examine excluded immigrants at port of entry, and provided for appeals of the Board decisions.

The Immigration Acts as far back as 1875 stipulated certain regulations for aliens. In 1875, the Act would prevent criminals and prostitutes from being admitted to the United Sates. That Act also eliminated Orientals from coming into the country without their free and voluntary consent mandating the use of "coolie" labor as a felony. That law was offset by the establishment of the

Chinese Exclusion Act of 1892. That regulation suspended Chinese immigration for a period of ten years. Any Chinese laborer who was previously allowed to be in the United States was allowed to return from a temporary absence. Chinese immigrants were not allowed to become naturalized citizens. Deportation enforcement for those illegally in the country took place (Summary of Immigration Laws, 1875-1918).

In 1882 a tax of fifty cents was levied on each passenger entering the United States. Additional restrictions by that Act excluded persons who would be classified as a public charge. The Bureau of Immigration was established by the Immigration Act of 1891. That law also restricted persons with certain contagious diseases, felons, and persons convicted of other crimes or misdemeanors. In 1893, those classified as "anarchists" or anyone who believed in or advocated for the violent or forceful overthrow of the United States Government, all government, forms of law, or the assassination of public officials were excluded (Summary of Immigration Laws, 1875-1918).

Pasquale had been told about Ellis Island. The initial group of Italian immigrants arrived at Ellis Island in 1892. The complexity of the alien arrival process was very confusing to the immigrants. Each immigrant was given a number. They were subjected to a series of inspections. Mental and physical fitness examinations took place. If an immigrant could not pass an eye exam or was determined to be physically unfit for potential employment that individual regardless of being part of an arriving family or not could be sent back to their country of origin. That fear labeled Ellis Island as the Island *L'Isola dell Lagrime*—the Island of Tears (Immigration - L'Isola dell Lagrime).

Pasquale was very concerned about the inspection process. What if he couldn't pass the eye exam? How would the immigration officers treat him? If they did not speak Italian what would they do to him as he could not speak English? Questions kept racing through Pasquale's mind. His fear and anxiety caused some restless nights. He kept his thoughts to himself. His dream could be shattered and he would be returned to Italy in disgrace. How would he explain this to Raphelia and his sons? Still, he tried to remain positive.

America meant prosperity. Pasquale would pray for strength. He decided to focus on his family during the trip so he could to keep his spirits up. He concentrated on his sister, Maddalena, because he was confident that all would turn out well when he was reunited with his sister. She had been through the inspection and was admitted to the United States. In his head, he imagined the inspection process and began to feel calmer. He pretended to be an immigration officer and asked himself similar questions from the manifest. Then he imagined he was the doctor performing the examination. He performed those roles over and over hoping that the inspection process would mimic his thoughts.

Maddalena and her husband Antonio had settled in Gloversville, New York in 1895. The United States was in the middle of an economic recession. Jobs were hard to obtain. The unemployment rate was around twenty percent. Immigrants were not a welcome sight for many American's who were struggling to survive. Maddalena and Antonio remained optimistic. They had sought their American dream and knew, despite the economic situation, that they would make it.

Antonio was a master mason, a trade he had learned in Italy from his father. Antonio's first job in America came about two months after settling in Gloversville. Antonio was hired as a construction laborer, a job he continued to apply for after being turned down many times. Within one year, and about the time the recession was winding down, Antonio found steady work in the area as a master mason. Construction began to boom in the growing community and skilled trades were in demand.

Maddalena and Antonio had been living in a two room apartment. In the summer of 1898, they had secured a very nice five-room bottom-story flat. The accommodations included a kitchen and a bathroom. There was a separate living room and dining room, and two bedrooms. Maddalena and Antonio did not have any children. The flat was perfect for the couple with room to spare. Maddalena and Antonio planned to have a large family, but a medical condition that was not well diagnosed at the time, prevented Maddalena from conceiving.

Maddalena was very excited that Pasquale would be in Gloversville soon. She had not seen her brother in three years. Pasquale and Maddalena were very close as children. Maddalena was three years older than Pasquale. Maddalena was preparing a huge welcome for Pasquale. She knew Pasquale would be ready for some good Italian food. Her voyage also was as a steerage passenger and she remembered how bad the food on the ship was.

Homemade pasta *(cavitelli)* with sauce made from Antonio's garden-grown tomatoes, and sausages, seafood, and the abundant fruit from local Italian grocers would make Pasquale feel at home right away. Maddalena had planned the grand Italian meal as a celebration of a family coming together for the new beginning in America. With Pasquale's arrival, the only missing piece would be Raphelia and the children, who would soon follow Pasquale's path to Gloversville.

Maddalena knew that the long journey would be very tiresome for Pasquale. She would let Pasquale rest for a few days before introducing him to the neighbors. Maddalena also knew that Pasquale would be eager to find work. Pasquale was a glove cutter. She knew about the many glove shops that would hire

Pasquale. She was also aware that Pasquale and his good friend Angelo, who was also coming to Gloversville with his family on the same ship as Pasquale, were inseparable and would seek work together. She would encourage and support that as well.

The Italian immigrants in Gloversville were a close knit group. Just like in Naples, family, friends, and neighbors would share meals, spend time playing cards or bocce, and always with great Italian music and entertainment. The Italians in Gloversville worked hard and were proud to be in America. They maintained their Italian traditions including the large gatherings after church on Sunday's. The heritage of the Italian culture was very much present in Gloversville.

Most Italians resided on the south and west side of the city. Many of the factories were located in the residential areas and typically workers could walk less than one mile from home to get to work. That made it easy for those who worked at the factories. They were also allowed for a period of time to maintain the Italian tradition of going home for the mid-day meal and then returning to the factory to finish the workday in the early evening hours. Most factories ultimately did away with that practice requiring the Italian workers to adjust to a straight ten-hour workday during the week along with a five-hour day on Saturday's.

Getting used to not having the large mid-day meal and break was quite an ordeal for some Italians. They did comply and did their best to work with the American culture. Even the Italians who were proprietors of glove shops adjusted to the American workday. Italian immigrants desired to hold onto the culture and heritage but also desired to fit in with American society. Most made the transition. There were others who could not adapt and decided to return to Italy.

Others came to America to earn as much money as they could with the plan to repatriate to Italy. That was true mainly for Italian farmers who desired to become landowners in Italy. The majority of laborers and those who had trade skills stayed in America. Most of the immigrants who settled in Gloversville did not return to Italy. The work was plentiful, the wages were good, and the Italian population created a community within the community. Although many missed the homeland, the closeness of their community in Gloversville provided sufficient reason to remain in America.

The Italians in Gloversville, similar to other locations in the United States, would experience some issues with discrimination. Many Italian families over the years, in all areas of the United States, would change their first names, and in other situations surnames to lessen the possibility of job discrimination and other circumstances that would lead to prejudicial treatment. Pasquale would ultimately be known as Charles DaCorsi. His son Francesco would be called Frank. Eduardo was Edward, and Arturo would be changed to Arthur. The commonality of this would be prevalent in America for Italian immigrants. Many Italian women were named Maria. The majority of them would take the name Mary. Unfortunately, some of the traditional Italian identity was lost in this process.

Two

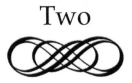

Occupations were as varied as the final destinations for the immigrants. The manifest listed an individual's calling. There were laborers, barbers, tailors, shoemakers, farmers, and a variety of other trades. Usually women were listed as housewives. Skilled tradesmen were sure they would all find work and that their talents would be welcome in the new world. Some of the trades required years of apprenticeship to qualify as a master in a specific trade.

Pasquale was a leather glove cutter by trade, a fairly elite and well respected career in Napoli. The manifest lists Pasquale's calling or occupation as a "glover." The listing also represents Pasquale's final destination as Gloversville, home to many Italian immigrants who brought the glove manufacturing industry with them to upstate New York. That industry would establish the city of Gloversville as the glove manufacturing capital of the world for many generations. Leather tanning, a sister industry of the glove trade would also become a leading industry in the community and adjoining towns.

Gloversville was originally called Stump City. The town was covered by trees which in the early 1800s had been largely cut down giving the area the peculiar name. In 1828, the village was officially named Gloversville attributing to the significance of the glove manufacturing industry in the community. Industrial leather tanning in Gloversville began in the early 1800s. By 1819 glove manufacturing had commenced. By the mid-1800s there were a number of glove manufacturing companies in Gloversville. The village of Gloversville was officially incorporated in 1853 (City of Gloversville, 2015).

Pasquale's glove cutting trade usually required three years as an apprentice before achieving the title of glove cutter. Pasquale completed his apprenticeship in a little more than two years. He began his apprenticeship at the age of seventeen. Pasquale was hired by fifty-three year old Luigi Amato. The small shop was a few blocks from Pasquale's childhood home. Pasquale would visit Luigi on a regular basis. Luigi would show Pasquale the leather hides in the shop and how the material was used to make gloves. Pasquale's interest led Luigi to an offer of apprenticeship. Pasquale willingly accepted after getting approval from his father. Pasquale's glove cutting career was briefly interrupted when he was drafted into the Italian Royal Army. He was almost twenty at the time.

The glove leather was cut by hand. Gloves were cut on a flat table. The process included using shears. The pattern templates were made of wood. All sizes and styles from short gloves to long elbow length gloves were produced. The leather was typically a doeskin or lamb. The advent of the use of hair sheep hides, mainly a breed known as Cabretta or Cape, revolutionized the industry. The soft but strong and supple leather was perfect for use as glove and garment leather.

In the two years it took for Pasquale to become a master glove cutter, his work became well known in the region. Pasquale had a natural ability to work with the hides. His hands moved quickly. The glove pattern layouts were always precise. He wasted no time and was a diligent and hard worker. Pasquale enjoyed his work and was most happy when he was cutting gloves. The work, however, made Pasquale's hands aged beyond his years.

Upon the completion of his military service, Pasquale went back to work for Luigi. He worked hard to perfect his craft and became one of the best glove cutters in the region. He soon was one of the best again and he began to teach others the glove cutting trade. As many as five apprentices were assigned to him at a time. The art of the craft was to know exactly how to properly stretch and trim the hide to obtain the maximum number of glove parts from each hide. Pasquale was an expert and always had very little hide trimmings left over. As he taught others, he shared his techniques with the goal of improving their skill levels to be similar to his.

Table cutting gloves using shears was the only method of glove cutting for many years. Becoming a master cutter was something to be very proud of. Perfecting the craft took more than completing an apprenticeship. Each cutter established their technique. Pasquale was not only one of the best table cutters; he also looked for ways to keep improving the process. Innovation was not widely accepted in the industry. Pasquale focused on hide stretching techniques on small portions of the hide that would actually smooth the skin where the leather would become softer. That special touch took a great deal of effort. Pasquale showed other cutters how to do the stretching in that manner. The result was a much higher quality glove.

Over the years a large solid cylindrical mallet was developed to stamp out the glove cuts. The patterns were made of metal. The entire leather hide would be stretched by hand and the patterns placed on the hide. The leather could not completely hold its shape in this method. The glove cutter would strike the metal jig template made in the shape of the pattern for the gloves with the mallet to cut out the leather. This block cutting technique was not appealing to the Italian table cutters. Pasquale, as a master of the table and hand cutting style, could cut the glove patterns faster and much better than the block cutters.

The art of tailoring the leather was a journey-level craft in Italy. Stretching portions of the hide and then cutting the gloves from the patterns produced a higher quality glove. The Italian glove cutters would bring that level of quality and craftsmanship back when they began working in the American glove shops. Production level of the Italian workers outpaced the block cutters. The quality of the products helped Gloversville become the leading supplier of fine leather gloves for men and women in America and a worldwide supplier.

Italians were proud of the work they performed and usually worked a minimum of five and one half days per week at their vocation. Hard working, dedicated employees, they gave great praise to the glove shops and owners they worked for. Workers would usually wear a shirt and tie with dress slacks for standard work apparel. Full aprons would be worn over their clothes in an attempt to keep their garments somewhat clean. The smell of finished leather was unmistakable and would permeate clothing. People could always tell who worked in the shops as the lingering odors of leather were ever present on the workers.

Although some working conditions were squalid, the majority of workers in the trade would do their best to make the environment more comfortable. Standing on your feet for the entire work day was the norm. Good Italian made shoes helped to ease discomfort. Breaks were infrequent but a welcome relief when they occurred. Most shops at that time were small, family-owned businesses with a few workers. Production was paramount as the demand for quality leather gloves was worldwide in the nineteenth century.

Naples was a major industrial center for glove manufacturing. The majority of the firms in Naples were small cottage-style industries. The shops employed a few workers. Women would be employed to sew the glove cutouts into the finished product. The advent of the sewing machine made that process much faster and with improved quality.

The sewing machine designed for use in glove manufacturing was an important advance for the industry. This machine made it possible for greater levels of glove production. The centuries-old process of sewing gloves by hand could take hours per pair of gloves. The machine made it possible to reduce that time to just minutes. A foot-operated level platform would propel the needle on the machine. So, in a sense, the faster one could operate the peddle platform, the greater the production rate. Much of the sewing work was performed by women. While some women worked in the cottage shops, many worked on the machines at their homes. This process allowed the women to keep pace with the work while tending to the home.

This tradition would carry over to the Italian glove workers who immigrated to Gloversville. Some shops in Gloversville were still cottage industries while others were larger more advanced businesses. The women could still work at home sewing gloves while being employed by the larger companies as well as small shops. Many would set their own time period for doing the work. It was not unusual for women to work very early morning hours or late night hours. The only deadline was to have the quota of work completed by the set day and time for the factory representative to pick up the finished products and return them to the factory for final checking and processing.

Pasquale had a true love for his craft. He would proudly display some of his work in his home. He would show his children how gloves were cut from leather. He would demonstrate the art of smoothing and stretching the hide properly. He would also show the children how to layout the patterns to get the most use of the hide. Pasquale's hands were calloused and had remnants of dark streaks from years of working with leather.

Pasquale would bring scraps of leather home with him and make leather toys for the children. He would weave some of the strips together to make braided arm bands. He would also take some larger and wider strips and make decorations for the home. He would use the leather strips to wrap the legs of chairs. He made a leather necklace for Raphelia one year for her birthday. He routinely made leather waistbands which resemble men's belts. His leather crafting skills from such small pieces of scraps was admired by all who visited his home.

Pasquale visited Luigi before his departure to America to say goodbye. Pasquale thanked Luigi for giving him a trade and occupation that would be welcome in America. Luigi was in his eighties now and wept openly when Pasquale said his farewell. Luigi was like a second father to Pasquale. There were many times when Luigi would visit the DaCorsi household to share the dinner table with the family. Luigi was also a generous man. He would bring gifts to the family and would frequently bring handmade toys for Pasquale's boys.

Some of the best times for the apprentice Pasquale was when Luigi would visit his home and tell the family what a good worker and talented tradesperson Pasquale was. Pasquale was deeply saddened when he left Luigi's home. The elderly father figure shedding tears brought Pasquale to tears as well. The two hugged tightly and they gave each other a kiss on both cheeks. Luigi in Italian tradition took his thumb and index finger on his right hand and pinched Pasquale's cheek while saying *"addio mio filigo"* (goodbye my son). Pasquale was forty-seven years old but he was still a boy to Luigi. In a sign of respect Pasquale responded saying *"grazie il mio maestro"* (thank you my teacher).

Pasquale knew he would never see Luigi again. Leaving his mentor and friend was one of the most difficult things Pasquale had ever done. Pasquale was with Luigi every day. He was concerned that Luigi would not have anyone visiting him once Raphelia and the boys left for America. Luigi's family would visit on occasion. Luigi had not been in good health and showed signs of aging. That also concerned Pasquale. Making contact with Luigi's nieces and nephews would be Pasquale's priority before leaving Italy. Pasquale cherished the memories of his relationship with Luigi. Pasquale had a picture of Luigi that he would bring with him to America. That picture would be placed in Pasquale's work station and would remain there for years as a reminder of his mentor, father figure, and his *amici per sempre* (friend forever).

Pasquale's tears continued to flow as he walked home. He would tell Raphelia about his visit with Luigi. Raphelia also had visited Luigi many times. She would bring him special Italian treats that she would make. Luigi's favorite was *biscotti alle mandorle* (almond biscotti). The cookie was baked twice to give it a crispy texture. Italians would dip the biscotti in a glass of sweet late harvest wine or in a cup of espresso. Luigi preferred the wine.

When Pasquale left for America, Raphelia brought Luigi some biscotti and wine. The two talked about America and how the DaCorsi family would have a new beginning. Luigi said he was excited for the family and told Raphelia to send some pictures of the family in America. Raphelia promised to send pictures. Raphelia also told Luigi that she would continue to visit often before she and her sons left for America. Luigi said *"portare I ragazzi con te quando si visita"* (bring the boys with you when you visit). Raphelia said she would do that.

Raphelia treasured Luigi's friendship. Like Pasquale she looked up to Luigi as a father figure. Luigi treated Raphelia's sons like they were his grandchildren. Luigi never married. The DaCorsi family was his family. Although Luigi had several nieces and nephews he felt much closer to the DaCorsi's than he did his own family. Raphelia also was saddened knowing that when she and her sons would leave for America they would not see Luigi again. She would hold onto the wonderful relationship the family had with Luigi and would always tell her sons how special Luigi was to the DaCorsi family.

Raphelia planned on writing to Pasquale before she would leave for America to tell him about her visits with Luigi. She wanted Pasquale to know that she and the boys were still seeing Luigi often and that he was doing well. Francesco would stop and see Luigi every day to see if he needed anything. Luigi really appreciated Francesco stopping by. Luigi usually told Francesco that he did not need anything. Raphelia would continue to make some biscotti and other type of Italian cookies for Luigi. Francesco would bring the cookies to Luigi a couple of times each week. It was going to be hard leaving Luigi. There would be many lasting memories that Raphelia and Pasquale would treasure from all the years with their beloved friend, Luigi.

Three

Pasquale settled into his third class quarters, a cramped six berth compartment, along with his good friend, thirty-six year old Angelo Guiliani and his wife, thirty-three year old Rosa. Their children, five-year old Giovanni and five-month old Leonardo accompanied them. Pasquale already missed his beloved wife and sons. Having Angelo and his family on the voyage provided some relief for Pasquale as their friendship is more like family than just good friends.

Every Sunday after church, Pasquale's family and Angelo's family shared a Sunday meal, a game of bocce, and, of course, some good homemade Italian wine. Sunday meals usually lasted all day. Multi-course presentations included antipasto, soup, fish or meat dish, the never-ending pasta dishes with the cooked for hours rich basil-infused tomato sauce, and loaves of homemade Italian bread.

Spending the entire day together was a true family affair. The festivities usually went late into the evening. Neighbors or other friends or relatives would visit. Most of the time the evening activities included the robust Italian card game, *La Scopa*. The term *La Scopa* means to sweep with the object being to clear the table, which is to play a trick that results in there being no cards left on the table. The men played cards while the women visited and did the routine chores. The children would entertain themselves with various games, and perhaps played with crudely made marbles, dolls, and handmade wooden blocks.

The evening activities also included more food. The remaining homemade bread, salami, prosciutto, cheese, figs, olives, grapes, and other fresh fruits, and the ever present wine would adorn the table. Italians love to cook and even more, they love to eat. With the second calling to the evening meal of the day, *"mangia bene"* (eat well), the evening festivities begin.

Life for third class or steerage passengers was less than accommodating. The SS Aller's third class section was somewhat more accommodating. The ship's third class area was designed and built for passengers. The four and six berth sleeping quarters were much improved over the typical steerage compartment. Many steamships used the steerage portion of the ship to haul goods and other commodities including livestock on one leg of a voyage and would carry passengers on the second leg of the trip. The SS Aller did haul goods but did not use the space for livestock transport which eliminated conditions that contributed to filth, disease, and foulness that humans should not have to endure.

The majority of the one thousand, two hundred forty SS Aller passengers were in third class. Only ninety passengers occupied in first class. Second class had one hundred fifty in the second with the remaining one thousand relegated to third class. Steamship companies made huge profits from steerage and third class passengers. The cost of feeding these passengers was less than one dollar per day. Many meals, especially in steerage, included a tin container with meager food supplies. Passengers would also bring small portions of food on the voyage. A thirty dollar passenger ticket resulted in thirty thousand dollars for the steamship company for boarding the steerage and third class passengers (The Immigrant Journey, 2008).

The third class accommodations were still a dark, crowded, unsanitary place with poor ventilation. Third class designs were not much better than steerage designs with the exception of the sleeping berths, a dedicated dining hall, and some daylight filtering into the area. The passengers were usually confined to quarters and did not freely move about the ship. During the voyage some third class passengers would chance the venture to the upper deck just for a breath of fresh air and a bit of open space. Most were turned back by the ship officers. Traveling in steerage, and in many situations in third class, was being imprisoned with little opportunity to move freely about during the long trip. Optimism still prevailed however for these immigrants in their confinement as America awaited their arrival.

As Naples faded from view, the smoothness of the Tyrrhenian Sea was a welcome start to the trip. As the hours progressed, the ship increased speed and moved into the Mediterranean Sea. The coarseness of these waters, although by no means overly rough seas on this first day of October, caused movement of the vessel that most passengers were not familiar with. Taking some time to settle his nerves with the rise and fall of the ship as it plowed through the sea, Pasquale was determined to ride it out and to do the best he could to enjoy the voyage.

Others had already begun to show some signs of seasickness. The sea worthy veterans helped those who felt queasy. Feeble attempts were made to cure the seasick passengers. From biting a piece of ginger root, taking doses of liquor as prescribed by the doctors on the ship, and swallowing a concoction made from the kola nut, a caffeine-based fruit, little relief was realized by those who had experienced nausea. With only two bathroom facilities in the third class section, the challenge to accommodate the ill, as well as all other passengers in the section was feeble at best. The foulness of the air was not easy to overcome. The cramped travel conditions put nerves on edge. Through all the unpleasantness, passengers would continue to encourage each other that the trials of the journey would be a fading memory upon arrival in America.

Traveling at approximately twelve knots or about fifteen miles per hour, five knots below the maximum speed of seventeen knots or approximately twenty miles per hour, the ship traversed the Strait of Gibraltar. Sixty hours into the voyage and more than one thousand nautical miles from Naples, passengers saw Morocco on the left horizon and Spain on the right. The view was a little more difficult for the third class passengers as visibility was limited.

Before entering the strait, the Rock of Gibraltar is visible. Passengers could see the icon stretching skyward and as a symbol of leaving the old world and venturing into the new world. Few third class passengers would see the sights. The ship blasted the steam horn as a salute to the Rock and as the signal that the true journey had begun. With nearly thirty-one hundred nautical miles of ocean before reaching the New York harbor, the traveling immigrants settled in and prepared for the long voyage to the North Atlantic Ocean.

The excitement was building and third class passengers who had not experienced the unpleasantness of being seasick began planning for a celebration. Passengers who brought meager portions of food aboard began to eat. The food they brought was mainly cheese and *salame* (salami). Some passengers would share their food with others during the celebration. Many others brought musical instruments and were accomplished musicians.

The combination of food and music was a welcome surprise. The celebration would wait however until most of the ill passengers began to overcome the seasickness. Helping those who had become ill was a priority.

Entertainment in third class was lively at times. Singing, dancing, energetic music from the instruments, and card playing filled the hours. Constant conversation was the order of the day with most talking about family and friends they were anxious to see, those they had left behind in Italy, and sharing stories of Italian history and traditions. They also talked about dreams and expectations once in the United States. Many had been planning this opportunity for years. The new world would bring the hope of prosperity, financial stability, and opportunities to build a better life for their children.

The fear for many, however, was being in a strange land with little or no English language skills. Their discussions were of concern if they could not be understood. How would they be treated? Could Americans speak Italian? They all decided that wherever they would reside the important thing was to keep close together as a community and to be there for each other at all times. Final destinations included New Orleans, Pittsburg, Buffalo, New York City, Montreal, Brooklyn, Hoboken, and numerous other locations throughout the United States.

Pasquale recalled a time when his oldest son, Francesco, had become very ill at the age of four. It was just a few weeks before Christmas when Francesco had complained of a very sore throat. He developed a fever, a mild rash, and soon had chills, body aches, and a swollen tongue. Pasquale and Raphelia knew that Francesco had come down with *Scarlatina* (Scarlet Fever). They knew that this sickness was contagious and carefully checked one year old Eduardo for symptoms. Eduardo seemed to be fine and displayed no signs of the sickness. Pasquale also knew that isolation and burning bed linens, toys, and Francesco's clothes had to be done to help prevent a spread of the infectious disease. Pasquale also knew that Francesco would be sent to an isolation hospital for patients with the disease.

Francesco was in the isolation hospital for more than two weeks. His symptoms started to subside. Fortunately, he showed no signs of rheumatic fever, a complication of a severe case of scarlet fever. Pasquale and Raphelia visited Francesco every day while he was confined in the hospital. Isolation however was just that. There was a glass screen that prevented family members making any contact with patients. Pasquale and Raphelia would do their best to console young Francesco from behind the glass wall. Francesco would wave and smile as his parents departed each day.

Francesco made a good recovery and was released to go home a little less than three weeks after coming down with the sickness. Pasquale and Raphelia were elated when their son was discharged from the hospital. Francesco would have some new clothes, new toys, and some candy waiting for him at home just in time for the Epiphany when the legendary Italian Witch, La Befana, would deliver the goodies to the children of Italy (Italian Christmas Traditions, 2016). Francesco was anxious knowing that La Befana would be making her annual visit that night.

The SS Aller was moving out of the Strait of Gibraltar and headed to the North Atlantic. Passing through the narrow Strait, the sights of land became distant. The North Atlantic would show no sign of land for nearly two thousand nautical miles. The vastness of the ocean would render the ship to a mere a tiny speck traveling to its destination. As the ship left the Strait the third class passengers would glimpse the Atlantic through the tiny portholes surrounding the third class compartments.

This leg of the voyage re-energized the passengers. Shouts of glee filled the third-class cabin. More music, singing, and joyous dancing took over the entire space. The famous 1880 Italian song, *Funiculì, Funiculà,* was played by the musicians and sung in unison by the passengers. The song was written about inclined railcars going to and from the famous Mount Vesuvius (Lisa Yannucci, 2016). The last verse of the song becomes louder than the other verses as the excitement for arriving in the new world recharges the immigrants.

Se n' 'è sagliuta, oì nè, se n' 'è sagliuta la capa già!

È ghiuta, pò è turnata, pò è venuta...sta sempe cà! La capa vota, vota, attuorno, attuorno, attuorno a te! Sto core canta sempe nu taluorno Sposammo, oì nè! Jammo, jammo 'ncoppa, jammo jà, funiculì, funiculà! (We've climbed it, my love; we've already climbed to the top! It's gone up, then returned, then it's back...It's always here! The summit revolves, around, around, around you! This heart always sings, my love, let's get married one day! Let's go up to the top, let's go, Funicular up, funicular down).

The sky was lit by a full moon that evening. The meal that night was a crudely-made soup served with bread. Most passengers would fill up on as much bread as they could gather or bring bread back to their berths to eat with the *salame* and cheese they had brought. The passengers filled the third-class dining hall. Long wooden tables and benches were the only furnishings in the hall. The soup was served from large kettles with the immigrants standing in line with tin bowls waiting their turn to be fed. The children were always fed first by the passengers. Some would share what they had not finished with others. Loaves of bread were passed table to table.

Bread became the staple of the meals with everyone receiving whatever portion they could eat. At least the ship owners recognized the need for bread and for them, it was a cost reducer as bread was easily made and for just a few cents per loaf. With the evening meal finished and passengers settling in for the night, the sounds of song and talk began to lessen. The peacefulness of the evening and the moonlit night brought a quiet only disturbed by the sounds of the engines and the movements of the ship.

Travel on the Atlantic could be a trying venture. The fourth day of the voyage was again filled with rough waters as a line squall or fast moving violent thunderstorm crossed the path of the ship. The passengers were awakened before dawn by loud thunder and flashes of lightning as a violent storm moved in. The experienced crew and captain of the SS Aller used all of their skills to keep the ship from being swallowed by the sea. The great steamship was able to maneuver the crashing waves of the Atlantic. The speed of the ship was purposely slowed significantly impeding the distance traveled. The reactions of the vessel kept passengers on edge. The constant swaying, bouncing, and seemingly sideways movement of the ship caused a great deal of fear for the passengers. The crew of the ship did their best to try and calm the passengers. The sounds of the waves smashing against the hull of the ship were deafening.

The passengers were in a panic as most were in an unfamiliar situation. Mothers held children tight. The men kept reassuring the group that the seas would soon calm. Howling winds and loud claps of thunder brought more fear to passengers. The light of day was replaced with vast darkness. It seemed that the ship was traveling in black clouds. Lightning filled the sky and brought eye-piercing bolts of bright light through the porthole windows. The violent movements of the ship once again made some of the passengers seasick.

The storm lasted for about nine hours before clearing. As the seas calmed and the light of day reappeared, the sun peeked through the clouds. The anxiety and nervousness of the passengers was replaced with sighs of relief and faint smiles. Some crew members began checking the ship for damages while others checked the condition of the passengers. The immigrants in third class began to pick up items that had been strewn about in the storm. The cleanup was in the fashion of the traditional Italian housekeeping. Everyone, including the children, pitched in. By early evening, order had been restored. The evening meal, soup and bread, was about to be served in the dining hall.

Pasquale and Angelo talked about the storm and wondered if there would be more to come. Angelo's five year old son had been very frightened by the storm. Pasquale picked up young Giovanni and placed the child on his knee. He told the boy that the storm was nothing to be afraid of. He reassured Giovanni that God would protect them and that no harm would come to them. Pasquale said that being frightened is a normal reaction. He told the boy that the ship was built strong and could withstand storms. Pasquale explained how the ship was constructed and how it moved through the water. Giovanni listened intently and seemed somewhat calmed by Pasquale's explanation.

Upon finishing the evening meal on that fourth day of the trip and with most filling up on bread, the immigrants were ready for some relaxation. There would be no loud, boisterous entertainment that night. The return to calmness was complemented by soft music of mandolins, violins, and accordions. These instruments also were treasured as a cultural possession. Immigrant musicians brought a piece of Italy, their instruments, with them on the voyage to America. The music from the instruments immediately made some homesick. It was a good feeling though as the music also brought a sense of serenity.

As the mandolins, violins, and accordions played, someone shouted "*Santa Lucia, Santa Lucia.*" The musicians began to play the popular Italian song and soon a group of men began singing in the style of the young, talented Neapolitan tenor, Enrico Caruso. As the men sang, most of the immigrants joined in. Santa Lucia is the story of a journey by boat and paying homage to beloved Napoli. "*Tu sei l'impero dell'armonia*" ("You are the kingdom of harmony"). The verses tell of the gentle breezes and waves and a silver star glistening off the water. The song invites passengers to come aboard the beautiful ship.

Sul mare luccica, l'astro d'argento. Placida è l'onda, prospero è

il vento. Sul mare luccica l'astro d'argento. Placida è l'onda, prospero è il vento.

Venite all'agile barchetta mia, Santa Lucia! Santa Lucia!

Venite all'agile barchetta mia, Santa Lucia! Santa Lucia.

(On the sea glitters the silver star. Gentle the waves, favorable the winds. On the sea glitters the silver star. Gentle the waves, favorable the winds. Come into my nimble little boat, Saint Lucy! Saint Lucy! Come into my nimble little boat, Saint Lucy! Saint Lucy).

As the song ends and the gaiety calmed down along with the lateness of the night, Pasquale and others were ready for some sleep. Pasquale prayed that the night would bring a calm and restful sleep. Having not slept well over the past nights, Pasquale was feeling the effects. His sleeping area was not very comfortable. The thin mattress laid on a hardwood frame was almost impossible to sleep on. There were the constant noises from the ship and from the other passengers, including crying children that kept Pasquale tossing and turning through the nights. Pasquale said a few prayers, stared at the ceiling in the berth from his bunk, and wondered what tomorrow would bring. As Pasquale laid his head on the not very comfortable pillow, he quickly fell asleep from the shear exhaustion even with the continuing noises of the night

Four

Pasquale awakened the next morning fairly rested but with a heavy heart. He was thinking about Raphelia and missed her desperately. Pasquale was twenty-eight years old and Raphelia was seventeen when they got married. Not unusual ages for marriage during the nineteenth century. During that time it was also not uncommon for marriages to be arranged by family members and many women were married by or before the age of eighteen. Italian men typically were many years older than their wives as was Pasquale being eleven years older than Raphelia.

Pasquale DaCorsi and Raphelia Santoro met at a church festival they both attended with their respective families. Raphelia was sixteen at the time. Over time Pasquale finally gathered up enough courage to approach Raphelia's mother, Giovana, to ask for Raphelia's hand in marriage. Italian tradition was to ask the mother first for the approval of marriage of her daughter. After the mother would approve, the father would be asked, and then the entire family would be involved to sanction the relationship for marriage.

With the approval of the family, Pasquale and Raphelia became engaged (*fidanzati*). An engagement period of about one year followed before Pasquale and Raphelia would marry. The engagement was also tradition and respected by the betrothed couple. Raphelia's family did all of the planning for the wedding. With the preparations for the wedding completed, the bride and groom were ready to set the date for their nuptials.

The *nozze* (wedding ceremony) was held on Sunday September 12, 1879 at the *Chiesa di San Benedetto*, a seventeenth century Roman Catholic Church. Wedding ceremonies were usually held on Sunday. Sunday was considered to be the best day for a wedding as other days were considered bad luck for wedding days. Sunday was considered a day of happiness and joy. The wedding would take place in the early afternoon.

San Benedetto Church was designed architecturally in the Italian Baroque style. The circular form of the nave, or the central part of the church containing the high altar, replaced the traditional long nave design with one main aisle and side aisles between the pews and each wall of the perimeter of the church. The numerous and beautifully decorated round windows brought rays of light into the church contrasting between shadows and brightly lit areas. The ceiling and walls were like an Italian artist's canvas filled with beautiful frescoes. The church exterior resembled a sculpture with curved walls, various column designs, marble statues placed in recessed alcoves in a framework-type setting, and an ornate dome spiraling above the gable style columned front façade.

That beautiful September afternoon was filled with bright sun, a slight breeze, and the sound of church bells ringing. The church was adorned with an array of beautiful red and white roses and yellow orchids, a symbol of joy and a new beginning. That sense of a new beginning would follow Pasquale throughout the years as he planned his *alba nuova,* the new dawn of his American journey. A large ribbon, tied in a festive bow, covered the top of the doors at the front of the church, signifying that a wedding was ready to take place.

The ceremony was attended by family and friends. Pasquale was nervous the morning of the wedding. He delivered a bouquet of flowers to Raphelia and as a special gift, white leather gloves he made for her as the final gesture of the boyfriend ready to welcome his girlfriend as his spouse. This was the day that Raphelia would become his *la mia bella sposa* (my beautiful wife). He had waited for this moment for one year. His nervousness was more of an anticipation of seeing Raphelia in her wedding dress with her face covered with a lace veil.

Raphelia was busy making sure, along with her attendants that her wedding dress and accessories were all in order. Raphelia was a detailed person who wanted everything to be perfect before walking down the aisle to meet her husband to be. Raphelia's wedding dress was made by her mother, Giovana. The silk and wool dress was ornately decorated but simple in fashion.

Wedding dresses at that time were usually black gowns. Raphelia decided that she did not want to be married in a black gown. Her dress was cream in color with fabric in a high neck fashion, a tight bodice, with hand sewn borders of white beads along the full length sleeves. The main body of the dress was filled with embroidered white roses. The dress flowed with the train cascading in pleated splendor. Wedding dresses of the time were also part of the women's wardrobe and would sometimes be worn during other special occasions.

The wedding guests took their place in the pews. Pasquale's eyes were fixed on Raphelia as she made her way toward the altar. As Raphelia's lace veil was lifted Pasquale gazed deeply into her eyes. Raphelia smiled as her eyes met his. The traditional Italian mass ceremony and rituals began. It soon became time for Pasquale and Raphelia to give their solemn assurance that their consent to be married is before God and His church. As vows are exchanged, and Raphelia has a ring placed on her finger, the priest signifies that the marriage of Pasquale and Raphelia is complete and they are now *marito e moglie* (husband and wife).

"A cosa stai pensando?" (What are you thinking about?) Angelo asked Pasquale. Pasquale replied, *"Mi manca mio Raphelia"* (I miss my Raphelia). Angelo sympathized with his friend. They began to talk about what life would be like in America. Pasquale

told Angelo that Raphelia and his sons would be coming to America when he had secured work and a home. Pasquale and Angelo knew they would have no problem getting a job as glove cutters. Their skills were among the best and they could both demonstrate how good they actually were. Maddalena had told Pasquale in a letter that there were many glove shops in Gloversville and that they were all looking to hire the best glove cutters from Napoli.

Since Angelo had owned his own small glove shop in Naples along with his brother he was able save enough money to bring his wife and children to America with him. Raphelia and her sons would have part of their trip to America paid by Pasquale when he got a job and sent some money to her. Raphelia's family would also pay for a part of the trip. Although Pasquale saved some money for the family, it costs about thirty dollars each for Raphelia and the three children, and it would take months for Pasquale to gather the funds needed to bring his family to America.

Pasquale worked an average of sixty hours per week cutting gloves. His average weekly wage was about nine thousand Italian Liras, or the equivalent of about four U.S. dollars. Living on that wage, attempting to save enough for the entire family to come to America, made it extremely challenging. Pasquale had heard that the average weekly wage for a fifty-six hour work week for a glove cutter in Gloversville was about twelve dollars. With eight dollars more each week than he made in Italy, he should be able to provide some money for Raphelia and their sons to make the trip to America.

Raphelia was adjusting slowly to the change at home with Pasquale being gone. She had waited for the day that Pasquale would leave for America with hesitant anticipation. Francesco was doing his best to keep Raphelia's spirits up talking about their leaving for America and the good times the family had together. Francesco and his brothers helped with the daily chores. Young Arturo would help his mother make pasta. Tomatoes were abundant and there was always the smell of tomatoes cooking.

Raphelia and her family also continued to make Sunday meals special. The food would always contain numerous dishes including seafood or meat, pasta, cured meats such as *salame* (salami), vegetables that were grown in the DaCorsi garden, cheese, and fruit. Pizza was also a regular food item. Authentic Neapolitan pizza included tomatoes, garlic, olive oil, and anchovies. Pizza was sold by vendors on the streets of Naples. Young Francesco worked as a part-time helper and beginning apprentice for a local butcher and on occasion would stop and buy pizza from a street vendor while on his way home. Raphelia also made pizza at least twice each week in the wood fired earthen oven that Pasquale had made.

The DaCorsi household did what they needed to do to maintain a fairly stable family life. Pasquale was a good handyman and could fix almost anything. His neighbors would ask for help on occasion and, although Pasquale never wanted anything in return, he would be given food, clothing, and other items for his work. Although Pasquale was content with home life and the stability of his family, he had other concerns.

The economy in Naples was suffering as a result of an outbreak of cholera that had turned into an epidemic. Tourism was nearly nonexistent. Large numbers of people died as medical treatments at that time were not very effective. The most vulnerable areas were the slums of Naples. Consuming contaminated mollusks contributed to the severe outbreak (Snowden, 1995). Fortunately the DaCorsi family escaped the epidemic. This was the time when Pasquale began to explore moving to America.

Pasquale was very concerned with the failing economy, the potential of his wife and his sons contracting cholera, and the radical decisions made by the government affecting the most vulnerable in the Lower Naples region in an attempt to control the disease. Pasquale and Raphelia and their families resided in the Upper Naples area which appeared to be less susceptible to the outbreak.

These concerns made Pasquale even more determined to go to America. In conversations with many men in the neighborhood, many had the same concerns and also planned to leave Italy. Pasquale had first thought about immigrating when he watched groups of Neapolitan families leaving from the Port of Naples for America in 1883. He knew the Italians were being charged fifty cents per person as a tax for immigration. He was familiar with the Immigration Tax imposed by the 1882 Immigration Act. This was a topic of much discussion among Neapolitan men.

Increased Italian immigration to America began in the early 1800s. Each year less than one thousand left Italy; however, a few years before 1880 more than one thousand six hundred left for America. More than twelve thousand would arrive in America in 1880. By 1890, the number exceeded fifty two thousand and the following year, more than seventy six thousand left Italy for America (Molnar, 2010).

In 1890, after years of hesitation, Pasquale finally began working on his plan to leave America. Little did Pasquale know that it would take eight years to complete his plan before his actual departure to the New World. Pasquale thought that he just needed to raise the money, file a few papers, and he would be on his way. The immigration process was laborious. Pasquale, like many Italians, had little formal education. He was however able to read and write in Italian. Gathering the paperwork, obtaining approval from the Italian authorities, and meeting the requirements of the U.S. Immigration Laws took its toll on Pasquale. There were many times when he felt like giving up on his dream. Raphelia was the one who kept Pasquale motivated.

When Pasquale was eighteen, he obtained his Italian passport. The practice in Italy was for citizens to have a passport to relocate to other areas within Italy. This requirement was put in place to ensure that Italian men were not immigrating to other countries to avoid being drafted into the military. Pasquale served three years in Royal Italian Army as a light infantry soldier. He entered the military in 1870. With the numerous Italian involved wars and conflicts subsiding following Italian unification, Pasquale was fortunate because he did not in serious combat situations during his military service.

On this fifth day of the journey and with the prior weather issues the ship continued to travel at a reduced speed and moved about ten miles per hour for the remainder of the trip. Although the SS Aller had two masts, the captain would not set the sails for this trip. The ship had been retrofitted with the original four masts reduced to two. The steamship company wanted the engines to do the work for this voyage. The captain was given orders for this and also to see how well the ship would perform using only the engines.

The slowing of the ship was a safety decision made by the captain as the unpredictable roughness of the ocean could damage the ship if the speed was pushed. The captain was almost ready to defy orders and set sail. The conditions however were not ideal for sailing. The ship continued on its voyage under mechanical power and would remain so for the rest of the trip. While closing in on half way to America Pasquale began to get very excited about the next leg of the excursion.

The Atlantic was beginning to provide some calm travel as the weather was clear, at least for now. The vastness of the ocean with no land in sight was daunting. Even with the limited visibility from third class on the ship, all one could see was water. Third class passengers were feeling much better with the uncommon smoothness of the Atlantic after that rough experience with severe weather. The captain knew that the calmness would be short lived. This sea was mysterious and could change without notice.

With a fairly pleasant day on the ocean, Pasquale took out a satchel he brought with him. The satchel contained several pieces of leather. He also had shears and other sharp cutting tools. He took out some of the leather and trimmed it into thin strips. He then braided the strips and made a leather waistband. The waistband was for his friend, Angelo. Pasquale also made a drawstring purse for Maddalena. He cut oblong shapes from the leather, made slits along the edges, and weaved leather strips through the slits to form the purse. He cut small vertical slots in the top edges of the purse for the drawstring.

Angelo was always amazed by his friend's handicraft. He thanked Pasquale for the handmade gift. He told Pasquale that together they should make leather waistbands and purses when they settle in America. As a small business owner in Naples, Angelo had already been working on a plan for starting a business in America. Knowing that he had good business experience and Pasquale had the best skills and talent together they would become good American businessmen.

Angelo had also traveled to England many times to experience how British leather companies operated. Although the British had small locally operated glove shops similar to those in Italy, they also had thriving larger companies that employed hundreds of people. Angelo decided that is what he was going to do in America. Creating a large company that employed many people was all part of his dream. Pasquale was a little hesitant about Angelo's plans. He also wanted to achieve great success in America but his first objective was to get a job so he could bring his family to America.

The two men began to discuss the possibility of having Angelo start a leather business in Gloversville. Angelo had the contacts for bringing in the raw materials. He had done some research of the leather businesses in Gloversville. His small shop in Naples was still in business and being operated by his younger brother, Alphonse. Pasquale told Angelo that he would be willing to come to work for him once the business was up and running. Both men were concerned about supporting their families. Angelo had little doubt that there would be no problem accomplishing that. Pasquale was confident but not as positive as Angelo.

Angelo was always a mover and shaker. Being eleven years younger than Pasquale he relied on Pasquale's advice. Pasquale was like a big brother to Angelo. When Angelo wanted to open his own glove shop he first consulted with Pasquale. Angelo had a grandiose vision for his glove shop in Naples. He would carefully prepare to discuss his ideas with Pasquale. The plans for the shop were finally completed and Pasquale had guided Angelo all along the way. Angelo wanted to repay Pasquale by offering him a job, but Pasquale had a strong allegiance to Luigi and had been teaching others to cut gloves which gave Pasquale a great sense of accomplishment. Pasquale declined Angelo's offer but said that he would continue to help Angelo with business needs. Angelo was grateful and told Pasquale that someday the two would be together working.

The fifth day was coming to an end. Pasquale was ready for a good night's sleep. There was a sense of peacefulness felt by Pasquale that night. Perhaps it was realizing that the voyage had about seven days left before he would be in New York and seeing for the first time that wonderful *Signora Liberta,* (Lady Liberty). He knew all about France's gift to America. He knew that the tablets held by the Statue of Liberty were a symbol of independence and had the date of July 4, 1776 inscribed on the tablets signifying American independence. He also knew that the Grover Cleveland, President of the United States, had dedicated the Statue in 1886. He was eager to see the illuminated torch when the SS Aller moved its way into the New York harbor.

As Pasquale waited for sleep to come, he thanked God in a silent prayer for taking care of the family and for the chance to begin a new life in America. Pasquale, a devoted Roman Catholic, prayed every day. He and Raphelia took their children to Mass every Sunday. A highlight for Pasquale was the first communion of his three boys and Francesco's and Eduardo's confirmation. He thought to himself that Arturo would be the first in the family to be confirmed in America. He wondered about the churches in Gloversville. Did they have Italian traditions? Were the priests Italian? Did they celebrate Italian holidays? He was pleased that at least he would be able to attend church with his sister. Pleased and humbled he drifted off in sleep.

Five

Something was again amiss on day six aboard the SS Aller as the roughness of the Atlantic returned. There was no storm in sight. The ocean was holding true to its character. The captain still held the speed at a slower but steady pace. Atlantic crossings could be a nerve-shattering event. The uncommon smoothness of the previous day was met with the familiar harsh movements of the ship. Even with the third class deck being less susceptible to the movements due to being located partially below the water line, the side to side and rolling effects of the ship were still unsettling. For a few of the third class passengers, the resulting seasickness would return.

Pasquale's lungs ached for fresh air. He was fortunate that he did not suffer from seasickness but the foulness of the air made him feel nauseous this day. He also felt claustrophobic. Even with the harsh movements of the ship Pasquale decided that he would make his way to the upper deck. Seeing the sky, the daylight, the openness of the sea, and breathing fresh air was worth the risk. As he made his way there was a clear passage to the stairway. He began climbing the steps. A ship crew member stopped him and asked Pasquale in English and in German where he was going.

Pasquale did not respond. The two stood silent for a minute. Another crew member approached. Pasquale was asked the same question by the other crew member but this time in Italian. Pasquale responded and passionately pleaded with the crew to let him have five minutes of fresh air. The compassionate Italian speaking crew member took Pasquale by the arm and escorted him to the upper deck telling him *"cinque minuti"* (five minutes).

Reaching the upper deck, Pasquale immediately took a long breath. It was the sweetest breath he ever took. The bright sky, the cool October breeze, and the wonderful smell of the sea refreshed him. The choppy sea did not bother Pasquale. The ship's motion on the upper deck actually felt relaxing to Pasquale. His head cleared. The nausea went away. He gazed around the beautiful ship and imagined where he would stand when arriving in New York. He pictured the Statue of Liberty in his mind. The crew member approached Pasquale and told him that his five minutes were over. *"Torna a quarti"* (back to your quarters). The directive from the crew member was gentle but straight to the point. Pasquale complied and said *"grazie, sei un gentiluomo"* (thank you, you are a gentleman).

Pasquale did not tell anyone where he went. He thought he may cause an uprising if he told anyone. He did not even share his good fortune with Angelo. Many third class passengers would go up the steps from third class but many never got as far as the upper deck. They were either stopped by the crew or they stopped on their own and returned after reaching the second class deck. When other passengers saw Pasquale return the assumption was that he went to the second class deck.

Pasquale was feeling refreshed after his excursion. He kept thinking about the Statue of Liberty. As he walked around the third class area he picked up a small block of discarded wood he had found. The block was about four inches wide and ten inches high. Although Pasquale did not know where the wood was from, he was certain it has no specific use as it was lying on the floor next to a trash bin. The wood block was just the right size for carving. He decided that he would try to carve the Lady Liberty statue with the block. He went to his berth to work on the carving. With a small peasant knife that he carried he began to shape the block. Pasquale, with his many talents used to make toys from blocks of wood for his sons. He would spend hours cutting and carving the toys. The statue replica would be much more challenging and time consuming but one thing Pasquale had at the moment was time.

Pasquale worked from what he had committed to memory from the many pictures and drawings he had seen of the Statue of Liberty. He roughly sketched an outline of the statue on the block. He started by shaping the base of the block. From there he worked from the top down. Using his peasant knife, which was a simple pocket knife with a blade that folded into the handle, the statue slowly began to take shape. He worked for hours on the base of the statue before starting to carve the Lady. Chipping away small sections and shaving the wood with his knife, he carefully completed a crude rectangle shape for the torch.

He worked slowly and methodically on his piece so he would not make any significant mistakes with his only wood block. As he was shaping the raised right arm of the statue he wondered if he could actually trim the block for the statue's crown and head portion. That would be the most demanding and would really test his carving skills. He thought that if Michelangelo could chisel blocks of marble and create beautiful lifelike statues then he could make the Lady Liberty from a block of wood. Pasquale worked on his masterpiece until his hands ached. With a part of the raised arm completed and nearly time for the evening meal he stopped for the day. He placed the partially carved block in his satchel for safekeeping.

That night was different than the previous five nights. The passengers were told by a few others not leave the dining hall after the evening meal as a special event had been in planned for all the children. There was a group of Italian thespians in third class. The group had acted in plays and performed throughout Italy. The event that evening was a presentation of *Cenerentola*, the story of Cinderella. This version was the creation of Giambattista

Basile, a sixteenth century poet, short-story writer, soldier in the Neapolitan Army, and a public official, who published his rendition of the tale in 1634 in the *Lo Cunto de le Cunti* (The Story of Stories) and included the Italian adaptations of Rapunzel, Snow White, and Puss in Boots (Giambattista Basile Italian Author).

The play was a huge success. For about one and one-half hours the children were in awe. The adults also enjoyed the presentation. The actors, without the benefit of scenery or costumes, kept the audience entertained. Children laughed, watched with amazement, and watched intently as the actors made their characters come alive. Cinderella in Basile's story is named Zezolla, the daughter of a widowed prince. The character is abused by the six daughters of the governess, who married the prince, Zezolla's father, and became the wicked stepmother. Zezolla was made a servant and given the name Cenerentola by her stepmother. In the story Cenerentola plants a date tree from which a fairy appears. The fairy grants Cenerentola's wish to leave the house without her stepsisters' knowledge.

Cenerentola attends the king's feast where her stepmother and stepsisters' also attend. In a rush to leave the feast before being discovered as Cenerentola, she loses one of her slippers. The king picks up the slipper and searches for the one it belongs to. The king travels to the prince's castle to meet with the governess and her daughters where the king attempts to fit the slipper on the feet of the sisters without success. The king then places the slipper on Zezolla's foot. The slipper fits. The king then sets a crown upon her head as queen of the kingdom (Bogue, 2007). At the end of the production the children all applauded loudly with shouts of *"bravo, bravo"* echoing in the dining hall.

When the children went to sleep, some of the adults talked late into the night about the wonderful play and the joy that it brought. For a brief moment in time the immigrants were able to forget about the trials of the voyage in third class. Most did realize that the bonds they made on the ship were likely not to continue when they arrived in America as they would be settling in different locations in the United States. Some would have New York City as their final destination and friendships formed on the voyage for those making that city their home would continue for many years.

The lifestyle for those who came from the southern Italian villages was one of clustering together. The social and political climate of the time led to an isolation where neighbors remained close, watched out for each other, and formed a bond that lasted for generations. The immigrants living in the New York City boroughs would maintain that same bond and lifestyle. It would be common for groups of Italian immigrants to live in the same tenement building or on the same city block. A traditional Italian spirit of kinship and bonding was known as *campanilismo*. This was an allegiance to the area within the sounds of church bells. The *campanilismo* would be maintained by a majority of the immigrants living in New York City (Immigration – A City of Villages).

Pasquale and Angelo wondered aloud about the living conditions and the lifestyle in Gloversville. They knew that the village was not like New York City where that population exceeded three million by the late 1800s (Centennial Classroom). In 1859 there were three thousand residents and five hundred homes in the Gloversville. By 1870 the population had grown to five thousand. By 1898 the population increased to about eighteen thousand. The need for additional dwelling units created a construction boom. Many homes in the area were built from the late 1800s to the early 1900s to accommodate the increasing population. (Menear, P., & Shiel, J. 2000).

Pasquale and Angelo knew about the two-story flats in Gloversville and that the row houses or tenement homes that filled New York City's immigrant areas did not exist in Gloversville. Pasquale hoped that when his family arrived in America he could have a flat near his sister. Pasquale wanted a *campanilismo* type living arrangement in Gloversville. He could hear the sounds of church bells in his mind as he pondered if Gloversville would be like Naples. There were two Roman Catholic Churches in Gloversville. Italian immigrants, along with other ethnic groups were served by Saint Mary's Parish and Saint Francis DeSales Parish.

The Italian community was growing much larger and a new church was established to meet the need. Our Lady of Mount Carmel Church was created in 1890 for the immigrating glove worker Italians in the community. The Italian Mass services by Our Lady of Mount Carmel would be mainly held at Saint Mary's. The growing Italian population prompted the pastor of Saint Mary's to purchase land and construct a larger church building. The first Mass in the new building was celebrated in 1893.

It would be twenty-eight years before the Italian catholic congregation would have a church facility that they did not have to share with others. After World War I with the Italian population continuing to grow, Mount Carmel needed a much larger and separate facility for the parish. Finally in 1921, the Bishop of the Archdiocese designated Father Dominic Ottaviano as the Mount Carmel Parish priest to serve and care for the Italian community. The task would also include buying land and building a new church. It would take until 1930 before the new church was finished and Italians would have a dedicated parish to call home (Church of the Holy Spirit, 2012). Mount Carmel would become the predominate Roman Catholic Church in Gloversville for meeting the customs and language needs of the Italian community for decades. Father Ottaviano, also an Italian immigrant, was forty-three years old when he was appointed as the Mount Carmel parish priest. He would serve the community for nearly forty years.

Pasquale and Angelo were still talking about the housing possibilities in Gloversville and soon realized the lateness of the hour. Deciding they should try to get some sleep they departed for the berths. Pasquale was not sleepy, and as he lay in his bed he started to pray once again. Pasquale carried his rosary beads with him constantly. He made sure he brought them before stepping foot on the ship. He received the rosary beads from his mentor Luigi, as a gift upon completion of his apprenticeship as a glove cutter. He took out his rosary, prayed the Apostle's Creed, and the Our Father, and began to recite the Hail Mary prayers.

Over and over, he scrolled through the rosary, alternating and praying as taught and always with the sequence of ten Hail Mary's. He repeated:

"Ave maria piena di grazie il Signore con. Te Tu sei benedetta fra le donna e Benedetto è il frutto del tuo seno Gesù. Santa Maria, madre di Dio, prega per noi peccatori adesso e nell'ora della nistra morte Amen." (Hail Mary full of grace Our Lord is with thee. Blessed art thou among women and blessed is the fruit of thy womb, Jesus. Holy Mary, Mother of God, pray for us sinners now and at the hour of our death, Amen).

Pasquale made it through about five sets on the rosary or about halfway through the recitals as he drifted off in sleep, rosary still clutched in his hand. At times Pasquale and Raphelia would say the rosary together before going to bed. Pasquale and Raphelia also prayed for their children every night. They also made sure they prayed with their children before putting them to bed each night.

Pasquale felt that prayer was a guiding principle in maintaining strong family relationships. As the spiritual head of the family he also felt that it was his duty to set the example for his wife and children. Faithful, God loving, and dedicated to his Catholic upbringing is who he was as a man, husband, and father. Pasquale always made the sign of the cross with his thumb making the sign on his forehead whenever he passed by a church. It was his way of honoring his God. This was a practice that he would pass onto his sons. He frequently would tell his sons the story of the crucifixion of Jesus and the significance of that sacrifice. Pasquale knew that one of his first duties when he arrived in Gloversville was to go to church and thank God for his safe trip and for the opportunity to begin his life anew in America.

Six

Pasquale awoke refreshed on this seventh day of the long trip. The nights of restless sleep finally caught up with Pasquale. Falling asleep without finishing the Rosary had not happened ever before. The sheer exhaustion of the first six days of the voyage would be replaced by a more invigorating feeling this day. Opening up his satchel, he took out the partially finished Statue of Liberty and decided to do more carving today. He wanted to complete his masterpiece before the end of the voyage. He planned on giving the statue to his sister as a gift. To signify the work he crudely chiseled his name and the date the ship was scheduled to arrive in New York, 12 *Ottobre* 1898 (October 12, 1898) on the bottom of the statue base.

The SS Aller left Naples just before noon on Friday, September 30, 1898. Still with more than one thousand miles to go, the ship was making steady progress. Some passengers had lost track of time and asked each other what day it was. Pasquale had just come back from the morning meal when he heard the question. As he walked by them he said *"è una bella venerdì"* (It's a beautiful Friday). Pasquale was excited that the journey was more than half way over. There were some who looked somewhat puzzled at Pasquale as they said *"grazie"* for his comment.

Pasquale smiled and continued on his way back to his berth to work on the statue. Angelo greeted Pasquale and asked *"perchè sei cosi felice oggi?"* (Why are you so happy today?). Pasquale put his hand on Angelo's shoulder and said *"arriveremo America il Mercoledi"* (we will arrive in America on Wednesday). *"Si dovrebbe essere felice troppo"* (you should be happy too) Pasquale told Angelo. To which Angelo responded *"Si, sono e sono pronto per il viaggio di fine"* (yes I am and I am ready for the voyage to end). Pasquale nodded in agreement.

The statue had a partially rough carved raised right arm with a rectangle block for the torch at the top of the arm and hand. Pasquale sharpened his knife and began working on the head and crown. Shaping this part of the statue would take a steady hand and precise cutting. Pasquale started each part of the carving by making a block in a size he thought worked for the scale of the piece. After about two hours of work, the block for the head part and a flatter more round, disc like portion was completed for the crown.

Pasquale worked his way down on the statue by shaping the shoulder area, the left arm bent at the elbow, and the tablet held in the left arm and hand, all in block form. This work was tedious. Pasquale, determined to finish his work, kept carving for hours. Pasquale had all of the block sections done. It had taken a total of eight hours to complete those sections. He could actually see a shape that resembled the Statue of Liberty.

The block parts needed to be transformed into a more complete and finely carved shape for each portion of the statue. Pasquale decided to continue his work late into the night after taking a brief period of time to have an evening meal. Pasquale decided that he would finish the robe of the statue first. Since the robe was the largest part of the statue and could be shaped easier than the other parts, he felt that he could make faster progress on his work this way. It was a struggle to keep the knife sharp. Pasquale used a leather strap that he had made to sharpen his knife. He also used the strap for keeping his straight razor sharp.

Pasquale decided that he would need to use his straight razor in addition to his knife to complete the statue. He figured that if his straight razor was ruined by the carving of the statue he would forego shaving for the remainder of the journey. Pasquale sported a full but neatly trimmed moustache. So a little more facial hair with a partially grown beard that would be a few days old wouldn't look too bad, he thought. If Maddalena saw him in a scruffy beard what would she think? Pasquale quickly rejected that thought and decided that the carved statue he would present to his sister would not bring a comment about not shaving from Maddalena.

Carving the robe was a little easier than expected. The flow of the garment was created by gouging out long straight wide areas with the knife. Pasquale then used the straight razor to trim the wide areas into an overlapping flowing design resembling the drapery style garment. It was more challenging to make the sleeve portion that covered the raised right arm of the statue. Pasquale used the straight razor to shape as best as he could that piece of the garment. The clothing on the statue also contained a tunic undergarment. Pasquale fashioned that part by undercutting the drapery to reveal an undergarment look that cascaded down from the left knee to the right foot of the statue.

It was nearly midnight when the work for the day was done. Pasquale was very pleased with the progress he made on the statue. He would need to finish the arms, hands, facial features, tablets, right leg and right foot, and the crown of the statue. He knew that would take the most time and many more hours of detailed work that would require fine carving and shaping of the features. Without having the benefit of smaller tools, Pasquale would have to use the very end edge of the straight razor and the tip of the knife to complete that work. Pasquale was ready to retire for the evening. His hands again ached from the work he did that day. It was a good ache, he thought, as his work was looking more like the Lady Liberty he had pictured in his mind.

Pasquale awoke around four in the morning on day eight of his voyage. He had a dream about Raphelia. In his dream Raphelia had arrived in America and had come to Pasquale's work. Pasquale was surprised to see her because he did not know she had left Italy. Raphelia told Pasquale that she could not wait any longer and decided to leave Italy because there were no more ships coming to America. Pasquale thought that was strange as ships left Naples regularly for voyages to America. Pasquale woke suddenly and wondered if Raphelia was actually on a ship to America. He realized he had been dreaming and knew Raphelia was still in Italy. He was bothered by the dream and wished he could talk to Raphelia. He missed her voice and he just wanted to hold her in his arms. The feeling of loneliness surrounded Pasquale. He could not go back to sleep and spent the rest of the early morning hours thinking about Raphelia.

It was around six o'clock and still feeling depressed about the dream Pasquale was unable to gather strength to get out of bed. He had been so happy the previous day. He was not hungry. He did not feel like working on the statue. He stayed in bed and just laid there. Angelo sensed something was wrong and asked Pasquale what he needed. Pasquale shared the dream and how he felt. Angelo tried to reassure Pasquale that in a short period of time he would be reunited with Raphelia and his sons. Angelo also told Pasquale that when they started work in Gloversville that would be the turning point where Pasquale could actually set the timeframe for his family to leave Italy for America. Pasquale understood and thanked Angelo for his compassion. Pasquale felt a little better with Angelo's reassurance but the separation from Raphelia left a void in his heart that was not easy to mend.

Angelo convinced Pasquale to get some food. Together they went to the dining hall and had some coffee. Unfortunately, but not unusual for food on the ship, the coffee was not very good and nothing like the good Italian espresso they both loved. They had a few pieces of bread that was always available and some nice *taralli* that other passengers brought on board and had left in the dining hall for others to share. *Taralli* is usually made by twisting two pieces of rope formed dough together to form a circle. The dough rope pieces are about the width of a soft pretzel. The unsweetened leavened dough is made with flour and lard, and contains course ground black pepper. The dough is baked until the dough ring is crispy. *Taralli* is an Italian treat that was readily available to the poor and working class society.

Pasquale and Angelo had enough to eat to feel full. The *taralli* made Pasquale feel a bit better and a little more energized. It was around eight o'clock when Pasquale and Angelo left the dining hall. Mealtime on the ship was nothing any of the passengers in third class looked forward to. The only thing the food on board did was to satisfy hunger. Mostly tasteless and poorly prepared, the food was only minimal sustenance that would get them through the day. The time Pasquale and Angelo spent together that morning with that traditional Italian treat made up for the bad food. They also knew that a good, home cooked Italian meal was only a few days away.

Returning to his berth Pasquale lay in his bed for a while still thinking about Raphelia. He knew Raphelia would want him to be in good spirits on the voyage. Although his heart ached for Raphelia he knew that he needed to be strong and ready for the last leg of the voyage. Pasquale decided it was time to get back to his task. It was later that the morning when he again began to work on his statue.

The remaining portions of Lady Liberty would be the most delicate carving. Pasquale focused on the crown portion of the carving the rest of the day. He knew that one mistake could be a disaster. He worked slowly and meticulously on each segment of the crown carefully making each extension the same size. He knew that the crown had seven spikes that represented the seven seas and each of the continents. Pasquale had studied the contents and history of the statue so well he had the image emblazoned in his mind.

Pasquale surgically removed wood material to form a rough cut of each spike. He then took each spike and shaved the wood so slowly that the remnant of carvings was like sawdust.

Pasquale thought to himself that if he shaved his face that slowly his beard would regrow and he would be constantly shaving. Pasquale had a good sense of humor and that thought literally made him laugh out loud. He hoped no one heard him or they may think he had just gone a little *pazzo* (crazy).

Pasquale worked steadily for more than seven hours. Angelo told Pasquale to take a break as food was being served in the dining hall. Pasquale was actually quite hungry as he had not eaten since early morning. The meal that evening was different than previous nights. The passengers were served pasta with marinara sauce. The sauce was not true Italian or Neapolitan style but it did represent a tomato sauce with a good amount of garlic. There was plenty of pasta and everyone had a good serving of the food as well as the always present bread. This was the first time that the third class passengers felt somewhat satisfied with the food.

After the meal that night, a group of men, including Pasquale and Angelo, stayed in the dining hall and shared their stories of why they chose to go to America. Final destinations varied. While many planned to stay in New York City, others were headed to New Orleans, Detroit, and Philadelphia. Some were going to Canada as a final destination. Pasquale was amazed at the wide variety of locations where the immigrants planned to settle. He was most curious about New Orleans.

One of the men, Luca Campisi, who would settle in New Orleans, explained that like him, many Sicilians were encouraged to go to there to escape the turmoil and poverty that plagued Sicily at that time. Work was available on sugar plantations or on the docks of the city (Maggi, 2014). Luca also described living conditions in New Orleans for immigrants and how he would need to overcome what was told to be significant discrimination against Sicilians and Italians. He described an incident that occurred in 1891 that took the lives of eleven immigrants.

New Orleans for the Sicilian immigrants was filled with prejudice and outright hatred of the nationality. Sicilians were considered to be lawless, dirty, and laced with disgusting and poor habits. One of the worst atrocities in the United States was the 1891 lynching of Sicilian and Italian immigrants. Nine of the immigrants were tried and found not guilty of the murder of the New Orleans police chief.

Following the trial a mob broke into the jail and took the nine not guilty Sicilians and two other Italians who were being held on non-related charges. The mob hanged the eleven individuals. This became the biggest mass lynching in American history. What followed the lynching was a wide-scale arrest of Sicilian and Italian immigrants in New Orleans. That action would contribute to a number of attacks nationwide against Italians during that period (Falco, 2012).

Pasquale was visibly disturbed about the incident. He could not imagine the suffering and injustice that took place. He knew of issues in Italy and Sicily where atrocities had taken place but in America, the land of new beginnings? He wondered if there would be prejudices and discrimination in Gloversville. Many Italians had already made Gloversville their home. There was no indication of such issues from letters he received from his sister. Perhaps she did not want to tell of those problems he thought. In any case, Pasquale was determined to make it and if he had to deal with the situations as they may arise.

Pasquale wanted to end the conversation with his fellow Italians that night on a positive note. He told the men that America would prove to be the new beginning they all sought. He went on to say that the dream they all shared of a better life for them and their families would be worth any trials or tribulations that they might have to endure. Pasquale left the men with his heartfelt feelings as he said in a very serious tone and with conviction, *"al mattino guarde l'orizzinte é verder il sol che sorge. Questa é la nostra alba nuova, il nostro destino."* (In the morning look at the horizon and see the sun rising. This is our new dawn, our destiny).

Seven

The Atlantic Ocean on day eight was once again making for a wild ride on the SS Aller. There were no heavy storms. A series of recurring squalls throughout the day created very heavy waves. The ship was listing because of the waves and the passengers were alarmed. A few thought the ship was about to lie over on its side and capsize. The crew did a great job in controlling the ship. Crew staff came to third class after hearing some screams and cries for help. The crew did what they could to reassure the passengers that the ship was fine and in no danger of capsizing and that the sea would calm shortly. Despite the crews attempt to reassure the passengers, many of the passengers were in near panic again.

With the ship listing and with the constant battering of waves, the forward progress of the vessel was drastically impeded. Struggling to keep the ship on course and in a constant forward movement took all the skills and techniques of the SS Aller crew. The captain barked orders constantly keeping the crew alert and on task. With the winds coming head on the captain ordered the crew to steer the ship at an angle to the waves. That would keep the ship in a more stable position. The maneuver would result in correcting the severe listing and would make the ship less susceptible to the violent actions of the sea. That action would require a zigzag movement of the ship to maintain the course. The ship would only travel about one hundred miles on the eighth day due to the path the captain had to take to keep the ship in one piece and to ensure the safety of the passengers.

As the seas began to calm and the winds subsided, the captain minimally increased the speed of the ship. The speed of the ship by order of the captain would be less than ten miles per hour at this point in the voyage. As the ship encountered the rough sea, the captain determined that a slower but steadier pace would be most beneficial to the crew, passengers, and for the ship. The mechanical systems had been pushed to their limit on this voyage.

The captain would not compromise the safety of the passengers and would not cause a situation where the ship would experience a severe mechanical breakdown. Overworking the steam engines could cause a catastrophic failure. If the ship travelled at full speed for the entire duration the voyage would take about seven days. This was not practical as the Atlantic was treacherous and unpredictable. The experienced captain was well aware of the issues with the Atlantic. The ship's chart outlined every segment of the voyage in advance. Charting this trip was something this captain had done more than fifty times.

Controlling the speed with changing ocean conditions ensured the trip was successful and the mechanical systems functioned and operated at peak levels. The captain's knowledge of the Atlantic and of the SS Aller was invaluable. The passengers were in good hands with this captain as he looked out for each and every passenger whether first class passengers or third class voyagers.

Pasquale did not work on the statue this day. The movements of the ship prevented any type of intricate carving. He was not about to ruin his masterpiece. Like most passengers, Pasquale spent the majority of the eighth day just trying to keep from getting bounced around. The passengers were told to stay in their berths that day. Pasquale took advantage of the time by praying the rosary. He would purposely took his time with the rosary. Normally Pasquale finished the rosary in one hour but this day, he spent more than two hours to finish the rosary. He did this as more of a devotion than just slowing down. After finishing the rosary, Pasquale felt a little queasy. He had not been seasick on the voyage. He thought it may be from something he ate. The ship had been rocking and swaying for hours. He soon concluded that his ailment was a seasick condition.

Pasquale hoped the nausea would subside quickly. He left his berth and went to the dining hall to see if he could find a few pieces of bread. He had not eaten for quite a while and thought the bread might ease his symptoms. He sat with a few others who also had been experiencing the same effects. The crew did have some bread for those who had asked. One of the passengers had some pieces of ginger that was shared among the group. Pasquale did not really like the taste of ginger but the way he felt at that moment he was willing to try some. He ate a small piece of ginger with a slice of bread.

After finishing the bread and ginger Pasquale returned to his berth. The harsh movements of the ship had begun to lessen somewhat. That was a welcome event for Pasquale as he lay down in his bed. He was feeling less queasy now. The bread and ginger seemed to have helped the symptoms. He thought that if he could go to sleep for a while that may also help. Sleep did not come and Pasquale lay in his bed with his eyes closed. That at least calmed him as the ship was not listing and the zigzag path taken by captain's orders had returned to a straighter pattern. There were still some heavy waves moving the ship up and down but the violent movements were no longer occurring.

Late that afternoon, Pasquale left his bed to check the contents of a small canvas bag he had brought with him. His trunk contained most of his clothing and other personal items in a compartment beneath the third-class area where the passengers stored their luggage. His canvas bag held a couple pairs of trousers, three shirts, an extra pair of shoes, a tin of blackening (shoe polish), a leather vest, a woolen flat cap, and a pair of handmade leather gloves. The bag also had a deck of Neapolitan cards used to play the traditional *La Scopa* card game, and his prized possession, a handmade wooden crucifix that had been given to the DaCorsi family by Luigi Amato.

The crucifix had a removable back with a hollowed out compartment that held a two small candles and two glass vials that contained holy water. The rear of the crucifix also had a hole on each side of the horizontal portion of the removable back that would hold the candles snug in an upright position. The DaCorsi family displayed the cross on the wall of their living room. Pasquale would take the cross down during holy days and place it back side up on the top of a bureau that was located at the wall that held the crucifix. He placed it that way so he could insert the candles in the holders. He put the vials of holy water on each side of the cross.

The family would recite the rosary together on holy days. Following the completion of the rosary, Pasquale would light the candles and wet his index finger with the holy water to make the sign of the cross on the foreheads of his sons and Raphelia. As he made the sign of the cross on each person, he would say, *"il Signore sia con voi"* (the Lord be with you).

Pasquale put the leather vest on and placed the flat cap on his head. Angelo had just returned to the berth when he saw

Pasquale sitting on the edge of the bed and noticed the vest and hat. He told Pasquale that he looked ready to have a photograph taken. Pasquale thought that was actually a good idea. He could send the picture to Raphelia.

Pasquale knew that one of the officers on the ship had a camera. He saw the officer taking pictures when he spent those few minutes on the upper deck. The camera was the kind that had a roll of film in the box. This fairly new invention allowed photographers to take pictures, and then ship the camera to the company that manufactured them where the film would be processed. When the pictures were produced the company would load another roll of film in the camera and ship the equipment with the completed photos back to the photographer.

Pasquale and Angelo wondered if they could convince the officer to take some pictures. But how could they approach crew members and ask to see the officer with the camera? Since Pasquale was allowed to spend a few minutes on the deck he would ask to see that officer. Fortunately many crew members spoke Italian so they though it should be easy to ask to see the officer who helped Pasquale.

Angelo and Pasquale went to the dining hall and asked a crew member they knew to approach the officer on their behalf about coming to third class to meet with them about taking their picture with his camera. The crew member said he would ask but could not guarantee it would happen. Pasquale and Angelo thanked the crew member and returned to the berth. They both became a little concerned that they might be in trouble for making such a request. They discussed for a moment that if the officer became upset or angry by the request they could be deported back to Italy. They concluded they would just be truthful about why they wanted a photo taken and would wait to see the reaction of the officer.

It was around five that afternoon when the dining room crew member came to see Pasquale and Angelo in the berth and said the officer had agreed to meet with them. Angelo's wife was concerned about the two plotting, but this had happened before in Italy that she knew somehow that Angelo and Pasquale would succeed in getting the officer to take their picture. She actually looked forward to having a photo taken with Angelo and her sons.

Pasquale changed his shirt and put on his leather vest back on to be ready for his picture to be taken. The first service of the evening meal was about to begin. Pasquale and Angelo decided they would wait for the second service. Neither was very hungry and Pasquale was just beginning to feel much better after his bout with seasickness. Angelo's wife also decided to wait for the meal as well.

Pasquale was a little concerned what Raphelia would think when she saw the picture because he had not shaved in a few days. Pasquale was always clean shaven except for his moustache. Pasquale had grown the moustache when he was eighteen so he had that feature for twenty-nine years. Raphelia liked the moustache but Pasquale was not so sure she would approve of a full beard. In any case, Pasquale could not shave as because he needed his straight razor to complete the statue. He knew Raphelia would understand when she saw the statue.

The officer showed up around seven that evening and had his camera ready to go. The officer told Pasquale and Angelo this would have to be done quickly as he needed to get back to his duty station. Taking Pasquale's photo first, the officer positioned Pasquale where there was a blank wall inside the berth as the backdrop. The officer took two pictures of Pasquale. He then proceeded to take a family photo for Angelo. The entire process took about five minutes. Pasquale gave the officer his sister's address so the photo could be sent there. Angelo provided an address as well. They both thanked the officer for his kindness. The officer told them that it was unusual to take individual photos of third class passengers but he knew how important it was for them and he was happy to accommodate them.

The second meal service was about to begin. Heading to the dining hall Pasquale and Angelo made a pact that they would tell no one about the photos. They did thank the crew member who made it possible. Still not very hungry, Pasquale took mostly bread for his meal. Some of the passengers had brought some *salame* to the dining hall and shared with others. Pasquale took some of the *salame* and placed two thick slices in his bread. It tasted so good. No need for watered down soup tonight. The bread and *salame* was the meal that night and just what Pasquale needed.

After finishing the meal, Pasquale and Angelo joined two other men to play *La Scopa.* The Italian card game is played with a forty-card deck. The game consists of capturing or matching cards. The games are always lively and filled with loud conversation. Pasquale would play *La Scopa* at least once per week in his village. There were groups of men who played the game each week. The men would set up tournaments where players would be eliminated until one was left to be crowned the champion. The game required good skills but also required a bit of luck. Pasquale became the champion many times as he was an accomplished player.

The *La Scopa* game ended around eleven that night. Pasquale had a great time playing cards. He always enjoyed the game. Although Pasquale was a competitive player, it did not matter tonight whether he won or lost. He just enjoyed being part of the group and the fellowship. Pasquale and Angelo talked for a while after the card game. They both mentioned how much fun they had playing cards. For a moment they almost felt like they were not on a ship but in a village with friends.

It was a long day for Pasquale and he was ready for some sleep. After overcoming the illness of earlier that day and having the good fortune of having his photo taken and ending the day with some good card games, Pasquale was feeling good about the day overall. As he walked back to his berth with Angelo, one of the passengers was softly playing *Ave Maria* on a mandolin. This is the song of Hail Mary. Pasquale and Angelo stopped to watch and listen. The mandolin was such a sweet sound to them. That brought some tears to Pasquale. *Ave Maria* was his and his mother's favorite song in church services and he always cried when it was played or sung. The song reminded him of his mother. Pasquale's mother died when he was ten years old. She fell victim to consumption (tuberculosis). Although death rates from the disease declined in the mid-nineteenth century, the disease was still devastating and took many lives. *Ave Maria* was sung during his mother's funeral service. As he lay in his bed he ended the day by saying a Hail Mary prayer for his mother.

Eight

Pasquale awoke on day nine with the song *Ave Maria* still in his head. He was in good spirits. Today was going to be a day to spend working on the statue. There were biscuits in the dining hall for the passengers today. That was a refreshing change from the routine bread served at every meal. Pasquale had the bisquits with some honey and some of the not-so-good coffee. He really had a craving for some good espresso but knew that was not possible on this trip.

The Atlantic was being somewhat cooperative today. Although there was some slight rough spots that morning, it was nothing like conditions of the previous day. There were only a few passengers in third class who still suffered from seasickness. These passengers had been ill throughout the voyage. Most were confined to their berths and were visited by the ship's doctor only a couple of times. Like most transatlantic voyages there was only one doctor for every seven hundred to eight hundred passengers. Seeing the doctor was nearly impossible unless there was a serious health issue. Seasickness was not considered to be serious or life threatening. The staleness of the air in third class was sometimes overwhealming, especially when many passengers had been aflicted with seasickness. Disinfectants were used abundently but even that did not clear the air sufficiently.

By this time in the voyage Pasquale had either built up a tolerance for the stale air or just did not let it bother him. He was used to the smell of animal hides in the leather shops. The leather tanneries that he frequently visited in Italy had smells so putrid that the odors on the ship were mild in comparison. Leather tanning was considered to be a vile industry. The process created odors so strong that many factories were located on the outskirts of towns to avoid constant lingering odors.

Leather tanning was a major industry in Gloversville during this time. The factories in Gloversville were located thoughout the town. Some were in residential areas. Others were more remotely located. In the late 1800s , there were nearly forty tanneries in Gloversville (Morrison, 2008). An economic slowing in the late 1890s closed many tanneries in Gloversville. The industry would still survive and remain a major employment base for the community for many years.

The processing of animal hides is a centuries-old craft. The ancient Hebrews and Egyptians tanned hides using oak bark and babul bark. This vegetable tanning method remained unchanged for thousands of years. The late nineteenth century brought about the use of chemical materials into leather tanning such as chromium salts (Tanning, 2016). The tanning system is a multi-step process. The hides are treated in a fashion that cures the skin, removes the hair and fatty layers while maintaining the outer, thinner layer of the skin. The hides are pickled to preserve, soften, and cleanse the material. Tanning also allows the fibers of the hide to meld together creating a nondecaying material (Leather, 2016).

Supporting the scores of glove manufacturing firms in Gloversville kept the tanneries alive. Gloversville produced nearly ninety percent of men's leather gloves and other fine leather gloves in America in the mid-to-late nineteenth century and into the twentieth century (The Keys, 2016). The tanneries produced glove leather and garment leather. From processing the raw hides to completing the finished leather, many tanneries included the entire manufacturing process. Once tanned, the leather had to be finished by adding the final color to the hide. That process included adding dye to the hide to the desired color and placing the final color on the surface of the skin. The final color process was known as swabbing which literally painted the finished side of the hide.

The material was then stretched and further heat treated in a process called toggling. This process used metal clamps that workers attached to the hide, stretching and smoothing the material. The toggle clamps had a hook on the bottom side that fastened into one of the hundreds of holes that were on a large perforated steel board. The hides were placed on the metal board. The tightly stretched hides on the horizontal steel boards would be turned to a vertical position. The boards would then be slid into a large enclosed steel box to be treated with the heat. The final finishing of the leather would include plating or pressing the material for a smooth surface, embossing the hides for a printed surface, and polishing the leather for a glossy finish.

Some tanneries focused on the tanning of the material only. Smaller cottage-style leather finishing shops would complete the process by producing the final product ready for glove or garment manufacturing. The economic turmoil impacted production, but with the high demand, large quantities of hides were produced daily. The timing for Pasquale to come to Gloversville was just at the end of the downturn in the economy. The glove shops still were at a steady production pace. As the economy improved, tanneries would resurface. The outlook coming into the twentieth century was promising for Gloversville.

Pasquale had a small quantity of camphor that he kept in a small tin box in his scatchel. He also had some antisceptic and cloth pads in the box. He would have the box at work while cutting gloves to use to treat minor cuts. While injury was not frequent, there were occasions when the sharp shears would nick the skin and cause some bleeding. Pasquale would use the antiseptic to wash the wound, the camphor to spread on the wound, and bits of cloth to cover the injury.

Although Pasquale was not overcome by the odors on the ship this day, he dabbed camphor under his nostrils to eliminate the any unpleasant odors. With that accomplished, Pasquale took out the statue and began to work. With the spikes of the crown finished, he started notching out the windows in the crown. The windows allowed rays of light to shine through the crown. Pasquale would not completely carve out the windows but instead created indentations that represented windows. Not as tedious as carving the spikes but just as demanding. Pasquale wanted to make sure that each window was the same size. It would take several hours to complete this task.

It was about four in the afternoon when he finished the windows. His next step was to carve the hair and facial features. While doing this portion Pasquale thought of the detail that was on the statue David carved by Michelangelo. Pasquale had visited Florence where that statue was displayed. He was in awe of the realism of the statue. He would use that memory as the inspiration to make the face of the statue as real as possible. He sharpened his razor and peasant knife.

He slowly began to make fairly even curved notches for the hair portion of the statue. He first shaped the rough outline of the hair and smoothed the part that would become the forehead of the statue. This was done to make the hair prominent with an ending point at the forehead. The sides were a little more challenging as Pasquale had to do a rough cut of the ears to allow the hair to slightly overlap the ears. He also cut wavy lines for the top part of the hair, the same for the back part and to shape and extend the hair half way down the neck area of the statue.

Pasquale finished that part of the statue just as the second call for the dining hall meal was announced. His appetite returned and he no longer felt ill. Tonight's menu was a stew made with beef, potatoes, carrots, and the ever present bread. The food actually had some flavor as compared to the bland soup typically served. Pasquale was quite hungry and devoured his meal. He also ate about a half a loaf of bread. He was not sure if the food tasted better that night or if he was just that hungry. It was tasty enough.

After the meal Pasquale joined Angelo and his family outside of the dining hall. There was a row of benches near the dining hall where they gathered. The Guiliani children were playing nearby with other children. Pasquale, Angelo and Rosa talked about the end of the voyage and their excitement to see family in Gloversville. Angelo and Rosa were meeting Angelo's cousin Luciana and her husband Vincenzo Leoni. The Leoni's immigrated to America four years earlier. Vincenzo had a shoe repair shop in Gloversville. He was a master cobbler who learned his trade in Naples. His services were in demand as the quality of his work was the best in the area.

Leatherworking was a tradition in the DaCorsi, Guiliani, and Leoni families. Vincenzo was about the same age as Pasquale. The two became friends when they were both learning their respective trades as apprentices. Luciana was five years younger than Vincenzo and six years older than her cousin Angelo. Vincenzo and Luciana have four children: Maria, seventeen, Fausto, fifteen, Giuseppe, thirteen, and Angela, twelve. Luciana is a homemaker although she also was a glove maker in Italy. Luciana and Vincenzo live near Pasquale's sister in Gloversville.

Luciana and Maddalena would talk constantly about the arrival of Pasquale and Angelo. Maddalena was especially excited to see the Guiliani children. The last time she saw little Giovanni he was two years old. She was very anxious to see the baby. Luciana and Vincenzo's children considered Maddalena an aunt. They called her *mia zia* (my aunt). The affection and respect of adults by the children was an expectation of the elders by all Italian children. Children would greet adult relatives or close family friends with a kiss on both cheeks. This tradition, usually a ritual of men greeting men or women greeting women in Southern Italy is a sign of loyalty. Children were taught the tradition at a young age.

The tradition somewhat got a little more attention on the voyage. In the dining hall it was not unusual to see this greeting taking place before the dinner was served. With the one thousand third class passengers it was common to not see someone on a regular basis. The kiss was a significant sign of respect and meant that we are here for each other covering each other's backs. Men would also ask *"come stai?"* (how are you?). Responses aboard ship would include *"sto bene"* (I'm well), *"non sto bene"* (I'm not so well), *"cosi, cosi"* (so so), and a variety of other statements including some that were a little comedic, such as *"mezzo morto"* (half dead). Pasquale would use that phrase on occasion and would add *"ma non mi posso lamentare"* (but I can't complain). He would also say *"la mia bocca è morto"* (my mouth has died), which meant he had nothing to say.

This night the music would resume because it had been absent during the rough sea events. Everyone was ready for some entertainment. The musicians all played together. The melodic sounds were refreshing to the third class passengers. The music was lively. As the music continued, a twenty-year old young man asked the violinists to accompany him and his twenty-two year old female companion while they sang.

In 1896, Giacomo Puccini completed a new opera that he called *La Boehme*. One of the duets in the opera, *O soave fanciulla* (Oh gentle maiden) is sung by the main characters, Rodolfo and

Mimi. This song becomes a love song between the two. The young man and the young woman on the ship sang this duet. While they were performing there was total silence in third class. The sweetness of the voices mesmerized the passengers. When they finished shouts of *"bellissimo, bravo, bravo"* filled the cabin. Pasquale loved opera and was in awe over this presentation. Pasquale looked at Angelo and said *"che spettacolo"* (what a performance). Angelo responded, *"si, era meraviglioso"* (yes, it was wonderful).

Many passengers had tears in their eyes from the outstanding duet. The passion of the performers was like being in an opera house. Even the musicians were amazed by the performance. The passengers wanted more. The young man obliged and performed Ruggerio Leoncavello's *Vesti la guibba* (put on the costume) from the opera *Pagliacci.* That was followed by a soprano solo from the young lady singing *Quando me'n vo* from *La Boehme.* This aria, also called Musetta's waltz, is a risqué song that details her perceived beauty. The passengers gave the performers rousing applause and again the loud *"bravos."*

Before the performers left the area to return to their berths, some of the passengers asked them why they chose to go to America. The young man told the others that they wanted to perform in operas in America. Like the others, the dream of America compelled these young people to take the risk to achieve their dream and potential success. The opera performers were pleased that they could bring some happiness to the passengers during the long and arduous voyage.

It was about ten o'clock when the musicians finished playing. As most of the passengers were headed to the berths, Pasquale and Angelo stayed behind and talked more about the performance. Pasquale wished that Raphelia was there. She loved opera as much as Pasquale. They had attended the opera at the famous *Teatro di San Carlo* in Naples. The theater, built in 1737, hosted some of the region's most well-known composers of the time (Teatro). Naples also became known as the center of the comic opera. These operas were produced with local dialects, and in a manner that depicted everyday life.

The sea was cooperating that night and the light from the moon lit the sky. Pasquale figured that he could finish the statue in the next two days if he worked steadily. He had his plan laid out for the next carving sequence. With the hair completed he would next work on the facial features, then the hands and arms, the tablets, and the final details of the robe and tunic. One last challenge would be carving the right leg of the statue. The leg was angled back in a walking motion. The majority of the leg would be covered by the tunic but needed to show the foot with a raised heel. Pasquale was not sure how he would accomplish that feature. He knew, however, that to replicate the statue in proper form, he would need to show that detail.

With his plan in place Pasquale climbed into his bed, silently talking to Raphelia for a while telling her about the day. He thought about his sister who he would see in the next few days. He was looking forward to a train ride that would take him from New York City to Gloversville. He wondered what the scenery would be like. Pasquale finished the night with a prayer thanking God for the good fortune to be traveling to America. He also prayed for his wife and children for their comfort and safety in his absence. He finished his prayers with the sign of the cross saying *"nel nome del Padre, del Figlio e dello Spirito Santo, Amen."* Before he went to sleep, he said *"buonanotte amore mio, la mia dolce Raphelia"* (good night my love, my sweet Raphelia).

Nine

It was around seven in the morning on day ten when Pasquale awoke. He immediately freshened up, had a quick bite to eat, and began working on the statue. Sharpening his tools again he made sure that the knife and razor were ready for the day's work. The facial carving was underway. Working from the forehead down he began to transform the small square block into the face of Lady Liberty.

With the forehead already completed the day before he rounded the rest of the block that would form the head to create the facial features. He scooped out the wood to make the indented eye sockets. He then carefully began shaping the nose portion. He knew the nose was prominent but he did not want to make it too large. He laughed to himself as most Italians have fairly large noses. Pasquale figured since the Lady replicated a Roman Goddess in design, he would give her an Italian nose.

He very carefully and with great precision made the shape of the nose and blended the wood at the eyes areas to create the proper dimensional look. Moving to the lip area, he removed material from the sides of the rounded block to allow the lips to be easier to carve. Using the straight razor, he scraped the face portion a little at a time to make the feature as smooth as possible.

He also finished the carving of the ears at this time. With the lips, nose, and eyes completed, he worked on the front neck area and again smoothed that portion with the razor.

He turned his attention to the right arm and torch. The arm and torch had been roughly shaped previously. Using the smoothing technique gave the final shape to the arm. He used the knife to cut the flame part of the torch. This was similar to how he shaped the hair. He cut the round torch base and then notched the wood to form the hand and closed fingers that grasped the torch handle. Finally, he shaped the bottom area of the torch handle. He gave one final smoothing of the right arm.

That work took nearly ten hours to complete. He worked almost non-stop. Pasquale's calloused hands ached again from holding the tools so intensely. He stopped working for about an hour to rest. He would grab some food and bring it back to his berth. He was intent this day to work late into the night on the statue. He only had about one full day left to finish his work. The SS Aller was scheduled to arrive in the New York harbor before ten o'clock in the morning on the twelfth of October.

After a meal of the same bland soup and lots of bread he resumed his work on the statue. Focusing on the right foot, he knew this would be a challenge. The angled right leg was covered by the tunic. The exposed right foot was partially covered by the tunic. He cut a flowing drape-like shape for the rear portion of the tunic. He shaped raised and indented sections to make the tunic look like it was in a walking motion with the right leg. He also completed carving the right foot and toes. He shaped the sandal and smoothed everything with the razor. Although four hours of work on this portion had worn Pasquale out, he figured he would carve for about another two hours before calling it a day.

He moved to the left arm area of the statue. He had previously shaped the left arm again in rough form. He shaved that portion to a smooth finish finalizing the shape of the arm. The left arm was bent forward at the elbow. The arm was covered to the forearm area by the sleeve of the robe. He found that carving the robe and tunic was a little easier than he thought it would be. The details of hands and fingers took the most time. For the left hand he had to work simultaneously on the rectangle of the tablets and the hand and fingers. The tablets rested on the left forearm at the elbow with the fingers wrapping around the middle of the tablets. Pasquale had all the rough cuts done when he decided to end the work for that day. It was nearly one in the morning when he stopped working.

Unable to sleep through the night mainly due to the excitement of the near end of the voyage, Pasquale was ready to finish the statue. He got up at six o'clock on the eleventh day of the voyage and immediately took out the statue. He checked his work from the previous day. The statue looked good and only needed a few minor touchups on the completed portions. That would make the final carving of the left arm, left hand and fingers, tablet, and left foot the real focus of the day.

Pasquale decided he would finish the left foot first. The foot was mostly covered by the draping robe with only the toes exposed. He carved indentations to form the robe covered left shin. Since he had already completed the right foot he knew exactly how to shape the left foot and toes. He notched out the area for the sandal first. He then proceeded to shape the toes. Pasquale's razor blade now needed more frequent sharpening. He only had his leather strap to sharpen the blade and although that worked, what he really needed was a sharpening stone to put a fine edge on the blade and to properly hone the blade. He figured he had just enough edge left on the blade to complete his work. He would need to get a new straight razor when he got to Gloversville so he could shave the beard he had grown on the voyage.

Pasquale was getting hungry. The mid-day meal was being served. As this was the last day of a full day at sea the food for the day included spaghetti *aglio e olio* (garlic and olive oil), baccalà (salt cod), fruit, potatoes, olives, prosciutto, and cheese. Pasquale loved baccalà. He would make baccalà, calamari (squid), anchovies, mussels, and other varieties of shellfish on special occasions and during the Lenten season. The Bay of Naples was abundant with many varieties of fish and there were many fish markets located near Pasquale's village.

The meal was considered a feast by the third class passengers. The poor food during the voyage was becoming normal to the passengers. The food on this day would be served for both the mid-day meal and the evening meal. That was fine with the passengers. Although not cooked the exact Italian way, the food was flavorful enough to taste good. The prosciutto was the surprise of the day. No one expected this cured ham delicacy. Since the meat was cured, it was not a problem keeping it on the ship. Prosciutto is made from the rear leg of a pig. The meat is first covered with salt and left in cool place for about two months. The salt is removed and the ham is placed in a temperature-controlled room to air dry and cure. That process can take as much as two years. The dried, uncooked ham is cut into very thin slices for serving.

Similarly, the *baccalà* is salted and dried. The fish would also do well on the ship as it was kept in open oak barrels. The fish could be maintained in that state for many months. Once ready to prepare, the fish is soaked in water for a few days making it ready to cook. The fish for the meal was cut into about four inch pieces. The fish was boiled. Garlic, tomatoes, olive oil, and potatoes were added to the fish. The finished dish was like a fish stew. The salting process gives the baccalà a sweet-like taste. Adding the other ingredients complemented the taste of the fish.

Spaghetti *aglio e olio*, a traditional Neapolitan dish, is a lighter fare compared to pasta with a rich tomato sauce. The dish was served throughout the year in Naples, and was also a staple during Lent. The spaghetti with the garlic and olive oil sauce was served along with a main course of fish, such as baccalà, in Naples. The passengers were delighted to have this dish on the menu today. Many third class passengers were from Naples, so this was a special treat for them. Even those on the ship from other regions knew the dish and would enjoy this pasta dish today.

Pasquale ate two full servings. He enjoyed the change of pace and for the first time on the voyage ate less of the bread and more of the main meal. Although wine was available for sale on the ship, the majority of third-class passengers had just enough money with them to buy train tickets and other necessities for the trips to their final destinations once the ship reached New York. On this day, it was announced that the captain would allow one glass of wine for each adult third class passenger compliments of the ship's owners. The wine was a welcome addition to the meal. Pasquale drank his glass of wine slowly. He wanted to savor every drop. He would look forward to a good glass of homemade Italian wine when he arrived at Maddalena's house. Like most

Italians, Pasquale enjoyed a glass of wine with his main meal each day. Pasquale made his own wine in Italy. He had a limited supply of red grapes that he would purchase from a local friend who had a small vineyard.

Pasquale made his own wine press. He had a steel screw forged with a perforated plate at the bottom. He attached the screw to a wooden framework that he made. The screw and frame were then attached to an old oak barrel that Pasquale acquired in exchange for a few leather hides that Luigi gave to Pasquale. The barrel had been cut in half making it the perfect size for a grape press.

Rotating a horizontal wooden handle that was made to work with the screw shaft and the framework, would push the plate downward into the barrel. The plate compressed the grapes and the liquid flowed from an opening on the front lower portion of the barrel. The barrel was raised to allow room for a pail that was placed partially under the barrel. The juice of the grapes would then fill a pail from the opening in the barrel. This process would be repeated until all the juice was extracted from the grapes.

Pasquale would remove the stems, crush the grapes and let them sit in the pressing barrel for about seven days. That would be the fermenting time for his wine. He stirred the mixture daily. He would then press the grapes multiple times to extract the juices. Pasquale would then fill one gallon jugs with the juice. He capped the jugs and placed them on their sides on racks in a cool shed that was located next to his home. The filled jugs remained on the racks for a minimum of thirty days before the wine was ready to drink. Pasquale would turn and rotate the jugs every two days to allow the sediment to settle. The wine usually aged well beyond thirty days as Pasquale would usually make about five gallons of wine at a time.

It was about two in the afternoon when the mid-day meal was finished. Pasquale was ready to finish his work on the statue. Taking a look at the piece to make sure he was satisfied with the detail, he did a few more minor touchups on the tunic and robe before returning to the areas that needed carving. He began working on the left arm. That work was less intense that what he endured shaping the right arm. It only took about one hour to complete that part. He then worked on the tablet before finishing the left hand and fingers. Doing the work on the tablet would allow the proper proportion in scale for the hand and fingers.

The tablet was a rectangle with a v-shaped cutout in each upper corner of the tablet. In about an hour and a half the tablet was done. The tedious work of carving the hand fingers was next. Pasquale shaved the wood for the backside of the hand that was the exposed portion holding the tablet. The hand was slightly bent at the wrist to allow the fingers to grasp the tablet and for the tablet to rest on the palm side of the hand. Another hour went by before the hand was completed.

The fingers were now being shaped using the peasant knife. Cutting the spaces between the fingers required just a little material being removed at a time. As the fingers began to look lifelike, Pasquale used the razor to remove wood from each finger and to carve the area of the fingernails. He finished the details of the fingers with the knife. He was pleased to see how well the fingers looked. He then completed the final detail work on the sleeve of the robe.

The work on the fingers took the most time. It was close to eight in the evening when Pasquale finished that work. Pasquale quickly went to the dining hall to fill his bowl with more of the special food of the day. He returned to his berth with the food so he could eat quickly and do the final touch up work on the statue. After eating, Pasquale did the last bit of detail work on the statue. With his peasant knife, he carved the date *Luglio* (July) 4, 1776 on the face of the tablet. Pasquale knew this date signified American independence. He also knew the day and year on the tablets on Lady Liberty were in roman numerals. So after carving the word July, he carefully carved *IV* for the fourth day and *MDCCLXXVI* for 1776.

The final work on the statue was to smooth some imperfections. Pasquale had saved some of the larger wood cutouts and used that material to rub over the finished piece. He did that to remove any additional rough spots. That treatment would make the wood statue very smooth. Pasquale wanted to give the statue a finished look instead of just the unfinished wood. He took out his tin of blackening polish and toned the polish color down using his camphor. The camphor was white. Pasquale mixed the two materials together until they had a light grey appearance. He took a piece of scrap leather strip and used that to cover the statue with the polish and camphor mix. Pasquale figured the camphor odor would dissipate in a short period of time.

He rubbed the statue with the mixture and blended it in to create highlighted areas and shadows. He used the inside portion of the leather to dull the finish that gave the completed statue a hue that resembled the patina look of the actual statue. One final check of all the details and Pasquale declared his work *finito* (finished). He marveled at the work. He was proud of the statue and how it looked. The proportions were good. The features pleased him. He was especially very satisfied with the tunic and robe. That part actually had a flowing characteristic that was typical of loose fitting garments. Pasquale placed the statue on the bed and stood back to look at it. As he gazed at the statue, he said *"quello che un capolavoro!"* (What a masterpiece!).

It was in perfect timing that the statue was finished because it was exactly midnight. It was now the final day of the journey. In less than ten hours, Pasquale's eyes would be fixed on Lady Liberty in the New York Harbor. Pasquale wondered if he would be able to sleep. His excitement of this last day on the ship made him both nervous and filled with joy. His dream of coming to America was a few hours away.

His mind raced with the thoughts of America. He was so anxious to see his sister and the new land. All the planning and preparations to make the trip to America had been worth the effort Pasquale thought. Pasquale held the statue again and said, *"Domini vi vedrà. Arriverò a New York. Tenere la torcia alta signora maestosa e benevenuto Pasquale vostra terra"* (Tomorrow I will see you. I will arrive in New York. Hold your torch high majestic lady and welcome Pasquale to your land). Pasquale put the statue in his bag and was prepared to go to sleep for the night.

Ten

Pasquale dozed on and off throughout the night. It was the twelfth of October, the day of arrival in New York. Pasquale began getting ready at six in the morning. The passengers would all be summoned to the main deck of the ship around nine o'clock. Pasquale was so excited he could not eat. He carefully packed his satchel and his canvas bag placing his masterpiece statue in the bag. He wrapped the statue in one of his shirts to make sure it would not be damaged. He polished his shoes. He put on his best pair of trousers, a white shirt, his leather vest, and his woolen flat cap. He wanted to look his best and also wanted to impress the inspection officers who would be processing the immigrants.

It was a beautiful October day. The sky was clear, the sun shining brightly, and the temperature was cool making this autumn day perfect for arrival at the harbor. The call to go to the main deck came at eight thirty. With so many third class passengers the process of going to the main deck would take more than thirty minutes. The crew members on the ship made sure that the passengers stayed orderly. Everyone was excited and relieved that they would no longer be confined to the third class compartment. Fresh air, sunshine, and a cool breeze would be a welcome change for the immigrants as they reached the main deck. Although it would be crowded on deck, that was a minor inconvenience compared to the isolation of the third class area.

At nine fifteen, all passengers on the ship were assembled on the main deck. This would be the only time first, second, and third-class passengers would be together. Once they arrived in New York, the first and second class passengers would be immediately processed. The inspection for this group was a quick process that took place on the ship. Only the third-class passengers would endure the entire inspection routine that included legal and medical checks. Although similar inspections were conducted when the third-class passengers boarded the ship, the entry into the United States required a quarantine-type inspection on the incoming ships. The ship did not actually dock at the harbor until all third-class passengers had been examined and released to a barge that took them to the United States entry point (Bateman-House, 2008).

At the mouth of the Hudson River the SS Aller approached New York harbor. It was just after ten o'clock on October 12, 1898. Twelve days after leaving Naples the journey was ending. The sun was glistening off the still waters of the Hudson. The magnificent Statue of Liberty came into view. The passengers were in awe of the statue. Pasquale exclaimed, *"La Vedo!"* (I see her!), *"mio Signora Liberta"* (my Lady Liberty). Then he said, *"sono arrivato!* (I have arrived!). As the ship moved closer to Lady Liberty, the passengers cheered in unison. The captain of the SS Aller always enjoyed this moment. Delivering passengers to America was not only his job, he had a personal sense of accomplishment knowing these people would have the chance of changing their lives.

Pasquale's joy, excitement, and amazement was shared by Angelo and his family. They all had tears of joy in their eyes. Pasquale cannot take his eyes off the the Statue of Liberty. Staring at the statue caused more tears flow. The stories of how the statue welcomes immigrants has become reality. Pasquale stretched his right arm and hand above his head imitating the raised arm and torch of the statue. Although it was far above his head he gazed into the statue's eyes. He sees the tablet and the crown with its seven spikes. He is amazed at the size of the statue. He becomes even more proud of his wooden statue knowing now that he truly captured the features of Lady Liberty. Pasquale lowered his arm, wipes his tears and smiled. He was ready to enter America.

The symbol of the Statue of Liberty was a significant moment for the immigrants. The Emma Lazarus sonnet, *The New Colosus*, penned in 1883 truly captures the arrival of the immigrants (The Statue of Liberty, 2016).

The New Colussus

Not like the brazen giant of Greek fame,

With conquering limbs astride from land to land;

Here at our sea-washed, sunset gates shall stand

A mighty woman with a torch, whose flame

Is the imprisoned lightning, and her name

Mother of Exiles. From her beacon-hand

Glows world-wide welcome; her mild eyes command

The air-bridges harbor that twin cities frame.

"Keep ancient lands, your storied pomp! cries she

With silent lips,"Give me your tired, your poor,

Your huddled masses yearning to be breathe free,

The wretched refuse of your teeming shore.

Send these, the homeless, tempest-tost to me.

I lift my lamp beside the golden door!"

The lamp is lifted, the huddled masses arrive, they are the tired and the poor. The exodus from the native land is complete and the arrival in the new world, America, is now, to breath free.

As the ship passes by the statue, Pasquale looks in the distance to the area of Ellis Island. There are no buildings on the site. Pasquale was unaware that Ellis Island immigrant station had a devastating fire that started just after midnight on June 14, 1897. The fire left most of the buildings in ruin and burned to the ground. Fortunately no one was injured and there was no loss of life from the fire. More than two hundred immigrants were rescued and trasported to Battery Park (The Museum of History, 2008).

Pasquale is troubled that Ellis Island is not where he will set foot on American soil. Fear came upon Pasquale as he was uncertain where he would be processed and what the procedure would be. He was also confused as to why the passengers were not informed that Ellis Island would not be the place where the immigrants would enter the United States. Pasquale wanted answers but knew that if he showed signs of agitation that could be reason to reject his approval to enter the country.

The SS Aller docks in the Hudson pier just off the southern tip of Manhattan at Battery Park, the alternate processing center, a temporary replacement for Ellis Island. As the ship passed Ellis Island the devastation and reconstruction that had begun was evident. Barge boats approach the SS Aller. First and second class passengers are allowed to disembark after a cursory on board medical inspection and are ready to be on their way to their destinations.

The third-class passengers are tightly packed on the barge boats and taken to the Barge office for the long ardous procedures for processing. The Barge office was crowded, noisy, and very uncomfortable. The immigrants are put into groups, each wearing a card identifying them by manifest number. There are about thirty immigrants per group (The Immigrant Journey, 2008). The card worn by each person also identifies what line they must stand in for processing. Waiting in the long lines is stressful.

There are interpreters assisting the immigrants with the process. Each person is inspected by a medical examiner in the presence of the interpreter. Some passengers have been detained and not admitted. Others are required to have an inquiry hearing to determine their fate. Those who fail inspection for medical reasons have their clothing marked with chalk with a letter of the alphabet identifying the ailment. These passengers would be deatained for a second medical inspection. One of the most feared inspections was the eye exam. Doctors would flip the eyelid of the person being examined. The doctor would use a finger or a button hook to conduct the exam. Physicians would look for a condition know as trachoma, a serious eye disease that could result in blindness, and in most severe cases, it could cause death. This condition could lead to deportation (The Immigrant Journey, 2008).

It was not uncommon for families to be separated due to individual medical or mental conditions. Even children were isolated from parents and could be deported and returned to their country of origin without their parents if they were older than twelve years of age. Younger children would be required to be accompanied by a parent. Families would have their dreams shattered as some would be allowed to stay and others would be returned to the port where they departed (The Immigrant Journey, 2008).

Those immigrants who successfully passed the medical examination were then subjected to a two-minute questioning by an immigration officer. The officer would have the ship's manifest with the data that was completed by the ship captain for each immigrant during the initial insepction upon boarding the ship. Although this process could take many hours of waiting in line, the majority of immigrants would pass the inspection and the questioning (The Immigrant Journey, 2008).

Pasquale had been waiting in line for the medical exam and was quite nervous. He knew he was healthy but he did not know what the doctor would think. He was not looking forward to the eye exam. He was watching other passengers as they had the exam and their anxiety was evident. Having a button hook flip your eyelid had to be extremely uncomfortable. Pasquale would try to remain positive and he hoped the doctor would use a finger instead of a button hook for his examination.

As Pasquale went through the various medical exams all was good so far. No chalk mark on his clothing. He was healthy and passed that portion of the exam. He also had no problem with the mental examination and was cleared for the remaining tests. It was now his turn for the eye exam. The physician looked into Pasquale's eyes. The doctor then propped open Pasquale's eyelids using only his fingers. The procedure lasted a few seconds and it was over. Pasquale breathed a sigh of relief. The interpreter who was at that station looked at Pasquale and said, *"benvenuto in America"* (welcome to America). Pasquale, again with tears in his eyes replied, *"grazie, io sono felice di essere qui"* (Thank you, I am happy to be here).

Pasquale then had the quick routine legal review. The officer asked questions that were on the ship's manifest. After checking Pasquale's manifest number to match the number on his card, the officer fired questions at Pasquale. The interpreter did a great job helping Pasquale understand each question. The process took less than two minutes. With a nod from the immigration officer Pasquale had successfully completed all his inspections. Pasquale now waited for Angelo and his family to complete the process. Pasquale and the Guiliani's would be traveling together to Gloversville. It was about another hour when the Guiliani's would be finished with their inspections. The entire process took about five hours. They all gathered and were ready for their next adventure, a train ride to Gloversville.

They made arrangements for their luggage trunks to reach their final destination. The next step was to exchange their Italian lira's for United States currency. Once completed, they made arrangements for the trip to Gloversville. It had been a long day already and Pasquale suggested that they get something to eat before buying the train tickets. Box lunches were available and that was good enough for a quick bite to eat. Pasquale and the

Guiliani's were anxious to get to the train station to get their tickets.

After eating, Pasquale and the Guiliani's made their way to the train station. It was after seven o'clock when they arrived at the train station. The crowds were large but with six ticket sellers they obtained their tickets in about thirty minutes. They would travel from New York City to Schenectady and then onto Gloversville. It would be another long journey, but this would be the final leg of the trip. The next train to Schenectady would not be leaving until eleven that night. They had some time to rest and relax before the train ride.

While they waited, Pasquale and Angelo talked about the voyage. The issues with the rough sea, weather, seasickness, and other factors that made most of the trip in third class uncomfortable were overcome by the excitement of arriving in America. New York City was such a large city. They were amazed at the number of people, the pace, and the buildings. The population in New York City at that time was over three million. They knew Gloversville was much smaller. They were overwhealmed by New York City and had no desire to settle there. Gloversville is where they had family. Pasquale was more excited now to see his sister, Maddalena and Angelo was ready to meet up with his cousin, Luciana. In just a few hours the family reunion would begin.

Before they knew it the conductor announced "all aboard!" Pasquale and Angelo did not understand what the conductor said but they knew by the announcement it was time to get on the train. The boarding began around ten thirty and was right on schedule. The distance from New York City to Schenectady was about one hundred and seventy miles. The trip, with a few scheduled stops, would take about five hours. The train from Schenectady to Gloversville would leave at nine in the morning. Pasquale figured he could get a few hours sleep on the way to Schenectady.

The train left the station and with a blast of the horn, the final leg of this trip was underway. The horn blast reminded Pasquale of the departure from Naples on the SS Aller with the steamship horn announcing its departure. The train in the same fashion just announced its departure. Pasquale felt relaxed. He was in America. His dream had become reality.

He missed Raphelia more than ever now. She would be so happy for him. Pasquale knew that it would be many months before they would be reunited. As he had done so many times before, he took out his rosary. This time, however, he did not recite the prayers. He kissed the crucifix on the rosary. He wrapped the rosary around his hand and held it tight. He closed his eyes and silently prayed. His only prayer that night was to thank God for the safe arrival in America and to keep Raphelia and his sons safe.

It was just after four in the morning and the train signaled its arrival in Schenectady. Pasquale had been sleeping soundly and awoke with the sound of the train's horn. He gathered his belongings and along with the nearly four hundred other passengers made his way to the depot. Pasquale and the Guiliani's sat on a bench in the depot to wait for the train to take them to Gloversville. With that train leaving at nine there would be plenty of time to get some food and to see some of the sights around the depot.

It is just before nine o'clock in the morning on Thursday, the thirteenth day of October in 1898. The sky is slightly overcast.The weather was cool but pleasant. The Fonda, Johnstown and Gloversville steam train was ready to board. The FJ&G Railroad had its beginnings in 1867 with the first trains running in 1870 (Parks, 2009). Pasquale and the Guiliani's along with a number of other non-immigrant passengers who are returning to Gloversville from Schenectady are boarding the train.

With everyone on board, the train slowly moves away from the depot. The thirty-mile trip would have two short stops: one in Amsterdam and the other in Johnstown. Pasquale's excitement is now about to burst. He cannot stop smiling. In less than two hours he would be reunited with Maddalena. He has so much to tell her. He has the carved masterpiece to present to her. He wonders what she will think when she sees his scruffy beard. He would tell her why he grew the beard and she will understand. Pasquale admitred the beautiful trees along the route. Everything was a so green in color. The majestic hills and the view of the Mohawk River was nothing like he had ever seen before. So different from Naples. Wide open spaces, a few farms in the distance, and the architecture of the buildings and houses have an immediate impact on Pasquale. He is really in America. This exquisite morning is Pasquale's *alba nouva*.

Eleven

The FJ&G has made its way to Gloversville. It is the end of the thirteen-day journey. At the train depot awaiting the arrival of Pasquale is his sister, Maddalena, and brother-in-law, Antonio. Angelo Guiliani's cousin, Luciana, and her husband, Vincenzo Leoni, are also there with two of their four children. The two older children stayed at home. The train comes to a complete stop at the station. Maddalena rushes toward the passenger cars looking frantically for her brother. Pasquale steps off the train and looks for his sister. As he walks toward the depot, he sees Maddalena. He runs to her, drops his satchel and carpet bag and embraces his sister. There are no words yet. They are both in tears. Pasquale looks into his sister's eyes and simply says, *"sono gui"* (I'm here). Maddalena replies, *"mi sei mancato tanto"* (I missed you so much). More silence and hugging. They did not want to let go of each other.

Antonio then hugs and kisses Pasquale and says, *"è cosi bello vedere il mio fratello"* (it is good to see you my brother). Pasquale is lost for words. He softly replies, *"si buona, io sono molto felice"* (yes good, I am so happy). Maddalena hugs Pasquale again and then looks at his face with surprise. She places both hands on his cheeks and says *"Maddona mia! Guardare il tuo volto. Si ha la barba"* (Mother of God! Look at your face. You have a beard).

Pasquale smiles and replies, *"si, e per una buona ragione"* (yes, and for a very good reason). Pasquale reaches into his carpet bag and pulls out the statue and the purse he made. Pasquale gives Maddalena the purse and places the statue in Maddalena's hands and tells her, *"ho fatto questo per vei"* (I made this for you). Maddalena gazes at the carved Statue of Liberty and is overtaken by tears of joy.

Maddalena looks at Pasquale and asks, *"quando hai fatto questo? È cosi bella"* (when do you do this? It is so beautiful). Pasquale told Maddalena that he made the statue during the voyage. He then told her that he used his peasant knife and his straight razor to carve the statue. He then said, *"per questo ho la barba. Il mio rasoio è stato il mio strumento per la scultura"* (that is why I have a beard. My razor was my sculpting tool). Maddalena laughed and rubbed Pasquale's beard saying, *"abbiamo bisogno di ottenere nuova rasoio"* (we will need to get you a new razor). Pasquale agreed. He was ready to shave the beard.

The group summoned a horse wagon driver to take them to Maddalena's home. The train station on West Fulton Street was only a few blocks away from the house. Angelo's cousin, Luciana, lives close to Maddalena. As they got on the wagon, Rosa handed Leonardo to Maddalena. She was so happy to see the baby. She held the child all the way to the house. Giovanni also sat next to

Maddalena. She was amazed how much he had grown. Maddalena told Rosa the last time she saw Giovanni he was two years old.

As they made their way on West Fulton Street toward Main Street, Pasquale was looking in all directions at the buildings. He asked what the small stream of water was that went under the street. Antonio told Pasquale that it was called the Cayadutta Creek. The creek is about seventy five miles long, runs through neighboring towns, and discharges into the Mohawk River (Mohawk River Basin). Pasquale kept looking at the buildings and commented on how many there were.

The horse and wagon turned left onto Main Street off of West Fulton known as the four corners. That intersection is where North and South Main Street and West and East Fulton Street bisect. North Main Street is lined on both sides with two to four-story brick and masonry buildings. Many of these buildings were constructed in the 1800s. The wide-paved street provides room for the trolley cars that cross paths with the horse drawn carriages and wagons.

The wagon turns left onto Spring Street where Maddalena lives. The home is a nice, two-story flat with wood lap siding. The house is painted white with light blue trim. Pasquale gathers his bags and takes his trunk from the wagon. He looks at the house, then to Maddalena and says, *"la vostra casa è bella"* (your home is lovely). Maddalena tells Pasquale, *"è la vostra casa ora anche"* (it is your home now also). Pasquale and Maddalena hug again. Maddalena invites everyone into the house. Once inside Pasquale takes in the smell of Italian food. Maddalena had prepared a feast for everyone. It was shortly after twelve noon and Pasquale was famished. He had waited for this moment for almost two weeks.

The inside of the house is nicely decorated. There are homemade doilies everywhere. Maddalena made all the doilies. She placed them on the dining room table, on the back portions of the sofa and chairs, on the shelves of the china cabinet, and on the stands that held her plants. The art of making lace with needles is a long standing tradition in Italy. Maddalena's mother, Maria, taught her how to make doilies before Maria died. Maddalena always puts the letters MD in the center of each doily as a tribute to her mother.

Antonio goes down to the cellar and returns with a gallon of homemade Italian wine. Maddalena heads to the kitchen to start bringing the food into the dining room. Antonio opens the jug of wine and pours a glass for everyone. Angelo and Rosa thank Maddalena and Antonio for their hospitality. With the glasses of wine poured, Antonio offers a toast. He raises his glass and says, *"la famiglia e gli amici, siamo tutti insieme per festeggiare un accogliente per l'America e per la vostra nuova casa – saluti!"* (family and friends we are all together celebrating a welcoming to America and to your new home – cheers!).

The others respond in unison, *"saluti!"*

Before Maddalena serves the meal, she places the Statue of Liberty in the center of the dining room table on a doily. Everyone is astonished with the detail of the statue. Pasquale tells the story of how he found the wood block and how he carved the piece over a period of days. He told them how he had to remember the details of the statue as he did not have a picture of the statue with him. Everyone agreed how well the statue resembled the Lady Liberty in the New York harbor. Angelo told them how much time Pasquale spent carving the statue and how he would spend many hours day and night to make sure the piece would be finished before the ship arrived in New York.

The meal is abundant. The homemade pasta *(cavitelli)*, sausages, mussels, *baccalà*, broccoli rabe *(broccoli di rapa)*, salami, prosciutto, fruit, and Italian bread fill the dining room table. With everyone gathered Pasquale offers a prayer of thanks for the reunion and for the wonderful food prepared by Maddalena. Plates are filled with the food and everyone is ready to eat and enjoy the fellowship. Pasquale sits next to his sister. Maddalena grabs Pasquale's hand and squeezes it tight. Pasquale looks at Maddalena and tells her that he misses Raphelia. Maddalena says she understands and that in a few short months Raphelia and the boys will be here and there will be another reunion at that time. Pasquale smiles and nods in agreement.

"*Il pasto è eccellente*" (the meal is excellent) says Angelo. Pasquale describes the meals served on the ship as mostly tasteless, except for a couple of meals. Pasquale also told Maddalena, Antonio, Luciana, and Vincenzo about the entertainment on the ship. The Cenerentola play that was performed by the actors in third class, and the opera pieces from the two talented individuals were outstanding. Maddalena told everyone that on their voyage the entertainment was lively but nothing like what Pasquale and the Guiliani's experienced. Pasquale also mentioned his venture to the upper deck. Antonio said that he and Maddalena spent their entire trip confined to third class. Luciana and Vincenzo recalled how extremely uncomfortable their voyage was four years ago. One thing they all agreed on how glad they were to be in America.

With everyone having a second helping of the feast the meal was almost over. Maddalena announced that she had made a special treat for everyone. She had prepared a *pastiera di grano* (wheat cake). Although this dessert was traditionally made during *Pasqua* (Easter) Maddalena knew this was one of Pasquale's favorite desserts and made it especially for him to celebrate his arrival in America. The *pastiera* is made with whole wheat that is soaked in water for at least one full day and mixed with ricotta cheese for the filling. The dessert also includes ingredients such as orange flower water, lemon zest, orange zest, eggs, and candied fruit known as glacé fruit, vanilla, and sugar. The mixture is placed in a pastry crust and finished with a lattice work pastry top. Once baked the *pastiera* is left to cool completely and dusted with powdered sugar before being served.

Pasquale was thrilled when Maddalena brought out the *pastiera*. The taste of the dessert was perfect. Even though he was full from the meal, there was no way he was going to refuse a piece of *pastiera*. Pasquale recalled that Raphelia made a *pastiera* every year for *Pasqua*. Everyone at the table thoroughly enjoyed the meal. It was after two in the afternoon when the meal was finished. The men excused themselves and went into the living room. Maddalena, Luciana, and Rosa put the remaining food away and cleaned the dishes. The men, completely full and relaxed, had another treat waiting for them.

Antonio opened a decorative wood box. Inside the box were handmade Italian cigars from Tuscany. Vincenzo, Pasquale, and Angelo took cigars as offered by Antonio. Pasquale would enjoy a cigar occasionally in Italy. Angelo and Vincenzo were both cigar smokers. The men lit their cigars and looked at each other with enjoyment. Pasquale said, *"ciò che un buon modo per concludere un ottimo pasto"* (what a good way to end a great meal). As they sat and smoked the cigars, Antonio took out his mandolin and played some music. Pasquale was completely relaxed now. He smoked his cigar, listened to the music, and thought about how good it was to finally be reunited with Maddalena.

Rosa, Luciana, and Maddalena joined the men. Little Giovanni sat by his mother. Rosa had put five-month old, Leonardo, in Maddalena's bedroom before the meal was served. He had been sleeping soundly since arriving at Maddalena's house. Luciana's two children took Giovanni outside to play after asking Rosa for permission. Pasquale and Angelo began asking questions about Gloversville. All they had seen of the city at this time was on the short trip from the train station to Maddalena's house. Angelo asked how many glove shops there were in the city. Antonio said he did not know for sure but guessed that there were at least one hundred shops. Vincenzo agreed and thought the number could even be higher. The city also had over two hundred stores, over thirty doctors and about the same number of lawyers all serving a population of about eighteen thousand residents (Menear, P., & Shiel, J., 2000).

Pasquale and Angelo figured with so many glove shops there should be no problem getting a job, especially for the two master glove cutters. Vincenzo said they could try the shop that was around the corner from his shoe repair shop. That shop employed about ten glove cutters. Business was so good there that the owner was looking for more glove cutters. Vincenzo said that having workers like Pasquale and Angelo would be a big help for the business. The work was plentiful and demanding. Vincenzo knew that the glove cutters there had been working about sixty hours per week and they still could not meet the quota. Vincenzo said he would see the owner and the foreman tomorrow and would let them know that Pasquale and Angelo were in Gloversville. Vincenzo's business was also very good. He was usually open six days a week. He closed his shop for the day to be with Pasquale and Angelo.

The conversation continued for a few more hours talking about everything from glove manufacturing to Antonio's masonry craft, Vincenzo's shoe repair business, and more about Gloversville and the neighboring communities. The children were all in the house now. Little Leonardo had woken up from a long and well needed nap. Pasquale was getting a little tired as this had been a long day but he was determined to spend much more time with everyone. Besides, since tomorrow was Friday, he could rest then and also over the weekend. He would begin his job search on Monday. He needed a few days to get acclimated to Gloversville.

About six that evening Maddalena again brought out the food. This time the portions everyone took were smaller. In true Italian tradition there was always a second meal served in the evening. Pasquale had a good helping of the *cavitelli*, some sausage and lots of the broccoli rabe, another of his favorite foods.

In Italy, he would place the broccoli rabe between two pieces of Italian bread and with a little olive oil. Pasquale and his sons loved eating broccoli rabe this way. Antonio filled everyone's glasses with the wine. Pasquale offered another toast. As he lifted his glass of wine he said, *"noi siamo I fortunate che sono stati autorizzati a venire in America. Dio benedica l'America e Dio ci bebedica"* (we are the lucky ones who have been allowed to come to America. God bless America and God bless us). Everyone responded with *"cento anni –saluti!"* (hundred years – cheers!) The response signifies a long life.

After another serving of the *pastiera* and a serving of Italian espresso, the evening was ending. Angelo and his family and Vincenzo and his family thanked Antonio and Maddalena again for the wonderful day. Angelo and Pasquale hugged as they said good night to each other. As Angelo and Rosa left to walk the few blocks to Vincenzo's and Luciana's home, they waved goodbye. The horse and wagon driver had delivered the Guiliani's luggage to Vincenzo's house earlier that day.

Pasquale, Maddalena, and Antonio went back into the house. They would spend another few hours talking about the voyage, Raphelia, and Pasquale's three sons. Maddalena offered Pasquale another piece of the *pastiera* which Pasquale gladly accepted. It was around eleven o'clock when Pasquale said he needed to get some sleep. He and Maddalena hugged tightly. She kissed him on his cheeks and rubbed his scruffy beard saying, tomorrow we will get the razor. Pasquale thanked his sister and told her how much he loved and missed her. He asked Antonio and Maddalena to pray with him before they went to bed. Together they recited a Hail Mary and the Lord's Prayer. Pasquale finished by praying for Raphelia and his sons. He asked for God's blessing on them, and for his sister and brother-in-law. Finally he thanked God again for his safe arrival in America. Together Pasquale, Maddalena, and Antonio made the sign of the cross saying, *"in nome del padre, figlio e spirito santo, Amen."*

Pasquale looked at Maddalena and says, *"buona notte mia sorella."* (good night my sister). Maddalena replies, *"buona notte mia fratello"* (good night my brother). Pasquale goes to his room and is so happy he will be sleeping in an actual bed for the first time since he left Italy. He had a wonderful time today with family and friends. He is glad however that the day is over. Exhausted and extremely tired from the long day, he lies down on the bed, stares at the ceiling, and within a few minutes is asleep.

Twelve

Pasquale did not wake up until nearly ten in the morning. Antonio left at six o'clock to go to work. Maddalena had already gone shopping. She bought a razor for Pasquale and she stopped at the Italian bakery to pick up some fresh *sfogliatella,* a Neapolitan pastry that has a flacky multi-layer crust filled with an orange-flavored ricotta cheese mixture. The rich pastry resembles a clam shell with the many layers of pastry dough when baked. Maddelana was going to surprise Pasquale with a nice breakfast that morning.

Maddalena returned home just as Pasquale was awakening. She asked him how he slept. Pasquale told her it was so nice to have a bed to sleep in and he felt good this morning. Maddalena told Pasquale that she was going to make him breakfast. Typically, breakfast in Italy was a quick biscuit or similar type food and a cup of espresso. That would not be the standard breakfast today. Maddalena placed the *sfogliatella* on a plate. She made some fresh espresso and told Pasquale that today's breakfast would also include *uova in buco con il pane* (eggs in a hole with bread). This dish was made by cutting a circular hole in the center of a piece of Italian bread. Butter is spread on both sides of the bread. The bread is placed in a hot frying pan and an egg was added where the hole in the bread was. The egg and bread are fried with a few slivers of red bell pepper placed on top of the egg. The bread and egg are then turned over in the pan just long enough to get a light toasting on the bread.

Maddalena finished cooking the dish and served it along with the *sfogliatella* and espresso to Pasquale. While Pasquale ate, Maddalena had a cup of espresso with him. Pasquale enjoyed the breakfast and ate two of the *sfogliatella*. They talked about how nice it was to have everyone together yesterday. Pasquale told Maddalena about the picture that was taken of him on the ship. He told her that when the picture came he wanted to send it to Raphelia. They talked about Pasquale's sons. Maddalena figured they must be real tall by now. She had not seen the boys in such a long time now. She told Pasquale how much she missed them. Pasquale responded that he missed them too and would work hard to bring Raphelia and his sons to America as soon as he could.

After finishing breakfast, Maddalena gave Pasquale his new razor. He was thankful for the razor and ready to shave the beard. Pasquale went to freshen up and shave. Maddalena, while finishing her espresso, picked up the statue and looked at all the fine details that Pasquale had carved. She marveled at her brother's talent with his knife. She treasured this gift from Pasquale. Maddalena decided she would make some special doilies for Pasquale and Raphelia. Maddalena was also anxious for Raphelia to come to America. She knew it would take time, but she was already anticipating Raphelia's arrival. When the time was right, Maddalena would suggest that sge, Pasquale and Antonio would go to New York when Raphelia's ship arrived. She thought that would please Pasquale.

Pasquale with his clean shaven face rejoined Maddalena. He felt much better without the beard. Although he kept his moustache, he vowed never to grow a beard again. Maddalena smiled as she looked at Pasquale and said, *"c' è il mio fratellino bello!"* (there's my handsome baby brother!). Pasquale blushed and looked at Maddalena and just smiled. Maddalena suggested that they go for a walk so Pasquale could see more of Gloversville. He agreed and was ready to see more of his new hometown.

The walk from Spring Street to downtown only takes a few minutes. Gloversville has a unique layout where many of the businesses such as the glove shops and tanneries are located in the residential areas. Walking toward Main Street, Pasquale and Maddalena passed two small glove shops. The smell of leather is evident. Pasquale stops for a minute to look at the buildings. The windows of one of the shops are partially open. He catches a glimpse of a glove cutter working. Maddalena tells Pasquale that there are more shops on the west part of Spring Street and virtually all areas of the city.

There were many buildings under construction in the downtown area. This is where Antonio was working as a mason. As Pasquale and Maddalena walked southward on North Main Street, they saw Antonio on a scaffold platform doing brickwork on a three-story structure. Antonio came down from the scaffold and greeted them. As he had to quickly get back to work, he hugged Maddalena and told Pasquale he would see him at home later today. Maddalena and Pasquale continued walking past the four corners down South Main Street. The trolleys were available but they both wanted to walk so Pasquale could stop and look at the stores along the way. They stopped at a grocery store to buy some fresh fruit and vegetables.

They turned west onto Cayadutta Street. There were more glove shops on that street. At the end of Cayadutta Street where it intersects with West Fulton Street, near the train station, was Vincenzo's shoe repair shop just around the corner from the glove shop Vincenzo told Pasquale about. That was also the same spot where Pasquale had asked about the creek yesterday on the way to Maddalena's house. Pasquale asked Maddalena why she did not tell him yesterday that it was Vincenzo's place. She simply replied, *"per sorprendere voi oggi"* (to surprise you today). *"Vedrai"* (you will see) she said.

They entered the shop and Vincenzo welcomed them. He then showed Pasquale all the tools and equipment used to repair and make shoes. He had Pasquale sit in a chair and told him to take off his shoes. Vincenzo then carefully measured Pasquale's feet. *"Che cosa è questo per?"* (what is this for?) asked Pasquale. Vincenzo replied, *"per le scarpe nuove che me accingo a fare per voi. Il mio regalo per voi"* (for your new shoes that I am going to make for you. My gift to you). Pasquale was visibly moved by the offer. He had not had a new pair of shoes in such a long time. Vincenzo asked, "when was the last time you had a new shoes." Pasquale replied, *"almeno cinque anni. Io continuo a inducendole riparato"* (at least five years. I just keep getting them repaired). Vincenzo said, *"allora è il momento un nuova paio"* (then it is time for a new pair). To which Pasquale replied, *"si, un nuovo paio per una alba nuova"* (yes, a new pair for a new dawn).

They left the shop and Pasquale told Maddalena that he wanted to send a letter to Raphelia telling her he had arrived in Gloversville and that all was well. There was a five cent store just up the street on North Main that sold stationery. After buying the writing materials, Pasquale and Maddalena stopped at an Italian bakery to buy some fresh Italian bread. They made their way back to Spring Street and home. It was about two in the afternoon. Maddalena made Pasquale a broccoli rabe sandwich. He also had some of the fresh fruit. Maddalena and Antonio has become accustomed to the American way of serving meals. Except for yesterday's feast and Sunday dinners, the weekly meals no longer included the typical Italian large mid-day meal. With Antonio's job the major meal of the day was served around six in the evening. This was a big change for Pasquale, but he was somewhat familiar with this as the meals on the ship were served in a similar fashion. He thought that it would take some time for Raphelia to get used to making larger evening meals. With all Italian traditions changing the meal patterns is a major modification.

Pasquale began writing his letter to Raphelia. As he finished the sandwich and fruit, Maddalena was busy in the kitchen preparing tonight's meal. She would make a hearty minestrone soup, *anguilla arrosto* (roasted eel), and *melanzane alla parmigian* (eggplant with cheese). Everything that Maddalena made reminded Pasquale of home in Italy. He especially loved *anguilla arrosto*. Raphelia would make similar dishes for the family. Raphelia and Maddalena would cook together quite frequently in Italy. Their cooking styles were similar. The handed down traditions from generation to generation were very evident in Italian cusine.

Pasquale continued writing. He told Raphelia how he missed her and that he would work hard to bring her to America soon. He also asked about his sons. He told Raphelia about the voyage and the statue. He explained the inspection process at the immigration office. He also told Raphelia about the Ellis Island fire and that she would be processed at the Barge Office in Manhattan when she arrived. He mentioned that Gloversville was a beautiful city and he knew she would like it here.

He decided he would wait until his next letter to Raphelia to tell her about how the American meal times were different that Italy. That way he could also share some other things about America after he had been in Gloversville for a while. The letter was about seven pages long at this point. Pasquale closed the letter saying, *"sei l'amore della mia vita. Sarmo di nuovo insime presto. Ti amo mia bella Raphelia"* (you are the love of my life. We will be together again soon. I love you my beautiful Raphelia).

Pasquale wanted to mail the letter right away. Maddalena helped him with the envelope. Antonio was just arriving home from work. Maddalena told Antonio about the letter. Antonio would accompany Pasquale to the post office to mail the letter. Instead of walking the entire way to the post office Antonio and Pasquale took the Main Street trolley south toward the post office that was located on the corner of South Main Street and Cayadutta Street. Pasquale enjoyed the trolley ride. He also thought it was so nice that people on the trolley greeted him and Antonio. One nice Italian gentleman asked Pasquale how long he had been in Gloversville. When Pasquale told the man he arrived yesterday the man said, *"benvenuto a Gloversville"* (welcome to Gloversville).

Pasquale replied, *"grazie. Sono felice di essere qui"* (thank you, I am glad to be here).

The man on the trolley introduced himself. *"Mi chiamo Emilio Savona"* (my name is Emilio Savona). Pasquale and Antonio introduced themselves as well. After exchanging some information about each other Emilio told Pasquale that there was a new Italian social and fellowship club just starting in Gloversville. He asked Pasquale and Antonio to come to the club to meet other Italians who live in Gloversville. Pasquale asked the name of the club. Emilio responded, *"Alba Nuova Cassetta"* (New Dawn Lodge). Pasquale looked at Emilio and asked, *"Alba Nuova?"* Emilio replied, *"si, Alba Nuova."* Pasquale looked at Emilio with surprise. Emilio asked Pasquale if there was anything wrong. Pasquale said no and that he liked the name of the lodge.

Antonio asked the location of the lodge and when the lodge was open. Emilio gave the address and replied that the lodge was open every evening from six to ten. He also told Pasquale and Antonio that a meeting would take place on Saturday at five in the afternoon. The purpose of that meeting was to invite Italian men to join the lodge. Emilio told the men that in addition to the forty or so members he expected about twenty other Italian men to be at the meeting. As Pasquale and Antonio got off the trolley they agreed that they would attend the meeting. They discussed having Angelo and Vincenzo to go with them.

After mailing the letter, Antonio and Pasquale decided to walk back to the house. During the walk home, Pasquale told Antonio that meeting Emilio was a miracle. Antonio asked why. Pasquale told Antonio of his conversation on the ship with other men about the atrocities that had taken place in New Orleans. Pasquale said he told his fellow shipmates that coming to America was fulfilling the dream of a new beginning, and the dawn of a new day, "*alba nuova.*" Antonio told Pasquale that this was a miracle, and the destiny of the new beginning has been confirmed by Emilio Savona. Antonio then said, "*andremo alla riunione do domani e si può comunicare a tutti il alba nuova*" (we will go to the meeting tomorrow and you can tell everyone about your new dawn).

The men shared their conversation with Emilio Savona with Maddalena when they got back home. Maddalena said this was no coincidence. This was destined to happen and that Pasquale's *alba nuova* was God's plan all along. Pasquale agreed. He knew that his immigration to America was God's plan for him all along. Maddalena had a shrine of the Virgin Mary in the corner of the dining room. She had Pasquale light a candle and together the three of them said a Hail Mary prayer.

After eating the wonderful dinner that evening, Pasquale and Antonio visited Angelo and Vincenzo and invited them to go to the meeting at the lodge tomorrow. Angelo and Vincenzo agreed to attend. Vincenzo said had planned to join the lodge and this was now a good time to do so. Pasquale told Vincenzo about the *alba nuova* conversation on the ship. Angelo recalled the conversation and how it inspired the men that night. Angelo was astonished that there was a lodge in Gloversville called *Alba Nuova*. Angelo said, *"Pasquale, il vostro sogno di una alba nuova e un nuova inizio è ora realtà"* (Pasquale, your dream of a new dawn and a new beginning is now reality).

The men had a glass of wine to celebrate the occasion. Vincenzo raised his glass and said, *"una alba nuova, di un nuova inizio!"* (a new dawn, a new beginning). Pasquale, Antonio, and Angelo all responded, *"una alba nuova, di un nuova inizio! Saluti!"* Rosa and Luciana were also very pleased about the good fortune of Pasquale and Antonio meeting Emilio. They were excited for the men and thought it was excellent that they would join the lodge and be in fellowship with other Italian men in Gloversville.

Luciana said, *"amicizia e fratellanza"* (friendship and brotherhood), *"fedeli al nostra patriminio Italiano"* (true to our Italian heritage). Pasquale looked at everyone, *amici, fratelli, sorelle, famiglia"*(friends, brothers, sisters, family) *"questo è ciò che siamo"* (this is who we are). Another final *"saluti"* is shouted by everyone. After kisses and hugs and wishing everyone a good night, Pasquale and Antonio left the others and returned home.

Maddalena was happy to hear that Vincenzo and Angelo will go to the lodge with Pasquale and Antonio. She had hoped that when Pasquale arrived the he and Antonio would have their friendship grow. They were close friends and like brothers in Italy. Having the family back together made Maddalena very happy. She had been waiting for this for a long time. When Raphelia and the boys arrive the family will be complete and all together again. She looked at Pasquale and says, *"la famiglia"* (the family). Pasquale kisses her hand and replies, *"la nostra famiglia"* (our family). Maddalena, Pasquale, and Antonio finish the night with a cup of espresso and *sfogliatella.*

Thirteen

It was early Saturday afternoon. Pasquale was a little nervous about sharing his story about his *alba nuova* vision with the others at the lodge. He wondered if they would even let him speak. The lodge was started by and for Italian immigrants. Surely they all must have their own stories about their dreams of coming to America. He was curious to find out how many of them were glove cutters. With more than one hundred glove shops in the area, he assumed that there would be a few who were employed in the industry. He also wondered how many came from Naples. He had so many questions.

Angelo and Vincenzo came to the house around four in the afternoon. The men left to go to the meeting about fifteen minutes later. They walked to the meeting location. The lodge was located at 24 South Main Street on the second floor. The building was constructed in 1880. The structure was an Italianate design. The features of the façade included cornices that were bracketed and projected outward from the building. The exterior design also featured dentils, arches, and round lintels, decorated horizontal bands known as friezes, and ornate projections under the cornices called modillions (Bryer, L. & May, C., 2009).

Arriving at the building, they walked up the stairs to the second floor. The room was decorated with the Italian flag and an American flag. There was a banner on the wall with the words, *Alba Nuova Cassetta* and *Benevenuti a tutti* (New Dawn Lodge – Welcome All). The room had seven rows of tables and chairs with seating for about seventy or so. There was another table with gallon jugs of homemade Italian wine and trays filled with salami, cheeses, Italian bread, and Italian cookies.

Pasquale, Angelo, Antonio, and Vincenzo had arrived a little early but there was already a group of men there. As they entered the room Emilio saw them and came over to greet them. He welcomed the men to the lodge and introduced them to some of the others who were there. Pasquale was hesitant to ask about sharing his story. He decided that he would talk to Emilio about that a litte later. Emilo told the men to get a glass of wine and some food and cookies.

More men began arriving. It was just before five and there were almost fifty men at the meeting. Emilio went to the front of the room and welcomed everyone to the meeting. He began the meeting by having everyone say *"viva l'Italia!"* He then proceeded to intoduce himself and asked everyone in the room to do the same. One by one each stood and told their names.

Emilio explained that the lodge had been started by a group of Italian men in Glovesville about a year ago. He said the purpose of the lodge was to bring together Italian men in the area for fellowship, brotherhood, and social activities. He also mentioned that *Alba Nuova* was established to help others who had recently immigrated from Italy in their transition to living in America. Emilio says, *"siamo tutti figli della patria che ha voluto un nuova injzio in America. Siamo qui per aiutare i nostri fratelli"* (we are all sons of the native land who desired a new beginning in America. We are all here to help our brothers).

A few other current members then spoke about joining the lodge and what lodge membership meant to them. It was evident by the various testimonies that the lodge had already made a difference for the men. Some men talked about the social activities that included playing Italian card games, bocce, family gatherings for banquets, and hosting Italian dance nights.

Emilio, who served as *Grande Venerable*, a title of respect and reverance for serving in a high office, then asked those who were attending for the first time to come up to the front of the room. There were about fifteen men, including Pasquale and the others who went to the front of the room. Emilio asked each person to tell about themselves and their story of coming to America. Each man took his turn. Some spoke for a minute or so and a few other spoke a little longer.

The last person to speak was Pasquale. He told his story and his vison of *alba nouva*. The room was silent as Pasquale mentioned the New Orleans incident and the statement he made to the others on the SS Aller about a new beginning and a new dawn in America. Pasquale mentioned meeting Emilio on the trolley and how when he heard Emilio say the name of the lodge he felt that his destiny had been fulfilled. Pasquale said he never imagined that when he came to Gloversville there would be a club called *Alba Nuova*. Pasquale said that he was ready to become a member of the lodge and continue on his path of a new beginning.

When all of the other men who were new to the meeting all agreed to join the lodge, the members in attendance stood and applauded. Emilio had each person raise their right hand and pledge to abide by the rules of the order, to uphold fraternity and brotherhood, to respect each other, to help those in need, and to agree to be good citizens in America. Upon completing the oath, Emilio shook each of the men's hands and in Italian and English he welcomed them as members of *Alba Nuova*. Emilio came to America five years ago. He learned English while attending the University of Florence. Everyone congratulated and welcomed the new members.

The lodge meeting was then called to order by Emilio. The meeting included reports on various activites, the financial status of the lodge, status of lodge membership dues that were established at five dollars per year per member, and recommendations for new social activities. The meeting lasted about thirty minutes. After the meeting the men enjoyed another glass of wine and some cookies. Many of the members had gathered around Pasquale. They asked him a number of questions about his *alba nuova* vision. They shared similar dreams about starting life over in America. A few men said they missed Italy but know their future is in America.

Pasquale asked some of the others what work they did. There were about ten others who were also glove cutters. They told Pasquale and Angelo that jobs were available in their shops. Some others shared that they worked as grocers, carpenters, leather tanners, painters, masons, road workers, tailors, and other skilled trades. It was apparent that the majority of Italian immigrants in Gloversville were skilled workers. In contrast, Pasquale found that many of the immigrants on the SS Aller who had planned on settling in New York City were laborers.

After the meeting Pasquale and the other men were anxious to go home and tell the women about the meeting and of joining the lodge. They were also ready for something to eat. Maddalena, Rosa, and Luciana made pasta with mussels for the meal. The men talked about the lodge meeting and Pasquale's heartfelt story of his *alba nuova*. The women were happy for the men and said they also looked forward to the dance nights and banquets. After the meal that night the men played cards, the children played a game similar to hide and seek, while the women talked, played with little Leonardo, and did crocheting.

At the end of the evening and just before going to bed, Maddalena told Pasquale that they would all be going to Mass together tomorrow at Our Lady of Mount Carmel. The Italian services for Our Lady of Mount Carmel were held at eleven in the morning at Saint Mary's Roman Catholic Church on Fremont Street. The original Saint Mary's Church was located on West Pine Street. The new church at the Fremont Street site was built in 1890 (Church of the Holy Spirit, 2012).

Pasquale was looking forward to attending Mass. He had not been to church since leaving Italy. Pasquale liked going to Mass and taking communion. He shared with Maddalena that he was concerned about communion because he had not gone to confession. Maddalena assured him that he could take communion and he could say his prayers tonight to prepare for communion tomorrow. Pasquale hesitated but agreed.

Pasquale was fairly rigid with the catholic rituals. He became an altar boy in Italy when he was eleven and served until he was sixteen. As an altar boy he had church doctrine instilled in him. Going against doctrine was sacrilegious to him. He would make an exception this time for communion. He served as an altar boy mainly at his local parish but would also serve at other churches in the village. He enjoyed being an altar boy and was curious to see the altar boys at Mass tomorrow.

As Pasquale walked into Saint Mary's and dipped his fingers into the holy water urn to bless him with the sign of the cross, his eyes are fixed on the altar and the ornate architecture in the sanctuary. The organist was playing music for the nearly two hundred or so Italians there for the Mass. The service would begin in about fifteen minutes. The altar boys entered the sanctuary and lit the candles at the altar. The black cassocks and white surplices worn by the altar boys are similar to the ones Pasquale wore when he was an altar boy. There were two smaller altars on either side of the main altar. Pasquale and Maddalena went to one of the small altar's that had a statue of the Virgin Mary. There are rows of candles in front of the altar. Pasquale and Maddalena each light a candle and kneel at the altar and say a prayer before returning to their pew.

Just before Mass begins a soprano, accompanied by the organist and the choir, sings *Ave Maria*. Pasquale is surprised it is being played and is visibly moved by the song. He grabs Maddalena's hand and tells her that *Ave Maria* was their mother's favorite song. Maddalena acknowledges and tells Pasquale that *Ave Maria* is sung before Mass here every Sunday. The song is beautiful and the soprano's voice is angelic. The church acoustics are perfect for the organist and the singers.

Father Alphonso DiGennaro is the celebrant conducting the Mass. The altar boys ring a bell and with the priest they enter the sanctuary for the Mass. The congregation stands as the priest enters. The Mass is performed in the traditional Latin. The priest makes the sign of the cross along with the altar boys and the Mass commences. The priest stands at the foot of the altar with the altar boys kneeling on each side of the priest. As the priest begins the prayers and the altar boys make their Latin responses, Pasquale silently says each of the altar boy responses in Latin. He remembers all the prayers and responses for the altar boys and all the church Latin for the Mass.

This is a High Mass meaning that after the initial prayers most of the service and the responses are sung by the priest with the choir and the congregation responding. About halfway through the Mass, Father DiGennero proceeds to the pulpit to deliver his sermon in Italian. His message today was from Leviticus 19:33-34 – [33] *"when a stranger sojourns with you in your land, you shall not do him wrong. [34]The stranger who sojourns with you shall be to you as the native among you, and you shall love him as yourself; for you were strangers in the land of Egypt: I am the Lord your God."*

The sermon was a message of encouragement to the Italian community in Gloversville. The priest mentions the atrocities and discrimination that had taken place against Italian immigrants and other ethnic groups who chose to come to America. Father DiGennaro came to America from Italy in 1892. He witnessed discrimination against Italians when he served as a parish priest in New York City. The discrimination was a result of American workers objecting to Italians taking laborer jobs. American workers felt that the Italians agreed to take lower wages for menial jobs just to have work. Italians had to take what was available to them for survival.

Father DiGennaro told the congregation to never forget their heritage and to always treat others respectfully no matter how others treated them. He then invited recent immigrants to Gloversville to stand and be recognized. Pasquale and Angelo along with about fifteen others in attendance stood up. Father DiGennaro welcomed them to America, to Gloversville, and to Our Lady of Mount Carmel. He then raised his right hand and gave the immigrants a blessing making the symbol of the sign of the cross for the blessing. Father DiGennaro prayed, *"il Signore vi benedica e le vostre famiglie e la pace sia si di voi nella vostra casa qui a Gloversville, Amen"* (may the Lord bless you and your families and may peace be upon you and in your new home here in Gloversville, Amen).

After the sermon was complete, the communion phase of the Mass began. The priest took the Eucharist and the Chalice with wine performing the ceremony in preparation for offering

Holy Communion to the congregation. The congregation assembled at the kneelers at the altar. Father DiGennaro gave communion to each of the recipients. Everyone in the church took communion that day. Upon receiving communion Pasquale returned to the pew and knelt to say a prayer. He thanked God for the day, for his family, and for the welcome he had received coming to Gloversville.

Vincenzo and Luciana were hosting the Sunday meal today. It was around twelve noon when Mass was over. Pasquale and the others walked to Vincenzo's house. The church location on Fremont Street is about a twenty minute walk to Vincenzo's home that was on Kent Street. Earlier that morning Luciana had prepared *pasta e fagioli* (pasta and beans), *braciole* (rolled beef stuffed with raisins, pine nuts and Italian parsley), *gattò* (a Neapolitan potato cake), and a endive salad. The meal as always included Italian bread and homemade wine. The *gattò* and *braciole* were in the oven. The food was ready to be served shortly after two o'clock.

This would be a typical Sunday Italian gathering with the afternoon meal being served first and then around seven that evening the food would be presented again. There was never a lack of food in Italian households. Being together to share meals with family and friends especially on Sunday's after church is an Italian tradition, just like Pasquale and Angelo and their families experienced in Italy. Pasquale was pleased that the tradition had been maintained.

After the meal, the men went to the back yard to play *bocce*, a centuries-old game that became a traditional Italian game hundreds of years ago. The game is played on grass court about thirteen feet wide and ninety feet long. The game begins by tossing and rolling a small white ball called the *pallino* down the court. Then players on two teams toss and roll their four larger balls each one in turn, down the court to try and stop that ball close to the *pallino*. The ball that comes closest to the *pallino* at the end of the round receives a point. The *pallino* at times is struck by the larger ball changing the dynamics of the game and requires a strategy for obtaining points. The game continues until one team has twelve points winning the match.

The men play bocce for about three hours. After the game some neighbors stop by to meet Pasquale and Angelo. One of the neighbors, Gaetano Picarelli, was at the *Alba Nuova* meeting last night. Gaetano greets Pasquale and Angelo and tells Pasquale how much he enjoyed what Pasquale said at the meeting. Antonio brings some wine for everyone. Vincenzo tells the neighbors about Pasquale's statue. Everyone wants to see the statue. Antonio goes in the house to get the statue. Pasquale briefly describes how he made the statue. Everyone is amazed how the statue looks and congratulates Pasquale on the great job.

With the darkness of the evening, the neighbors head home. Pasquale and the families go inside to have their evening meal. These long days of being with family and friends help to keep Pasquale in a positive mood. He thinks about Raphelia all the time but the fellowship and companionship with others keeps his morale up and takes his mind off of his loneliness. Pasquale thinks about tomorrow and looking for work. He is feeling good about his chances of getting a job. He talks to Angelo about the plan for looking for work. They agree that they will begin the job search at seven in the morning. They have a list of glove shops to go to that Vincenzo had prepared for them.

Pasquale wants to get a good night's sleep but is excited about going to work and he is not sure he will actually get a lot of sleep. Maddalena tells her brother that he will sleep well and that she will make breakfast in the morning. Antonio leaves early for work as well and Maddalena always makes sure Antonio has something to eat before leaving. Maddalena and Antonio are usually up around five thirty in the morning. Maddalena will wake Pasquale around that time as well. Pasquale was pleased about the great day he had. He enjoyed going to Mass. Although he was hesitant about taking communion, once he had done so, he felt blessed. He liked being with everyone today. The friendship, companionship, food, fun, and just being with his sister made Pasquale feel wonderful.

He thinks about Raphelia all the time and knows she will enjoy being with everyone when she is in Gloversville. Raphelia has a great personality and Pasquale knows she will adapt well to the people and to Gloversville. The others will also help with Raphelia's transition to America. Since each of them had been through the process and the uneasy first few months in America, they would be able to share their experiences with Raphelia. Pasquale knew that there would be a lot of help for Raphelia and for his sons. Pasquale's short time in Gloversville was much easier because of the help from everyone. Although being in a strange land is stressful, it was easier being surrounded by family and friends. Each day for Pasquale has been better than the day before since he arrived in Gloversville. Tomorrow will be a great day, he exclaims to himself, as he goes to bed for the night.

Fourteen

The next morning, Pasquale and Angelo take the list of glove shops and begin their job search. There are four shops that have been recommended to them. They arrive at the first shop at seven thirty. That shop, located on Forest Street, employs about forty people. After waiting for about thirty minutes, they are greeted by the owner who does not speak Italian. One of the glove cutters is Italian who serves as the interpreter for them. The glove cutter tells them that the owner wants them to demonstrate their glove cutting. Pasquale and Angelo cut the glove patterns from two hides. The owner looks at their work and thanks them for coming in to apply for a job. Pasquale and Angelo are not quite sure what to think about the owner's reaction but thank him for allowing them to demonstrate their work.

The next shop they go to is the Shipman Glove Company on Cayadutta Street. This is the one located near Vincenzo's shoe shop. Pasquale and Angelo are welcomed by the office clerk. They are given a tour of the small shop by the foreman, an Italian who has worked at this shop for five years. The foreman then introduces Pasquale and Angelo to the owner. They are asked to show the owner how they cut gloves. After seeing the first gloves being cut the owner has them work for one hour to see how many gloves they can produce and to examine the quality of their work. The foreman watches the men for the entire hour, checking the quality of the glove patterns as Pasquale and Angelo each finish cutting from each hide.

The foreman is impressed with their work and is especially impressed on how Pasquale stretches the hides to minimize the amount of scrap material left over and to produce higher quality product. Pasquale works fast but steady. He feels good about cutting gloves again. Working with the shears and doing precise cuts was the standard for Pasquale. When the hour was over Pasquale and Angelo had together produced one dozen pairs of glove pattern cuts which would make six pairs of gloves. The quota for this shop was enough cuts to produce two pairs of gloves per glove cutter. Angelo and Pasquale exceeded the quota.

The foreman had the owner check the quality of the work, how much scrap material that was left over, and the total number of patterns cut. The owner immediately offered Pasquale and Angelo jobs. He said he would pay them fourteen dollars per week. The work hours were seven in the morning to five thirty in the afternoon Monday through Friday and four hours on Saturday for a fifty-four hour workweek which is two hours per week less than Pasquale expected. The shop had been working sixty hour weeks and was still short of the quotas. The owner tells the foreman that he anticipates reducing all cutters to fifty-four hours with the addition of Pasquale and Angelo. With Pasquale and Angelo as the two new well experienced cutters, the owner believes quotas will be achieved with all cutters working the fifty-four hour weeks.

The amount of wages offered was more than Pasquale and Angelo thought they would be paid. In order to make that amount, they would have to meet the quotas. If they were short, the amount of pay would be reduced. They both agreed to accept the job. The job search took less than three hours and they were now employed. The owner told them to be at work the next day. The foreman congratulated them and told them they will like working at this shop. Pasquale and Angelo are overjoyed. They thank the foreman and the owner for the opportunity.

Pasquale and Angelo immediately go to Vincenzo's shop to tell him the good news. Vincenzo is happy for them and tells them he figured they would accept jobs at Shipman's. The reputation of that shop was excellent and the owner treated all his employees with the greatest of respect. Vincenzo tells Pasquale that his new shoes will be ready tomorrow just in time for the new job. Vincenzo also gives new aprons to Pasquale and Angelo for their new jobs. A new apron and new shoes, Pasquale is thankful.

Maddalena and Rosa are elated that Pasquale and Angelo got jobs and will be working together. Maddalena said she will make some *zeppole,* a deep fried Italian donut that is usually rolled in sugar. Maddalena will also fill the *zeppole* with a rich pastry cream made with ricotta cheese. Maddalena asked Pasquale if he had enough clothes for work. Pasquale said he did but that he would like to have some new ties. In Italy glove cutters wore ties to work every day. Pasquale and Angelo were glad to see the cutters at Shipman wearing ties. Pasquale thought it was important to dress professionally. He also felt that representing the industry and the trade showed in how you dressed for work. The glove cutters felt that dressing well reflected on the quality of gloves they produced.

Pasquale and Angelo went back downtown to shop for some new ties. There are a couple of clothing stores on North Main Street. They spend some time in each store and then decide to buy the ties in the second store. The ties in that store were closer to the style that both Pasquale and Angelo liked. They each buy three ties. Angelo also bought a new shirt. They both feel they are now set for work tomorrow.

That evening after dinner and some *zeppole* for dessert, Antonio opens a bottle of champagne that he had been storing in the cellar for a special occasion. Angelo takes his glass and raising it up says, *"nuovo lavora, nuova vita, nuovo inizio"* (new job, new life, new beginning). To which Pasquale replies, *"alba nuova!"* The celebration for Pasquale and Angelo includes a surprise from Vincenzo. He presents Pasquale's new shoes to him. Pasquale tries on the shoes and comments on how well they fit and how comfortable they are. Vincenzo's craftsmanship is evident in the quality of the shoes. Vincenzo's business has quickly gained a reputation in town for being more than a shoe repair shop. He has been making custom handmade shoes for many clients in the city including for some prominent businessmen.

Vincenzo then presents Angelo with a new set of glove cutting tools. Angelo is stunned. His tools are good but well worn. Luciana knew that Angelo liked his old tools and had used them for many years. Angelo appreciated his new tools. He says his old tools did their job well but for the new job in America, new tools will even do a better job. A glove cutter prides himself on the quality of his tools to perform quality work. After many years of using older tools as well, Pasquale invested in a set of new tools about a year ago. Both men express their gratitude for the gifts.

Tomorrow will be a busy day. After the long voyage, keeping very active the first few days in Gloversville, and becoming members of the lodge, it is time to get to the real reason for coming to America, a new job with new opportunities. Pasquale's mission from here on will be to save money to bring Raphelia and his sons to Gloversville. With fourteen dollars per week, more than expected, Pasquale figures he could save enough in less than four months to bring his family here. He also knows that Raphelia's family will provide some of the money for the trip.

Pasquale likes to keep very busy and along with the new job his plans include becoming active in the church, attending lodge functions, looking for a new home for when Raphelia arrives, resuming his hobbies of making leather belts and wooden toys for children, and volunteering to help others in need. Pasquale's sons are also very talented. Francesco seems to have a mind for business innovation proving himself to his employer. Working for the butcher, Francesco designed and built a storage area in the shop that featured a double wall with a cavity space between the walls. Similar designs had been used in Great Britain. Francesco's self-insulated, double wall area would keep meet cooler as ice blocks would last longer and provide a cost savings for the butcher.

Eduardo's passion was learning different languages. He was already fluent in Italian, French, and Spanish, and he was learning English. Young Arturo had a strong interest in mathematics. Arturo could already solve some complex math problems. Pasquale was very proud of his sons. The formal education system in Italy at that time was somewhat limited but a focus on science and mathematics was a part of every curriculum.

Tuesday morning had arrived. Pasquale wrote a note on a piece of paper that he begins work in America on October 18, 1898. He places the paper in his satchel. Pasquale and Angelo walk to work. They arrive about fifteen minutes early. They are welcomed by the foreman, Marco Carbone. He takes them through the entire shop. He brings them to the work tables. He explains the paperwork that tracks the hides and the glove orders. He also teaches them the company method for chalk marking the cutout glove patterns so the women sewing the gloves can place the proper pieces together when making the actual gloves.

After about an hour of training, Pasquale and Angelo are introduced to the other cutters. With Pasquale and Angelo, there are now twelve glove cutters. Pasquale and Angelo are taken to their work table and begin cutting gloves. Shortly after, Mr. Shipman comes to the work area and again welcomes the men to the company. He tells them he is glad to have such talented glove cutters in his business. With Marco interpreting Pasquale and Angelo again thank Mr. Shipman for hiring them. The owner tells them they will like working here. That night Pasquale would write to Raphelia and tell her about the job.

Angelo's new tools are just right for the job. Pasquale is working at his steady pace. Pasquale has a unique style of glove cutting. He moves and shifts his body and feet in a manner that almost looks like he is dancing. His hands and arms move fluidly. Every movement is done with a purpose. He is constantly surveying each hide as he lays out the patterns for marking the skin before cutting the gloves shapes. The meticulous stretching of each skin to ensure the best quality is performed like a conductor leading an orchestra. Pasquale is so focused on his work he appears unaware of his actions. However, Pasquale is consistently aware of his every movement and what he needs to do so he does not waste time. Meeting and exceeding quotas while producing top quality work is what Luigi taught Pasquale. That lesson has been Pasquale's guiding principal for all these years.

Pasquale and Angelo now have to get used to the American work schedules. There is no mid-day break for the main meal. They have prepared themselves for this from the time they boarded the ship. Around noon the crew takes a lunch break. Maddalena had prepared some salami sandwiches for Pasquale. The company provided coffee for the workers. Pasquale and Angelo get a chance to talk to the other cutters. They all tell a little about themselves. One cutter who had been there about eight months said he recently brought his family over from Italy. He wished Pasquale well in bringing his family over sooner and told Angelo it was nice that he had his family with him.

The day seemed to go by quickly. Before Pasquale knew it the time to go home for the day had arrived. Marco asked Pasquale and Angelo how they felt about the day. They were both positive and said it was a good day. They both had met the quota for the day. Pasquale had some troublesome hides but was able to work through the process without losing significant time. Sometimes a hide is a little stiff and needs some extra handling to stretch the skin properly for the glove patterns. Other hides have visible flaws that require taking time for the best layout to limit the waste of material. Pasquale was an expert at that but also wanted to make sure on this first day that he had no product returned for rework. That was successful and he had no cutouts returned to him by the checkers for rework.

Pasquale and Angelo were a little tired but they both looked forward to returning tomorrow for another day at work. When they left the shop it was getting dark outside. The October weather was getting quite cool. Pasquale had heard that winter in Gloversville could be harsh at times. He knew he would need some warm clothes for the winter weather. He was already calculating his finances. He was thankful that Antonio and Maddalena would allow him to stay in their home. That would help financially and allow him to save more money for Raphelia's trip to America and to have some money to purchase a winter coat.

The conversation at dinner that night included Pasquale's day at work and Antonio's job where the majority of the brickwork on the new building was done. Antonio said that two new buildings were under construction and he would be doing masonry work on those as well. Maddalena said she was going to start sewing gloves at home again next week. She stopped for a while to prepare for Pasquale's arrival. The glove company she worked for had asked her to resume working. She also sewed gloves in Italy. When she first started she sewed by hand. When sewing machines were introduced she transitioned to that method of sewing gloves. Like Pasquale she was one of the best in her trade.

The women were paid much less than the men in the industry. Maddalena would earn between three to five dollars per week in Gloversville. The work week was somewhat shorter. Working from home the women set their own hours but still had to meet their quotas. The shop worker would come to the home every other day to pick up finished work, deliver the next workload, and to bring back finished gloves that needed rework by the sewing machine operators. The rework was not compensated. So, if there was significant rework, the women would have to work additional hours for no pay and still work to meet the quota for the new work.

Antonio and Pasquale were happy for Maddalena's choice to return to sewing gloves. She enjoyed the work. The extra money would also come in handy. Maddalena and Antonio had their sights set on buying a home. They had found one they liked but it would be a few months at the earliest when they could actually offer to buy the home. Vincenzo and Luciana had recently purchased the home they live in. Many new homes were being built in Gloversville during this time. The need for housing was great. The population of the city was expected to continue to grow with the glove industry thriving.

Pasquale was ready to call it a day. He was very glad to be working again. He would need to get in a routine to make sure he was properly rested and ready for work each day. With a fifty-four hour workweek he would need all his energy to keep pace with the job and would also need the relaxation times. Spending time at the lodge, enjoying time with family, and going to church was relaxing and comforting for Pasquale. He was thankful to have a job at what seemed to be a good company. He was also beginning to really like Gloversville and the people. The transition from Italy to America has been a little easier than he thought it would be and his *alba nuova* dream is being fulfilled.

Fifteen

Pasquale has been working at Shipman's for about two months. The job experience has been good. He enjoys the work, his co-workers, and the company. The glove cutters have all increased production and have achieved the quotas working fifty-four hours per week. They have maintained a high level of quality as well. Marco tells the cutters that Mr. Shipman is very pleased with the production and quality of the work. Marco also tells them the owner will have a surprise for all his employees next week. Pasquale is a little nervous about what it might be. Marco settles Pasquale's anxiety by telling him there will be a gift from the owner. Pasquale is humbled by the thought of the owner of the company doing something like that for his employees.

Pasquale has become more accustomed to the the job and to the lifestyle in Gloversville. The routines have become almost normal, especially the transition of when meals are eaten. Long workdays are tiresome but rewarding. The owner shows great respect for his employees each day. The glove company even allowed the employees to take Thanksgiving Day off with pay. As this was a traditional American holiday Pasquale was very appreciative that the Italian employees were treated like all other employees including being paid for the day. Vincenzo had told

Pasquale that was the way the company was managed and that was how the owner treated employees. Pasquale now had experienced that first hand.

The streets of Gloversville are decorated for the Christmas season. The ornate appearance of downtown Main Street is so festive. A large decorated Christmas tree was displayed at the four corners. The decorations reminded Pasquale of Christmas in Naples. It had been snowing in Gloversville over the past few days. The snow made the city look even more festive. It was also very cold. The temperatures ranged between twenty degrees and thirty degrees during the day and as low as zero degrees at night. Pasquale was having a hard time with the cold. The temperatures in Naples this time of the year were not nearly as cold. Pasquale had bought a warm winter coat and had some new gloves. He always wore his flat cap as well. He had a wool scarf that Antonio had given him. He knew it would take time to get used to the winter weather.

The Italian Christmas holiday season begins eight days before Christmas in Italy and ends on the sixth day of January which was the Feast of Epiphany. Antonio and Maddalena have decorated the house and have put up the Christmas tree. They also have a *presepio* (Nativity scene) in the living room. All of the figurines for the Nativity display were brought over from Italy by

Maddalena. The figures of the Holy Family are all hand carved and beautifully designed.

Christmas this year is on Sunday. Maddalena tells Pasquale that she will prepare *La Vigilia* (the Vigil), a traditional Christmas eve Italian feast. The meal for the feast will include seven different seafood dishes. The seafood will consist of *baccalà*, *polipo* (octopus), *calamari* (squid), *vongole* (clams), linguine with anchovies, *insalata di mare* (seafood salad), and *anguilla marinata* (marinated eel). Roman Catholics have periods of the year when there is an abstinence from eating meat including the eve of Holy Days. Christmas eve is one of those periods.

Pasquale has begun to learn a little English. With a heavy Italian accent he can say good morning, good night, thank you, how are you today, it's a nice day, and he is learning how to say the days of the week in English. He can also count from one to ten in English. Marco, who is bi-lingual, has worked with Pasquale teaching him English. Many Italian immigrants have not learned the English language. Marco feels it is important for Italians to be able to communicate in English. He believes that immigrants will be less likely to experience discrimation, have better opportunities, and can more easily handle their affairs if they can speak English.

Mr. Shipman has encouraged and supports Marco in his efforts to teach the Italian workers the English language. Most of the lessons take place during the lunch break each day. Many of the Italians are interested and participate. Angelo was a little hesitant at first but Pasquale convinced him to participate. Pasquale told Angelo that if he still planned on having his own glove shop in Gloversville, knowing English would be very helpful in conducting business activities. Pasquale also told Angelo that Giovanni. who is now in school, will learn English. Pasquale said that Leonardo will definitely learn both Italian and English.

Pasquale received the photo that was taken on the ship. He looked at the photo with that scruffy beard and is not sure he should send it to Raphelia. He has been writing letters to Raphelia every week. Raphelia has sent two letters to Pasquale. After showing the picture to Maddalena she tells him to send the picture to Raphelia. She tells him that he can explain the beard in his letter. She also says that when Raphelia sees the Statue of Liberty that Pasquale carved while on the voyage, she would probably laugh as to how he used his razor to carve the statue instead of shaving.

The week before Christmas flies by. Pasquale had mailed the photo of himself and the letter to Raphelia. He also told Raphelia to start making the travel arrangements as he would have enough money in about one month to bring her and the boys to America. Raphelia in her letters to Pasquale tells him how much she misses him and that she is very excited to be with him in America soon. She told him that his sons were well and very helpful. They are also excited to go to America and to be reunited with their father. Pasquale had originally thought that it could take up to five months or more to save enough money to have his family join him. He was only about a month away from having the money to pay for his family's trip to America because Maddalena and Antonio assisted him with living expenses and he was frugal.

The last workday before Christmas was ending. Mr. Shipman gathered all employees together at four o'clock that afternoon. As Marco had told Pasquale, Mr. Shipman had a gift for his employees. Mr. Shipman thanked everyone for doing a great job and he told them that he was sending everyone home early today and giving them next Monday off to help celebrate Christmas with their families. He also had envelopes for each employee. He shook their hands and wished them a Merry Christmas. He even said it in Italian. As Mr. Shipman handed out the envelopes to each Italian employee said, *"boun Natale."* All of the Italian employees wished him a Merry Christmas in Italian as well.

Pasquale thought it was very nice that the owner let the employees go home early and to close the shop on Monday in celebration of Christmas. Pasquale did not open his envelope until he got home. He told Maddalena about letting the employees off early and that each one received a gift from the owner. Maddalena said, *"aprire la busta"* (open the envelope). Pasquale opened it and just looked at her. Maddalana asked what was wrong. With tears in his eyes, Pasquale showed her what was in the envelope. When Maddalena saw what it was, she hugged Pasquale and began to cry. There was one hundred dollars in the envelope with a handwritten note in Italian and signed by Mr. Shipman that said, *"grande lavoro che e Boun Natale. Grazie. Portare la vostra famiglia in America"* (great job and Merry Christmas.Thank you. Bring your family to America).

That was more than two months pay. What a generous man Pasquale thought. To give Pasquale money to have his family join him was beyond comprehension. Pasquale was overcome with joy. His tears flowed as he told Maddalena that with this money and what he had saved over the last two months he now had enough money to get the tickets to bring Raphelia and his sons to Gloversville. Pasquale told Maddalena that when he got to work next week he was going to ask to see Mr. Shipman in his office to thank him for his kindness. Pasquale and Maddalena shared the good fortune with Antonio when he came home from work. Antonio said he had heard good things about Mr. Shipman and how well he was respected in the community. Antonio mentioned that Mr. Shipman donated money for many good causes and was always there to help people. Pasquale said, *"Dio benedica questo uomo me raciglioso"* (God bless this wonderful man).

Angelo and Vincenzo came over to see Pasquale. Angelo was told by Marco that Mr. Shipman was going to give Pasquale money to help bring the family to America. Angelo shared that he had received fifty dollars from Mr. Shipman and how thankful he was for such a kind gesture. Vincenzo told Pasquale and Angelo that as he had said before Mr. Shipman treated all his employees with respect. He also agreed with Antonio about Mr. Shipman's reputation in Gloversville. Antonio poured a glass of wine for everyone. Pasquale needed a glass of wine after this. He was still numb from what had happened.

Pasquale woke up on Christmas eve morning still recovering from the kind gesture from Mr. Shipman. It was again snowing outside and the snow was beginning to accumulate. Pasquale liked the snow. He was not fond of the bitter cold however. When he went outside on these very cold days, he wore two shirts, wool trousers, a sweater that Maddlalena had knitted for him, his heavy winter coat, his wool scarf, flat cap and gloves, and a pair of rubber boots that Antonio gave him. Maddalena would laugh at him when he dressed like that to go outside. Today she told him, *"è freddo fuori, ma si dispone di cosi tanti vestiti su di voi probabilmente sciogliere"* (it's freezing outside but you have so many clothes on you will probably melt). Pasquale looked at her and took his flat right hand and struck the edge of his right hand against his left palm meaning "get out of here!" like he was saying, "you must be joking." Maddalena then took her index finger and pointed it at her head. This was telling Pasquale that he was *"pazzo"* (crazy). Laughing they both pointed to their heads telling the other you are crazy.

Pasquale went to see Angelo. He and Angelo had been discussing Angelo's idea about starting a glove shop. Angelo's plan was to work at Shipman's for about one year and then open his own shop. Pasquale supported the idea but wanted to continue to work at Shipman's. Pasquale asked Angelo if he would have enough money to open a shop. Angelo mentioned that the shop in Italy being run by his brother was doing well and that there would be enough money in about one year. Pasquale said he would think about working for Angelo but would not commit to working for him. Angelo understood and said Pasquale would always be welcome to work for him anytime he was ready.

The Christmas eve feast was underway at Maddalena's house. The dinner was served at seven. Luciana and Vincenzo along with their children and Angelo and Rosa with their children were there. The fish dishes were excellent. Although it was still snowing, everyone would still attend midnight Mass. For the meal Pasquale especially liked the *polipo* (octopus) and the *insalata di mare* (seafood salad). The salad had potatoes, onions, smelt, arugula, tomatoes, and endive with a olive oil and balasmic vinegar dressing. Maddalena finished the dish with some shaved parmesan cheese.

After dinner Maddalena served an assortment of homemade Italian cookies and espresso. She made *biscotti*, *bocconotti* (a crisp fried dough shell filled with almond paste), *pignoli* (cookies made with almond paste and pin nuts), and *biscotti di ricotta di Natale* (Christmas ricotta cookies). Maddalena also made *panettone* (a sweet bread made with raisins) to give as gifts to Angelo, Rosa, Vincenzo, and Luciana. Maddalena spent two days cooking in preparation of the Christmas eve celebration.

About eleven thirty, everyone arrived at Church. The church was filled to capacity. The midnight Mass was a very special service. There were three priests and seven altar boys conducting the service. The very formal yet traditional midnight Mass includes an array of special songs, each priest taking a segment of the service, the smell of burning incense, a full choir, and every person in attendance coming to the altar twice, once for communion and once to kiss the baby Jesus at the Nativity display.

Pasquale, Antonio, and Angelo were surprised at church. Emilio was there for the Mass. Pasquale introduced Emilio to Maddalena, Rosa, and Luciana. Emilio told the ladies that he would look forward to seeing them at lodge functions. Emilio also told Pasquale that he had heard about Mr. Shipman's generosity. He was pleased for Pasquale about being able to have the family come to America sooner than planned. He told Pasquale that the lodge would provide assistance for buying the train tickets when Raphelia and the boys arrive in New York. Pasquale was again amazed by this offer and thanked Emilio. He was told by Emilio this is what brotherhood and helping each other is all about.

The Mass lasted about an hour and a half. It was still snowing lightly when everyone left the church. Returning to Maddalena's house the night was finished with a glass of wine. Pasquale enjoyed the day and really enjoyed the midnight Mass service. With about eight inches of snow on the ground Christmas day would look special. Pasquale was ready for some sleep and also anticipating another nice day celebrating Christmas. It was after two thirty in the morning when Pasquale, Antonio, and Maddalena went to bed. With kisses and hugs, and Maddelana telling Pasquale he was still *pazzo*.They all laughed and then said *boun Natale* and *bouna notte* (good night) to each other.

Sixteen

Christmas day and another six inches of snow. The entire city is covered in a blanket of snow. It stopped snowing around noon. With nearly fourteen inches of snow on the ground clearing pathways, roads, and walkways is slow treacherous work. Horse drawn plows worked on removing snow from the main routes of travel. A battery of shovel bearing workers cleared downtown sidewalks. The majority of side streets were packed in with the snow. Some residents would gather together to shovel snow to create walkways. Since this was Christmas day, only a few sidestreets were cleared of snow. Fortunately, the winds were not blowing hard so snow drifts were minor. The temperature had risen and was hovering around twenty eight degrees.

A four-block area along Spring Street to Main Street on the east and to Spring Street to Orchard Street on the west was being cleared of the accumuated snow by about fifty residents who lived on Spring Street. Pasquale and Antonio helped clear the snow. Pasquale still had his heavy clothing on although the temperature was not bitterly cold. He had a hard time with the cold weather, even at the slightly higher temperature. The snow banks from the shoveled snow were growing. The children loved playing in the snow and especially on the tall snowbanks that lined each side of Spring Street.

Getting to know more neighbors was also interesting for Pasquale. With the language barrier, communication was an issue. There was one Italian family who lived about two blocks away from Pasquale and Antonio who spoke English. After introducing themselves, they knew Pasquale and Antonio needed help with communicating with some of the others who were removing the snow. They helped with translating for Pasquale. Antonio had learned some English but also needed translation help with much of the conversation.

It took about four hours of steady shoveling to move the snow off of the road and walkways. The work was hard and tiresome. It was almost five o'clock when the work was done. Pasquale and Antonio returned home tired and hungry. Luciana and Vincenzo cooked Christmas dinner. Pasquale, Maddalena, and Antonio walked to Luciana's. Part of the street they lived on had some snow removed but the majority of the snow was still in the roadway making walking a little difficult.

After Pasquale and Antonio told Vincenzo about the snow shoveling work, he offered them a shot of anisette to help warm them up. This anise-flavored liqueur is slightly sweet but strong. Pasquale and Antonio gladly accepted the drink. The liqueur is sipped slowly. It has a fairly low alcohol level. Anisette is usually served as an after dinner drink, but in this situation, Vincenzo felt a nice glass of the drink would be just what Pasquale and Antonio needed.

Luciana made lasagna for dinner. Her speciality of the dish was to make hundreds of tiny Italian meatballs that she would fry and then place in the layers of pasta and tomato sauce along with ricotta and mozzarella cheeses. Her lasagna was five layers thick. Vincenzo made *arancini di riso* (Italian rice balls). Made with rice, parmesan cheese, and eggs to hold the mixture together the rice balls are rolled in bread crumbs and fried. An antipasto that included a variety of Italian cheeses, proscuitto, salami, marinated olives, anchovies, and roasted red peppers was served before the main meal.

Maddalena brought the leftover cookies she had made for the Christmas eve dinner. Everyone enjoyed the cookies with some espresso for dessert. During dessert the conversation was about Raphelia coming to America along with the boys. Pasquale told the group he planned on purchasing the tickets tomorrow. Everyone was delighted that Raphelia would be in Gloversville soon. They knew how much Pasquale had sacrificed to leave his family behind.

Pasquale explained the details to everyone. He told them that he and Maddalena would travel by train to Albany where the steamship brokerage company was located. The brokerage firm would notify the steamship company who would arrange to have the ticket receipt and prepaid passage documents in Naples for Raphelia and the boys. He mentioned that Raphelia would be notified by the steamship company and that the entire process would take about two weeks to complete. Pasquale also told them he would write a letter to Raphelia explaining everything.

Mr. Shipman had gathered all the details for Pasquale for bringing the family to America. He had Marco write down this information and included it in the envelope with the money. The information included where to buy the tickets, the name and location of the brokerage company, the cost of the tickets and fees, information on how Raphelia would receive tickets, and the potential dates when Raphelia would leave Italy. The details were very specific and provided a step-by-step process for Pasquale to follow.

The third-class tickets would cost thirty dollars each. The brokerage company would charge another five dollars for each ticket for their services. Pasquale had saved forty dollars from working. With the one hundred dollars he received from Mr. Shipman, he would have just enough money to pay for the tickets and for the broker's fee. Raphelia's family would not have to help pay for the tickets. Antonio would pay for the train tickets for Maddalena and Pasquale to go to Albany. They hoped the snow conditions would not prevent the trains from running. The tracks were usually kept clear since train travel was a major source of transportation.

After processing the paperwork, including purchasing the tickets and using the information gathered by Mr. Shipman, Raphelia and the boys would be leaving Naples for America at the end of January. Pasquale figured his wife and sons would be in New York the second week of February. That time frame now placed another priority on Pasquale. He would need to find a place to live for his family. He would begin that search next week. Finding a home should not be a big issue. There are places available for rent in Gloversville and new homes are being built. Pasquale wanted to make sure he had everything set up before Raphelia arrived. The biggest challenge would be buying some furniture. Pasquale figured he would get the essentials so Raphelia could also choose most of the furnishings after she arrived.

The morning after Christmas, Pasquale was still thinking about all the things that he needed to do to prepare for Raphelia's trip. The train to Albany would leave at nine. Pasquale and Maddalena were at the train station at eight thirty. With the train tickets in hand, they waited for the boarding call. Pasquale had the paperwork that Mr. Shipman had prepared. He read it over and over again to make sure he would not forget any of the specific details that needed to be done.

The train station was very busy today. The snow had stopped and the main roads were passable. Travelers who had visited friends and relatives were headed back home. The train to Albany was fully packed. The trip only takes about one hour or so with one stop before reaching Albany. Mr. Shipman had the address of the brokerage company written on the paperwork that Pasquale had. The broker was only three blocks from the train depot. When Maddalena and Pasquale arrived at the brokerage location they had to wait another hour to see the representative as there were about fifty people in line to buy various tickets.

When they were at the ticket window, Pasquale had his paperwork in hand to make sure he did exactly what was listed. There was an intepreter there to assist. The ticket broker had to complete many pages of paperwork and Pasquale had to sign each document. The process took about twenty minutes. Pasquale made the payment and breathed a sigh of relief. The broker told Pasquale that the tickets would be issued by the steamship company in Naples. Maddalena hugged her brother and told him she was happy for him.

Pasquale and Maddalena arrived back in Gloversville late in the afternoon. Pasquale was very excited and talked about the tickets and about Raphelia the entire trip from Albany to Gloversville. Pasquale planned on telling Mr. Shipman about buying the tickets and to again thank him for what he did. When

Pasquale and Maddalena got home everyone was waiting and cheered when they walked in. More wine and another celebration was underway. Rosa and Luciana had prepared some pasta and a *lucciariello* (sausage and broccoli pie) for the celebration. With tomorrow being a workday the celebration would end early in the evening.

Tuesday morning at work started with Pasquale meeting with Mr. Shipman telling him about the tickets and thanking him for the time off to get the tickets. Pasquale thanked Mr. Shipman for all of his help. All Pasquale's co-workers were happy for him and congratulated him on getting the tickets for his family. Although it would be about another month before Raphelia would leave Naples, Pasquale was very pleased that the arrangements had been completed. He would now begin his search for a place to live. Vincenzo had some contacts that he provided to Pasquale for the search. Angelo and Rosa had moved into a flat next door to Vincenzo and Luciana. Pasquale was hoping he could find a place close to Maddalena.

A grand New Year's eve party was held at the lodge. Luciana's daughter, Maria, had the duty of watching the Guiliani children, her sister, and her brothers at the Leoni home. Rosa had put Leonardo to bed for the night. Luciana made *pasta e fagioli* and cookies for the children. Pasquale, Maddalena, Antonio, Luciana, Vincenzo, Angelo, and Rosa arrived at the party at nine.

There were over one hundred people at the party. There was a group of Italian musicians at the party to provide entertainment and music for dancing.

The party was well underway. A table was filled with Italian delicacies including bruschetta, focaccaia, salami, proscuitto, cheese, olives, a variety of fruit, and an assortment of Italian pastries. Wine was at every table. Lively music and dancing was almost non-stop during the night. The musicians played a *tarentella*, a traditional upbeat Italian folk dance. The dance was very popular in Southern Italy and continued to be as popular with Italian immigrants in America. Many other popular Italian songs were played. A few of the men attending sang Italian songs accompanied by the musicians.

The midnight celebration was even more lively. Another *tarentella*, numerous toasts, handshakes, kisses, and hugs. Emilio gathered the crowd together and announced that Pasquale would be bringing his family to Gloversville in a few weeks. Everyone cheered and congratulated Pasquale. Emilio also told the group that a new century was approaching and that there will be greater opportunities in the coming years for Italian immigrants. He mentioned how fortunate they all were, including himself, to be in America. He wished all of them a year of great prosperity.

The festivities at the lodge ended around one in the morning. The streets of Gloversville were still filled with people celebrating the new year. Pasquale and the others walked back to Maddalena's. It was a cold night. Snow on the ground was crunching under the footsteps. Some parties were still going on. Pasquale was surprised that so many people were outside after one o'clock in the morning. He wondered how many would make it to church services. He imagined most would not.

After arriving home and saying good night to the others Pasquale went to bed. He did not want to miss going to Mass. He had a good time at the lodge party and was glad that everyone went. Pasquale and Emilio had become good friends. Emilio had been a lawyer in Italy but found that his credentials were not accepted in the United States. Emilio had been serving as a law clerk for a local law firm. He also was attending Albany Law School to improve his knowledge of Amercian law. A combination of education, experience, and his law clerk work would prepare Emilio for the bar exam. Emilio was also helping Pasquale with learning some English.

Mass at Our Lady of Mount Carmel did not have as many parishoners as usual. Pasquale and Maddalena attended Mass while Antonio stayed home. Angelo and Rosa were there but Luciana and Vincenzo were not. After church Pasquale would spend the rest of the day relaxing. This was a busy couple of weeks with some late nights. It had been a while since Pasquale wrote to Raphelia. With all arrangements in place, he felt this was a good time to write a letter to Raphelia telling her more about his job, the travel arrangements and the tickets, the money from Mr. Shipman, and all about the lodge. Pasquale wrote for about two hours. This was the longest and most detailed letter yet. There was so much to tell Raphelia. The past couple of months had been so eventful. He told Raphelia about the Christmas and New Year celebrations. He described the crowds on the streets in the early morning hours after the New Year parties. He also mentioned that he was just taking time today to relax and to write the letter. Pasquale felt relaxed. He was also beginning to become more comfortable with the daily routine.

He did not plan on sending more letters after this since Raphelia would be on her way to America in a few weeks. He would have so much to share with her when she arrived in Gloversville. He would begin making preparations for seeing his family again. Each day he became more excited and began counting down the days when his family would be on the ship and finally in America. He knew that it would be soon that he and his family would be together never to be separated again. Together in America. The thought was still hard to imagine, but the reality was just a short time away.

Seventeen

Pasquale had been looking at places to live. He had not found a place that he thought Raphelia would like. He was told by someone at the lodge that there was a nice large three bedroom upper flat in his neighborhood and that he knew the landlord. He gave Pasquale the address and made arrangements for the landlord to show the flat to Pasquale on Saturday, the twenty-first of January. Although the house was not as close to Maddalena as Pasquale would have liked, a large flat would be very nice to have.

The house was on Third Street and not too far from Pasquale's work. Third Street is located off of Broad Street and three blocks south of West Fulton Street. Maddalena's house is a little more than one half mile away. Emilio went with Pasquale to translate for him. The landlord met Pasquale and Emilio at the house. The lower flat was occupied. The upper flat had three bedrooms, a large living room, a dining room, bathroom, and a kitchen large enough for a table. There is also a small storage room next to the dining room, and two large enclosed porches. One porch is located off of the living room area in the front of the house and the other is off of the kitchen area at the rear of the house. The landlord told Pasquale that the rent for the unfurnished flat will be twelve dollars a month. Pasquale would also have to pay for electricity. Pasquale knows Raphelia will like the flat and agrees to the rent. Pasquale said he would like to move in the following Saturday which the landlord agreed to. Pasquale would have time to partially furnish the flat and get it ready for Raphelia.

The house was built in 1892 and originally had gas lamps. The landlord had electric lights installed about a year ago. The house is one of the largest on the block. There is a nice size yard with some trees on the lot. There is a new home being built on the next block. Construction of new homes in Gloversville has continued in an effort to meet the needs of the growing population.

Maddalena is very happy for Pasquale. Finding a place now provides time to have all the preparations complete before Raphelia comes to Gloversville. Pasquale will take Maddalena to see the house Sunday after Mass. Emilio was especially happy for Pasquale. Emilio is the same age as Pasquale. Emilio came to America one year after his wife died. His wife had been ill for many years. They did not have any children. Emilio has no family in America. He considers all his lodge members his family. Emilio would do anything to help his fellow lodge members. As a lawyer in Italy, he was able to have a comfortable living. His dream of coming to America was also for a new beginning. He is financially secure and he offers to help others when needed. With his work as a law clerk and with his education at Albany Law University being completed in the spring, Emilio will be taking the bar exam to be allowed to practice law in New York state.

There are furniture stores on South Main Street, Church Street, two on West Fulton Street, one on North Main Street and another on Cayadutta Street near Pasquale's work. Maddalena offers to go to the stores to look at furniture since Pasquale will be working. Pasquale agrees and likes the idea. With that many stores Maddalena is confident that they will find what they need to furnish the flat. Pasquale tells Maddalena that she would probably know better what Raphelia would like. The plan is still to buy just some basic furniture now and then Raphelia can choose the rest of the furnishings when she arrives.

Sunday after church Pasquale takes Maddalena and Antonio to see the house. Maddalena likes the size of the flat. Antonio likes the two enclosed porches. Maddalena walks around the flat and starts to plan a furniture layout so she has an idea of what to shop for. The design of the interior is very nice. The walls in the bedrooms, living room, and dining room are painted a light beige color, all of the woodwork is white, and the hardwood floors have a light brown finish.

There is a floor-to-ceiling built-in cabinet between the dining room and kitchen that has access doors on the dining room side and access doors on the kitchen side. The storage room located next to the dining room has a separate closet space. The larger bedroom that is located in the front of the flat has a large closet. There is a second bedroom off of the living room and a third bedroom off of the dining room. The bathroom is behind the kitchen area. The living room has bay windows. The access to the front porch is at the living room. The access to the rear porch is at the kitchen. The large kitchen has a gas stove with an oven, a kitchen sink, room for a small table and chairs, and a spot for an icebox.

Maddalena tells Pasquale he made a good choice renting the flat. She says that Raphelia will love the flat. Pasquale is happy with the decision. Pasquale tells Maddalena that his next plan is to buy a house. He said that it will probably take a few years but he was going to achieve that goal. He also told her that he wanted to set an example for his sons that anything is possible in America if you work hard and make good decisions. Pasquale is proud of his sons and knows they will do well in America.

Maddalena visited all of the furniture stores on Monday. She spent much of the day looking at what the stores had available. After seeing the selections, one of the stores, the Gloversville Furniture Company, located at 34 West Fulton Street

(Morrison, J., & Shiel, J., 2008) had in her opinion the best furniture selections for Pasquale and his family. One of the store workers spoke Italian. She made arrangements with the store manager to have Pasquale look at the furniture after Pasquale got out of work.

Maddalena went to Shipman's to see Pasquale. She told him the store manager would meet them that evening. It was almost time for the workday to end. Pasquale put his work tools away, washed his hands, and grabbed his coat. The store on West Fulton Street is just a few minutes walk from Cayadutta Street. The store manager was waiting for them to arrive. The employee who spoke Italian showed Pasquale the furniture and asked if there was any specific items he was looking for. Pasquale explained that he was interested in just some basics for now and that when his wife arrived from Italy in a few weeks they would choose the rest of the furnishings.

Pasquale had a nice surprise for Maddalena. He told her Mr. Shipman had increased his weekly wage from fourteen dollars to seventeen dollars. Mr. Shipman was very pleased with Pasquale's quality of work and his consistant high level of production. Marco also told Pasquale that the company was expanding and Mr. Shipman would most likely make Pasquale the lead cutter. That would also provide additional money as

Pasquale would be in charge of the daily quotas for the glove cutters in his section.

After looking at the nice variety of furniture, Pasquale thought the best option for now was to select two Italian style tall back upholstered arm chairs with wood trim, a bed, and a small wooden kitchen table with four wooden bow back style chairs. Maddalena helped Pasquale with the selections. The total cost for these furnishings was seventy five dollars (about $2,500 today). The store was willing to take weekly payments from Pasquale. He would pay three dollars each week. The store scheduled the delivery of the furniture for Friday. Maddalena offered to be at the flat for Pasquale when the furniture arrived.

Maddalena also told Pasquale that she had plenty of extra linens, bed coverings, pillows, and extra dishes and other kitchen utensils that she would give to him. She also said that he would come to her house for dinner every day. Although Pasquale could cook, Maddalena felt it was best if Pasquale did not have to worry about meals. Maddalena told Pasquale how proud she was that his wages increased and that he was making a good impression for the owner of the glove company. Pasquale told her that Mr. Shipman planned to hire another five glove cutters. He said the business was expanding and the orders keep coming. The high quality of the gloves produced at Shipman's was the main reason why business was so good.

Pasquale has only been in Gloversville for three months. With the flat rented and some of the furnishings purchased, everything seemed to be in good order. Pasquale was pleased that he had so much accomplished before Raphelia's arrival. Pasquale was also looking forward to becoming the lead cutter at Shipman's. He was also calculating his finances. As a lead cutter Marco told him he would receive another three dollars each week. That would bring his earnings to twenty dollars each week. Pasquale would be one of the highest paid glove cutters in the area.

Angelo still planned to open his own glove shop. He and Pasquale talked about the plan on a regular basis. Angelo told Pasquale he had looked at a building that would work well for a glove shop. Angelo had been in contact with his brother and the shop in Italy was still doing well. That also produced additional income for Angelo. With the money he received from his brother, he would have enough to start the business in Gloversville in less than one year. Angelo was still interested in Pasquale working with him in the business. Pasquale was open to the offer but also wanted to make sure that the company had enough work to stay in business.

Pasquale reminded Angelo that there were some shops in Gloversville that had gone out of business. The reason Pasquale figured was that the shops were not well managed, did not have good quality products, and did not pay their workers well. Pasquale knows Angelo has good business experience but there would be some challenges in starting a new operation in Gloversville. Angelo understood and said he had been talking to other businessmen in Gloversville and was quickly learning the American way of conducting business. Pasquale told Angelo he had all the confidence in him and believed he would be very successful in his business.

The furniture was delivered on schedule. Maddalena began to arrange the furniture while the delivery crew set up the bed. Maddalena liked the furniture and thought it went well with the home. Maddalena had also brought some of the items she had told Pasquale about. She was still amazed how large the flat was. With the three boys, Pasquale and Raphelia, there would be plenty of room. She also liked that the location was only six blocks from Pasquale's work.

Pasquale went to the house right after work. Maddalena told him she would meet him there. He really liked the furniture. He sat on the bed and then laid down. He said it was very comfortable. He told Maddalena that if the bunk on the ship was that comfortable, he probably would have slept the entire voyage. Maddalena had put the bed coverings on and had two feather pillows for Pasquale to use. Tomorrow Pasquale would be living at the flat. Maddalena reminded him that he would come to her house for meals. Pasquale took Maddalena's hands in his and thanked her for everything she had done for him. He said a prayer and thanked God for the home.

On Saturday the whole group came to see the flat. Angelo and Rosa stopped by first. Then Luciana and Vincenzo came by later that day after Vincenzo closed his shop for the day. Emilio stopped by to let Pasquale know that after church on Sunday the lodge would be hosting a pasta dinner. The next surprise was a visit by Mr. Shipman and Marco. Mr. Shipman asked Pasquale about the furniture and where he purchased it. Mr. Shipman knows the owner of the furniture store. He asked Pasquale about his plan for getting more furniture. Pasquale told him about having Raphelia make the selections for the rest of the furnishings. Mr. Shipman told Pasquale before he bought more furniture to talk to him first. Mr. Shipman said his wife had recently purchased all new furniture and that he had stored his other furniture. He offered to give that furniture to Pasquale and Raphelia if she liked the furniture. Pasquale again was deeply touched at the kindness of his boss. He agreed to have Raphelia look at the furniture and again humbled by the offer thanked Mr. Shipman.

The spaghetti dinner at the lodge was very nice. Emilio had invited many others in the community to be at the dinner, including the mayor of Gloversville. The lodge and the name *Alba*

Nuova was beginning to be noticed by members of the community. Lodge members had been volunteering to help people with various projects in the community. The name *Alba Nuova Lodge* had been painted on the windows of the building where the lodge was located. Emilio was regularly meeting with businessmen in the city and had been promoting how good of a community member the lodge was. Emilio was determined to show and communicate that Italian immigrants were dedicated and hard working members in America society.

January 30, 1899 was a monumental day. This was exactly four months from the date that Pasquale left Italy for America. This was also the day Raphelia and their sons would be leaving Italy for their journey to America. The SS Napoli would leave the harbor in Naples at noon. Raphelia's family was there to see her and her sons depart. The ship carried fourteen hundred passengers with eleven hundred in third class. This ship, built in 1897, was scheduled to make the Trans-Atlantic crossing to New York in nine days and arrive late afternoon on eighth day of February.

Pasquale was so excited he had a hard time focusing at work today. He did his work and finished the day meeting his quota, but struggled to do so. After work he went to Maddalena's for dinner and to talk about being reunited with his family. Pasquale told Maddalena that the lodge was paying for the train tickets from New York to Gloversville for Raphelia and the boys. Pasquale would have to ask for the day off when the ship was scheduled to arrive so he could go to New York and meet his family.

Raphelia and the boys had their berth in third class on the ship. They had gone through the inspection process. Pasquale had detailed the entire inspection sequence in one of his letters to prepare Raphelia for what to expect. The only item he left out was the eye exam that would take place in New York. He knew he should have told her but he did not want to frighten her. Raphelia was aware of the voyage issues as Pasquale had explained that as well. She prayed that she and her sons would not get seasick on the trip. She brought some food for the boys. She had salami, tarilli, and four tins filled with Italian cookies. Raphelia was relieved that she was finally going to see Pasquale. Being separated for the past four months had been hard. She was ready for a new life in America and finally to have her family together again.

Eighteen

Before Raphelia and the boys left for America, they visited Luigi. This would be the final goodbye. Luigi was so happy to see Raphelia and her sons. He was also very emotional as he would not see Raphelia or the boys again. Raphelia brought some biscotti and wine like she had done many times when visiting Luigi. They talked for nearly two hours. Luigi asked about Pasquale. Raphelia told Luigi about his voyage and his job. He was pleased that Pasquale found work and was cutting gloves in America.

As the visit was ending Luigi began to cry and told Raphelia how much he would miss her and the children. Raphelia hugged Luigi and told him she would always remember what he did for Pasquale and the family. Francesco, Eduardo, and Arturo hugged and kissed Luigi. Francesco said, *"addio nonno"* (goodbye grandfather), to which Luigi replied, *"addio mio nipote"* (goodbye my grandson). The DaCorsi family treated Luigi like he was a father and grandfather to them. They had great respect for Luigi and loved him dearly. Raphelia kissed Luigi and said her goodbye.

As Raphelia and the boys left, Luigi said, *"che Dio sia con te. Bouna fortuna. La tua vita in America sarà prospero"* (may God be

with you. Good fortune. Your life in Amercia will be prosperous).
Raphelia thanked Luigi and said that God has blessed him and
will continue to do so. Luigi's tears continued to flow. He watched
Raphelia until they were no longer in sight. He blew a kiss and
said, *"la mia famiglia il mio amore. Il mio cuore si è rotto"* (my family,
my love. My heart has broken).

Raphelia cried all the way home. Her heart also ached. She
was excited to go to America, but was deeply saddened leaving
her family and leaving Luigi. She told her sons that showing
respect to others in the Italian culture is always expected. She said
how proud she was at the respect the boys had always shown to
Luigi and to her family. The boys always approached the elders
with a traditional kiss. Raphelia used to remind them not to forget
to kiss the grandparents and the aunts and uncles. The boys
always said they knew and always gave the kiss of respect. The
kiss they gave to Luigi was done without any prompting by
Raphelia.

Raphelia was pleased that the voyage would only take
nine days. With Pasquale's twelve-day trip she knew how
stressful that was for him. The conditons in third class were about
the same as Pasquale had experienced. Crowded, unsanitary, and
the food was there to fill the hunger but was not satisfying. Being
confined to third class was the hardest part of the voyage. The
typical, unpredictable Atlantic held true to its reputation. There

were some days of seasickness for Raphelia and her sons, but they recovered quickly.

Raphelia kept busy crocheting. The boys played with the other children in third class. They also read books that Raphelia had brought. Pasquale and Raphelia had made sure the boys could read and write. With some formal education, along with reading and writing at home, the boys did well learning. When they are in America, the process will have to start over again. Pasquale and Raphelia had agreed that the boys would need to learn English to have better opportunities in America.

Pasquale had been given time off of work to meet his family when they arrived in New York. Maddalena had begun to sew gloves at home again, but had worked extra hours and over the weekend to meet her quota for the week. Pasquale and Maddalena left for New York early in the morning on the day the ship was to arrive. Antonio was not able to accompany them. Traveling from Gloversville to Schenectady and then to New York would take about eight hours with the scheduled stops along the way. They would arrive in New York around three in the afternoon. Pasquale had the money from the lodge to purchase the train tickets from New York to Gloversville. Emilio met Pasquale at the train depot in Gloversville to wish him a good trip and to tell him he would also be at the train depot when he returned with the family.

Pasquale was told by Mr. Shipman before he left he was giving him the lead cutter job next month with the wage increase Marco had mentioned. Mr. Shipman also told him that he wanted to make sure Pasquale spent some time with his family. In addition to the day off to meet his family, Mr. Shipman gave Pasquale the rest of the week off with pay. The caring that Mr. Shipman had for his employees and their families was unprecedented at that time. To allow days off with pay was not something companies did. Pasquale was very grateful for Mr. Shipman's continued generosity and kindness.

Arriving in New York, Pasquale and Maddalena made their way to Battery Park. They went to the pier to look for the ship in the distance. It was just after four o'clock when Pasquale shouted, *"Lo vedo! Eccolo! Loro sono qui!"* (I see it! There it is! They are here!). He began to cry and held Maddalena. The ship made its way to the dock in the Hudson. The barge boats were stationed ready to take the third-class passengers to the immigration station. It took nearly one hour before the barge boats began to bring the passengers to Battery Park and the Barge office.

Pasquale frantically looked for his family. Then, as the third barge boat came to the pier, he sees Raphelia. He began shouting her name. He keeps shouting and as she is stepping onto the pier, she sees her husband. She points toward Pasquale and motions to the boys. Pasquale keeps calling her name. Raphelia and the boys begin waving with both arms raised high. Pasquale and Maddalena rush to the pier. He reaches Raphelia. They grab each other and hug tightly. Pasquale does not want to let her go. He says, *"La mia bella moglie, è cosi bello vederti"* (my beautiful wife, it is good to see you). Raphelia through her tears tells Pasquale that it is good to see him also. The boys give their father a kiss and a hug, also not wanting to let go.

Maddalena greets Raphelia and also gives her a long hug and a kiss. The boys kiss their aunt. They all make their way to the Barge office. Pasquale keeps stopping and hugging Raphelia. As they reach the Barge office Pasquale kisses Raphelia and explains the inspection process. He also describes the eye exam but for her not to worry as it only takes a few seconds. Pasquale checks the paperwork for Raphelia and his sons to make sure it is all in order for the inspection. Raphelia and the boys make their way to the assigned line. Pasquale and Maddalena find a place to sit near the inspection area. They now wait until the processing is complete.

It takes over two hours before Raphelia and the boys have their inspections. Station by station they are approved and sent to the next inspector. The last inspection is the eye exam. Raphelia is very nervous. The doctor checking Raphelia looks at her eyes and then uses the button hook to flip her eyelids to complete the examination. Fransceso's doctor does not use the button hook, but both Eduardo and Arturo are checked with the button hook. They are all glad that part is over quickly.

The question portion of the inspection goes smoothly, and as typical, only takes a couple of minutes. The interpreter for Raphelia and the boys congratulates them and tells them they are free to go. Pasquale and Maddalena have been waiting for them close by. Raphelia tells Pasquale that she is glad the inspection is over. She also tells him the button hook examination was very uncomfortable but that it did not hurt. With paperwork in hand the family is all set to get the train tickets to Schenectady. Just like Pasquale had done, they buy box lunches. Raphelia tells Pasquale how bad the food was on the ship. She mentions that she brought salami, tarilli, and cookies for the voyage. Pasquale was glad she had done that and told her his food on his trip, other than a couple of meals, was just as bad. He then tells her that home-cooked meals is all they will eat from now on.

They leave for Schenectady on the eight o'clock train. The railroad company recently added more trips to the schedule. Trains now leave every two hours and the trips have been shortened. There will be only two short stops on the way. They will arrive in Schenectady just after midnight. The first train for Gloversville will be at seven in the morning. The FJ&G Railroad had also expanded and created more frequent trips from Schenectady. Pasquale told Raphelia that it would be good to rest a while in Schenectady. He could tell she was exhausted from the voyage. The boys were like their father. They kept looking at everything within eyesight. They did not want to miss any of the sights. They had told their father about seeing the Statue of Liberty and were anxioius to see the carving that their mother told them about.

When they arrived at the train depot in Schenectady and found a large bench area where they all could sit. Pasquale had Raphelia lay her head on his lap. He told her to try and get some sleep. She did not want to sleep and just wanted to spend the time with her husband. After about thirty minutes, Raphelia fell asleep. Pasquale kept his hand on her shoulder and made sure she was as comfortable as possible. Raphelia slept for a little over two hours. Pasquale had not moved as he did not want to disturb her or wake her. Raphelia was a little refreshed when she woke up. She was still tired. Pasquale told her about the bed and the other furniture. He said that the bed was very comfortable and she would be getting some needed sleep in her new home.

Pasquale described the flat to Raphelia. She was curious about the kitchen. He told her about the gas stove and oven. She was surprised that it was not a wood burning stove. She asked if it was hard to use. He said he did not know, he had not used it. He said he eats at Maddalena's. Raphelia laughed and asked Maddalena if she had taught Pasquale how to cook. Maddalena said, *"guardare quelle mani. Sono le manu di un taglio guanto un cuoco"* (look at those hands. They are the hands of a glove cutter not a cook). Pasquale looked at the women and made a comment about how he would cook if he knew how to use the stove. Maddalena and Raphelia both laughed out loud. The boys also laughed. Eduardo told his father, *"quando si impara come utilizzare la stufa si può inseqnare è come cucinare"* (when you learn how to use the stove you can teach us how to cook). Maddalena and Raphelia laughed even harder. Pasquale was not amused. He told everyone he would cook them a big Italian meal when they all learned how to use the stove.

The boys were anxious to see Gloversville. Being in America was exciting but they told their father that they miss their friends in Italy. Pasquale told them about the lodge and that they would make new friends. He also told them they would be meeting Vincenzo's and Luciana's children and that they were all close in age. The boys asked about schools in Gloversville. Pasquale told them he had not looked into that but they would visit the schools together. Francesco had recently finished primary school in Italy. He had completed all the required course work. Francesco was interested in finding part-time work. Pasquale told him that there would be job opportunities in Gloversville for him. Francesco was not interested in glove cutting. He liked working as a helper and a apprentice butcher in Italy. Francesco wanted to find something similar in Gloversville.

It was just about time to board the train to Gloversville. Emilio,Vincenzo, and Luciana would be waiting at the depot in Gloversville. On the trip to Gloversville, Raphelia mentioned how beautiful everything looked. Pasquale told her that he had the same thoughts on his first trip to Gloversville. Raphelia asked Pasquale if all of America was this beautiful. Pasquale replied that he did not know and that only saw the parts from New York to Gloversville. Raphelia called him *"sciocco"* (silly). She said that she would not be surprised if all of Amercia was as nice as what she had seen so far.

The train pulls into the depot in Gloversville. It's a cold day in Gloversville. There is snow on the ground. Raphelia steps off of the train, looks at Pasquale and says, *"sono casa"* (I am home). Pasquale looks at her and says, *"siamo a casa. Siamo di nuovo insieme"* (we are home. We are together again). Pasquale and Raphelia hug again. Vincenzo and Luciana greet Raphelia and welcome her to Gloversville. They have the wagon there to take the DaCorsi family to their home. Pasquale introduces his family to Emilio. Raphelia tells Emilio that Pasquale had told her in his letters about him and she was happy to meet him. Emilio told her he felt like he already knew the family. Emilio told her after she settled in, the lodge would host a welcoming function for her and the children. Emilio mentioned Pasquale's *alba nuova* and that it was no coincidence that the name of the lodge was *Alba Nuova*. Emilio referred to that as a destiny for the DaCorsi family and how well things have progressed in just a few months. He said it will even get better as time goes on.

Raphelia asks about the cold weather and the snow. Maddalena tells her that this time of the year it is cold and that it usually begins to snow in December and can continue all winter. She also tells her it can get very cold but the clothing worn keeps people warm. Raphelia says she does not mind and will get used to it quickly. Raphelia is wearing a woolen shaw that she made that is helping to keep her warm now. Pasquale tells her and the boys they will buy some new coats later today.

With the cold weather, Raphelia and the boys are glad that the trip to the house only takes a few minutes. Raphelia likes the outside of the house. She comments on how big it is. Once inside, Raphelia is overcome with emotion. She loves the flat. She tells Pasquale he picked a perfect home for them. She tells him the place is so big. She likes the furniture. He tells her that Maddalena helped pick it out. Raphelia thanks Maddalena and said she knew exactly what she would like. Pasquale tells Raphelia that she will choose the rest of the furnishing for the flat. The boys are also very impressed with their new home. The all go to the kitchen and the first thing they all look at is the stove. Raphelia says she can learn how to use it in no time. Pasquale replies, *"questo è un bene ho fame"* (that's good I'm hungry). Maddalena slaps the side of her brother's head. Raphelia tells Pasquale, *"si vuole mangiare è meglio imparare a usare quella stufa nei prossimi cinque minuti"* (you want to eat you better learn how to use that stove in the next five minutes). Pasquale and Raphelia have always enjoyed joking with each other. They picked up right where they left off a few months ago. The boys thought both of their parents were a little *pazzo*.

Raphelia immediately fell in love with the bed. She agreed with Pasquale on how comfortable it was. The boys will sleep at Maddalena's for a few days until the rest of the furniture is purchased including beds for them. Raphelia is already thinking about how much furniture is needed to finish the flat. Maddalena tells Raphelia about the furniture store. She will take Raphelia there tomorrow to look at furniture. Raphelia is also interested in seeing all of Gloversville and where Pasquale works. She also wants to see the Guiliani's. Maddalena tells her that everyone will be at her home for dinner tonight.

Things were already moving very quickly for Raphelia. She figured she would be very busy and not have much time to rest or relax. She was not concerned. This was the beginning of a new life for her as well and she wanted everything to be perfect. She was just happy to be reunited with Pasquale. She missed him very much. She did not tell him how sad she was when he left or how lonely she felt when he was away. They had never been separated before. She stayed strong for her boys. She did not show any outward emotion in front of her children. Her sons knew, however, that she was lonely and missed their father.

Before going to Maddalena's for dinner, they stopped at a store to buy some winter coats. Maddalena again knew just what store to go to. Pasquale had also purchased his coat at the same store. The boys picked out the coats they liked. Raphelia tried on many coats before selecting one. Her coat was full length made of wool with a beaver fur collar. The boys coats were also wool and came just below the waist. The boys already had flat caps similar to their father's. Raphelia had a smaller woolen shawl that she would wear over her head.

Dinner at Maddalena's was another reunion. Seeing Angelo, Rosa, and their chidren was emotional for Raphelia. Rosa and Raphelia hugged for a long time. Raphelia held the baby. She could not believe how much he had grown. Rosa told Raphelia he has a good appetite, just like his father. Giovanni said, *"è bello vederti zia Raphelia"* (it is nice to see you aunt Raphelia). Although they are not related, that was a sign of respect to call Raphelia aunt. She told Giovanni it was nice to see him as well and that she had missed him.

They all talked about the voyage, and as usual, compared notes on each other's experiences on the ships. Raphelia's voyage was shorter in time than the others. They were surprised that the passenger ships had been made that much faster. Raphelia shared that the SS Napoli was a new ship and only had taken two previous trips to America from Naples. She also said she was real glad that the trip only took nine days. She said it was hard to imagine a twelve-day trip like Pasquale's or longer times for others. Vincenzo mentioned that their voyage took almost fourteen days. Maddalena said their trip was almost as long as Vincenzo and Luciana. Vincenzo also told the others that some Italians had returned to Italy permanently while others had gone back and then a year or more later returned to America. Pasquale said he could not imagine taking more than one trip in third class or the amount of time that it takes. Antonio said he had heard that within the next couple of years, the voyage time would be reduced to four or five days.

Everyone had a great time at dinner. The evening was getting late and Raphelia was very tired. Pasquale and Raphelia said goodnight to everyone. They kissed their sons and said they would see them in the morning. Tomorrow will be another busy day. The plan for tomorrow was to see the sites in Gloversville, meet Mr. Shipman, shop for furniture, meet Emilio at the lodge, and, of course, learn how to use the stove.

Pasquale and Raphelia walked back to the flat to spend some needed time together. Pasquale had his arm around

Raphelia's waist all the way home. As they got to the front door, Raphelia kissed Pasquale and said, *"ti amo il mio dolce marito. Sono così felice che siamo imsieme ancora"*(I love you my sweet husband. I am so happy that we are together again). Pasquale rubbed her cheek with the palm of his hand and said, *"la mia bella moglie. Siamo uno nuovo"* (my beautiful wife. We are one again). He led her up the stairs and said, *"ti amo"*(I love you) to which she replied, *"anch'io ti amo"* (I love you too).

Nineteen

Raphelia had the picture of Pasquale with his beard. He saw the picture and laughed. He remembered how it felt and what it looked like. She told him she was glad he did not have the beard now. He told her no more beards but he would not shave his moustache. She was fine with that. When Raphelia saw the statue last night at Maddalena's, she commented that it looked lifelike. She was very impressed with her husband's skills. She also knew why he had grown the beard using his razor to do the carving.

The next morning Pasquale and Raphelia went to Maddalena's to pick up the boys. The family went to see Mr. Shipman first and then planned to meet Maddalena at the furniture store. Mr. Shipman was delighted to meet Pasquale's family. He was very impressed with the children and, especially with Eduardo's English. Pasquale told Mr. Shipman that Eduardo speaks four languages. Eduardo said he was learning more languages and had begun to study the German language. Mr. Shipman welcomed Raphelia to Gloversville and told her that he had some furniture that is not being used at his house that she could look at and have if she liked it. He also told her if she needed anything he was there to help. She thanked him and said she appreciated all he had done for Pasquale.

At the furniture store Raphelia was taking her time looking at all of the furnishings. After about an hour she had made some of her selections. Her choices included beds for the boys, a sofa that matched the chairs that Pasquale had purchased, a dresser for her bedroom, and end tables for the living room. With the furniture purchased, the weekly payments were increased to five dollars. The furniture would be delivered later today.

They also shopped for an icebox. They were told that one of the stove and tinware stores also had some used iceboxes for sale. The iceboxes at the store were all in good condition. Pasquale chose a wooden icebox that had a larger storage compartment and was well insulated. The cost of the icebox was four dollars. Ice was delivered daily in Gloversville. Owners of iceboxes would place a card with the amount of ice needed in a window of the home. The iceman would see the card and make the delivery. For about two dollars a month, the icebox was kept full of ice.

Pasquale and Maddalena then took Raphelia and the boys around Gloversville to see the city. They took the trolley along Main Street. They also took a horse and carriage ride. Raphelia commented on how big the city was in comparison to her small village in Italy. She saw many of the glove shops and could not believe how many there were in the city. Maddalena told Raphelia that like in Italy, women sewed gloves for the shops at home. Raphelia was interested in that as she had done that kind of work in Italy. They returned home to wait for the furniture to be delivered.

Before dinner at Maddalena's that evening, Pasquale took his family to the lodge. Emilio was there along with a few others. Emilio told Raphelia about the lodge and activities that the lodge had. He said the lodge would be hosting a welcome party for her and the boys next Saturday. Raphelia was surprised at the kindness shown by everyone she had met. Emilio asked the boys how they liked Gloversville so far. They told him they liked it but missed their friends in Italy. Emilo said that they would meet many others, including the children of lodge members, and they would have new friends.

Vincenzo, Luciana, Angelo, and Rosa had a surprise for Raphelia and Pasquale at dinner. They gave Raphelia and Pasquale some new pots for cooking and a new set of china dishware. Raphelia was thrilled. She said now they really do need to learn how to use the stove. She was very thankful and expressed her appreciation for the gift. Maddalena then gave Raphelia some doilies that she had made for her. Raphelia's home was nearly complete with all of the gifts and most of the furnishings. She told everyone that having so much in such a short time was a true blessing.

Saturday morning was very busy for Raphelia. The furniture was in place and Raphelia was getting the house in order. Pictures of family and treasured knicknacks she had brought from Italy were displayed on the walls. She had brought a large cut glass bowl that just fit in the trunk for the voyage. She placed the bowl in the center of the dining room table on a doily that Maddalena had made. She also had purchased some fabric and lace to make drapes. She placed the crucufix that the family had in Italy and that Pasquale had brought to America on the dining room wall. She had set up a shrine of the Virgin Mary in a corner of the dining room. The flat was feeling like home.

Pasquale and Raphelia visited Mr. Shipman at his home to look at the furniture that Mr. Shipman had offered to give to them. Emilio went along to translate for Pasquale and Raphelia. There was a beautiful dining room set with a nice buffet and china cabinet that Raphelia loved. Mr. Shipman told Raphelia that it was hers and he would have his workers bring the set to Raphelia tomorrow afternoon after church. Pasquale was very thankful for the offer Mr. Shipman had made. Raphelia was also very thankful and gave Mr. Shipman a kiss on each cheek.

The first few days in Gloversville were like a whirlwind for Raphelia. So much to do and getting settled in the flat was stressful. She was glad that most of the tasks had been completed. There was still much more to do but she could take time now as there were no immediate needs. She had learned how to use the stove. She even showed Pasquale how to use it. Raphelia's home-cooked meals never tasted better. Pasquale was happy to have Raphelia's cooking again. He enjoyed Maddalena's meals but it was nice to have meals in your own home.

The DaCorsi family went to Mass on Sunday morning. This was a very special day for Pasquale. To have his entire family with him at church made the day complete. Raphelia liked the church. Before Mass she went to the side altar to say a prayer and to light candles for Luigi and for her family in Italy. Everyone was there that morning and all sat together. Maddalena sat next to her brother. Angelo and his family and Luciana and her children were in the pew behind Pasquale's family. Vincenzo was an usher at the service today. Before Mass the choir sang *Ave Maria*. Raphelia took Pasquale's hand and held it tight. Pasquale told her they sing *Ave Maria* every Sunday.

This day everyone would go to the DaCorsi's after church for the Sunday dinner. Raphelia did the cooking on her new stove. Maddalena brought an antipasto. Luciana made the dessert. Rosa made tarilli. Raphelia made minestrone, roasted pork, and spaghetti. Like always there was more than enough food. Spending the day with family and friends made Raphelia feel very good. She had missed these gatherings when Pasquale left for Amercia. Although she would spend time with her family on Sunday, she felt empty without Pasquale.

Pasquale was back at work Monday morning. That morning Raphelia and Maddalena visited the Spring Street school that Arturo would attend. They also went to the high school to enroll Francesco and Eduardo. Each school had intepreters to help Raphelia with the enrollment paperwork. Arturo would start school the next day. Eduardo and Francesco began attending classes the same day. Arturo was placed in a class with other Italian immigrant children. They had a bi-lingual teacher and learning English was part of the studies. With Eduardo knowing some English he had help from interpreters assigned to classes. There was also interpreters for Francesco and his Italian classmates. Raphelia was pleased that the boys were in school. She knew they would do well with their studies.

Francesco also went to some of the bucher shops after school in the city to look for a part-time job. There are five meat markets in Gloversville. Francesco visited each one. He was asked by a few to show his butcher skills. Others told him they did not need any help. One market on South Main Street was located in the same building as the lodge. There were two Italians working for the owner of that shop. The owner asked Francesco to come back the next afternoon when school got out to show his skills.

That night Emilio came to visit Pasquale and the family. He was told about the schools. He shared his education background with the boys and told them he was just finishing his studies to take his bar exam to be a lawyer in America. The boys were impressed. Pasquale mentioned how proud he was of his sons and that education was very important for their future. Francesco mentioned his appointment with the butcher shop owner tomorrow. When he told Emilio which shop it was, Emilio said he would meet Francesco there.

The next afternoon Emilio met Francesco in front of the shop. As they entered, the owner greeted Francesco. He also shook hands with Emilio and said he was good to see him again. Francesco was a little stunned. Emilio knew the owner. Emilio stayed to interpret for Francesco. The other two Italians spoke some English but not enough to interpret. The owner's brother spoke Italian but was not there that morning. Francesco told the butcher about his innovation in Italy to help keep meat products cooler. The owner gave Francesco specifics on what cuts of meat he wanted demonstrated. When Francesco had finished and presented his work, the owner looked at Emilio and told him to tell Francesco to be at work at after school tomorrow. The shop was open from nine in the morning until seven in the evening each day. Francesco thanked the owner and thanked Emilio. Francesco raced home to tell his mother he had a job. Raphelia congratulated him and told him that his father will be very proud of him. Francesco told his mother about Emilio knowing the owner. Raphelia said that Pasquale had told her that Emilio was very well respected and knows many businessmen in the community.

That next Saturday there were about eighty people at the welcoming party at the lodge. Emilio asked Francesco how the job was. Francesco said he liked it a lot and was doing well. Emilio had a banner made that welcomed Raphelia and the boys. Emilio talked about sacrifices that are made to make things better in our lives. He mentioned Pasquale's coming to America months before he was able to have his family join him. Emilio asked how many others had experienced a similar situation. More than half of those at the event raised their hands. Emilio said those sacrifices make families stronger and more determined to succeed in America.

Emilio went on to say that a new century was just a few months away. He told them just like those immigrants who are here now sought that new beginning, many more Italians would make the decision to come to America. He ended saying, *"buona vita, bouna amici, e una alba nuova. Siamo Italioamericani"* (good life, good friends, and a new dawn. We are Italian Americans). Emilio's uniqueness was that he inspired people. He wanted the best for everyone. He sacrificed his law practice in Italy for an opportunity to come to America. He sacrificed more after arriving to obtain the necessary education to fulfill his dream of becoming a lawyer in America. In a few months he would reach that goal.

Emilio sat with the DaCorsi family. He told the boys that they could be whatever they desired in America. Emilio was very impressed with Eduardo being multi-lingual and said that will help him greatly in the future. Emilio told Francesco he was very talented with a good business sense and that he could have his own business if he wanted that. For Arturo he said the options for him were limitless and to keep doing well in school. Pasquale appreciated the kind words and encouragement from Emilio.

The rest of the evening was filled with good food, some wine, singing, dancing, and getting to know the others who were there. Raphelia had a nice time and met other women who had experienced months of being separated from their husbands and taking separate voyages to America. The boys met other children and were quickly becoming aquainted. The closeness of the lodge members reminded Raphelia of the *campanilismo*, the bonding of people in villages in Italy. Being there for each other and creating that community would continue to be a guiding principle for this lodge.

Returning home Pasquale and Raphelia talked about the party and how the lodge was more than a social club. The lodge was becoming a gathering place for sharing life stories, encouraging success and prosperity in America, and a group dedicated to helping others in the community. Raphelia mentioned that the women had discussed working in America. A few of the women sewed gloves at home. Raphelia then mentioned that she had been thinking about sewing gloves at home and that she and Maddalena had talked about that. Pasquale said he was fine with that as long as Raphelia was comfortable with it. She said she wanted to work and that the extra money with her working and with Francesco working would help the family.

Pasquale told Raphelia of his goal to buy a home in Gloversville and extra money would help make that happen. She said she liked the flat but she would like to own a home. In the coming weeks, Pasquale and Raphelia would begin saving money for a new home. With new homes being constructed in Gloversville, Pasquale knew that there would be many options for selecting a home that would work well for the family.

Twenty

It has been almost five months since Raphelia arrived in Gloversville. Francesco, Eduardo and Arturo successfully completed their school courses. In September Francesco will be a senior in high school, Arturo will be entering the sixth grade and Eduardo will be a sophomore in high school. Eduardo has become proficient in English and has begun to learn German. Arturo has also learned some English. The boys are helping their parents with English. Eduardo is now the interpreter for Pasquale and Raphelia when they need help. Raphelia has been sewing gloves at home for a large local glove manufacturer. Pasquale was made the cutting room foreman in April after Marco left Shipman's for another job. Pasquale was now being paid thirty five dollars each week. Francesco worked full time over the summer at the butcher shop.

The family was notified in late May that Luigi had passed away. Luigi had been ill for some time and was not doing well when Raphelia left Italy. The family was deeply saddened by his passing. Raphelia received the news while Pasquale was at work. She cried for hours. She then told the boys what had happened. They were also very sad about Luigi. Pasquale wept when

Raphelia told him that Luigi had died. Pasquale recalled that both he and Luigi knew they would never see each other again when Pasquale left for America. He was forever grateful to Luigi for teaching him how to be a glove cutter. The skills he learned from that training allowed him to achieve the lead cutter and foreman jobs at Shipman's. He attributed his success to Luigi.

The family was now earning almost forty-five dollars each week with Pasquale, Raphelia, and Francesco all working. The furniture bill was nearly paid off. Pasquale and Raphelia had also been saving money toward purchasing a home. Pasquale had been talking to banks about loans for homes. With the family income, two banks in town said they would be willing to provide a mortgage for a purchase. Pasquale still needed to save more money, however, to have sufficient funds to make a purchase. It would be a few more months before Pasquale could actually be ready to buy a home.

Eduardo spent the summer learning German and working on Saturday at Shipman's. His job was cleaning the shop. On Saturday morning, he went to the shop with Pasaquale at seven in the morning. For an hour each Saturday, Pasquale taught Eduardo how to cut gloves. Eduardo would then clean the shop from eight until four. If needed, Eduardo would also work around four hours cleaning on Sunday afternoon. Mr. Shipman paid Eduardo three dollars for working Saturday and an additional one dollar and fifty cents for Sunday. Pasquale told Eduardo to save his money. He was allowed to have seventy five cents each week for spending money. Francesco also saved some money. He would give half of his pay to Pasquale and would save most of the rest. Francesco usually took two dollars each week for himself.

Pasquale taught the boys the value of money and showed them how important it was to save money. Young Arturo kept a ledger for his brothers showing how much they earned, what they had in savings, and the amount they took for spending money. Pasquale also told the boys that times could be unpredictable. He mentioned the prior economic problems in Italy. He also told them that having money when the economy was not doing well would help them get through those times.

As the summer was winding down, Pasquale was taking on more responsibilities at the glove shop. While he was still cutting gloves and performing his foreman duties, he was now put in charge of hiring new glove cutters. If a job applicant did not meet Pasquale's expectations, they were not hired. Mr. Shipman relied on Pasquale to maintain the high level of quality and workmanship of products that the company was known for. Pasquale did not like rejecting anyone but knew that some of the other shops would give the cutters jobs.

Raphelia began sewing long leather fashion gloves. The demand for these gloves for women's evening wear had been increasing. This work also paid a little more. Raphelia, like Pasquale, was known for her high level of production and her excellent quality of work. The production levels she achieved paid her a bonus for exceeding quotas. Raphelia liked this type of sewing. It was a little more challenging but she knew how to keep the leather pieces in perfect position.

Angelo was quickly putting his resources together for starting his own shop. Angelo's brother was sending money from the profits made by the shop in Italy. The business in Italy had grown and had doubled sales in the past few months. The shop in Italy also began to produce leather garments. That was a plan Angelo had put in place before he left for America. Angelo kept Pasquale informed of the status. Pasquale was still interested in joining Angelo but he was concerned about leaving Shipman's. Pasquale had been making very good money and he was not sure Angelo could pay him a similar amount.

It was late September when Angelo told Pasquale he was ready to start his own glove shop. He had funding to open the business. Pasquale was excited for Angelo but still made no commitment to go to work for him. He discussed that with Angelo who understood Pasquale's concerns. As Angelo had told Pasquale previously, anytime he was ready to join the business, he would be welcome. Pasquale always admired that quality in

Angelo. Pasquale knew that when the time was right he would go to work for Angelo.

Mr. Shipman called a meeting of all employees on the last Friday of September. That was almost one year to the day when Pasquale and Angelo left Italy for America. Mr. Shipman announced that he was going to retire and put his business up for sale. The employees were stunned and questioned what would happen to their jobs. Mr. Shipman told them he was retiring in January but would still operate the business until it was sold. Mr. Shipman explained that he was seventy-one years old and had been working since he was twelve. He also told the employees that he would look for someone to buy the business who would carry on the Shipman way of doing business and its values including how employees are treated.

All of the employees thanked Mr. Shipman for all he had done for them. They gave him a loud round of applause. He shook the hand of each employee thanking them individually for being such loyal employees. Mr. Shipman had grown the business from a three person operation to one that now had forty-seven employees. He started the business in 1875 when he was forty-seven years old. Yearly business revenues had grown from ten thousand dollars at that time to more than six hundred thousand dollars in 1898. The business manufactured about one hundred thousand pairs of gloves in 1898 or five percent of all gloves manufactured in Gloversville.

Angelo immediately began thinking about buying the Shipman Glove Company. Later than night, Angelo calculated the amount of funding he had available, what he thought he could offer to buy the business, and if he could borrow money to purchase the business. Angelo knew he would need some form of security for a loan, and would need to have sufficient capital to maintain operations. Interest rates were low and since Shipman's was an existing successful business he thought that may be enough to convince the bank to provide financing. Angelo was a good businessman with a very good reputation in Italy. His business in Italy was growing and doing well. He did not know if an Italian immigrant who had been in America for about one year would qualify for owning a business like Shipman's. He would continue to work on the plan and then schedule a meeting with Mr. Shipman.

Pasquale told his family about Mr. Shipman's decision to sell the business. Pasquale also said that they should not be concerned as Mr. Shipman would keep the business in place while it was being sold. Pasquale did not consider that Angelo might be interested in buying the business. Angelo did not say anything to Pasquale about the sale when they left work that evening. Pasquale did begin thinking he would talk to Angelo about going to work for him when he started his business. Pasquale did not approach Angelo at this time. He thought he would wait until he had a better sense of where Angelo was with his plan to open his business.

Angelo decided to talk to Emilio about his thought of buying Shipman's. He met Emilio alone at the lodge a couple of weeks after Mr. Shipman had made the announcement. Angelo shared his original plan with Emilio about starting his own shop. He told Angelo about the business in Italy. He discussed how much money he had now and what he thought he would need to buy Shipman's. He also talked about loans for the business and his concern about being an Italian immigrant and so new to America.

Emilio had recently passed the bar exam and was admitted to practice law in the state of New York. Emilio was now working for the law firm in town where he was a law clerk while completing his studies. Emilio listened intently and then began speaking to Angelo as a lawyer. He detailed how business operations work in America as compared to Italy. He explained that with a viable business plan and good start up capital even as an Italian immigrant he may have a chance of convincing financial institutions to loan money. Emilio also offered to assist with the necessary legal paperwork, the negotiations for buying the business, and to help talk with the banks. Emilio mentioned that with the success of the family business in Italy, Angelo was already in a fairly good position. They would need to convince the financial community that the risk is lessened since there is good business experience.

Angelo felt good about the meeting with Emilio and his willingness to help. He knew that he would have to pay the law firm for that work but having Emilio guide him and provide counsel would be worth the cost. Angelo would need a lawyer in any case so why not have someone he knew and trusted. Angelo would plan on talking to Pasquale in the next few weeks about the meeting with Emilio and the possibilities about purchasing the Shipman business.

On the twelfth day of October 1899, exactly one year since Pasquale and the Guiliani family had arrived in America, there was a celebration at Maddalena's to mark the anniversary. During the party Angelo asked Pasquale to walk outside with him. Pasquale thought something was wrong and asked Angelo if everything was alright. Angelo replied, *"le cose non poteva essere migliore dal caro amico"* (things could not be better my dear friend). Angelo told Pasquale that he was going to make an offer to buy the Shipman business. Angelo had already talked to the financial institutions. During the past few weeks Emilio had helped with the business plan and the financial information from the business in Italy including its history and profitability. Based on the success of the business in Italy, some good cash assets that Angelo had, and the experience that Angelo had as a business owner in Italy, there was one bank that was willing to provide a loan. Angelo's Italian business had also no debt. The lender would use the Italian company as the main source of collateral for the business in Gloversville. The business in Italy also had just secured a major contract for leather garments that would nearly double the revenues in less than one year. That was very pleasing to the lender as Angelo would have sufficient working capital to maintain business operations.

Angelo explained all that to Pasquale. Angelo then said, *"tutto ciò che resta da fare è fare un'offerta per acquistare il business"* (all that is left to do is to make an offer to buy the business). Pasquale did not know what to say. He looked at Angelo and just nodded. Angelo told Pasquale that if Mr. Shipman agreed to sell to Angelo the current business operations would continue for a short period of time unchanged. Angelo told Pasquale that the worse that could happen was that Mr. Shipman rejects the offer. Angelo said if that were to happen then the plan of starting a new glove shop would happen. He said either way there would be a Guiliani Leather Company in Gloversville.

The two went back into the house and did not share the information with the others at this time. Maddalena talked about Pasquale's beard he grew while carving the statue. Pasquale told them about his excursion to the upper deck to get some fresh air and how accommodating the ship crew was. Both Angelo and Pasquale shared their feelings when they saw the Statue of Liberty. They all agreed that coming to America was good for them and their families.

Raphelia sensed that Pasquale seemed to be a little tense. She asked Pasquale if something was wrong. Pasquale told her everything was fine and things may even get better soon. She looked puzzled by his answer. Pasquale told her not to worry and that he and Angelo would be sharing some news with the families soon. Still concerned, she kept asking Pasquale what it meant. Pasquale responded, *"la mia bella moglie presto vedremo il miracolo del sogno Americano"* (my lovely wife soon we will see the miracle of the American dream). Raphelia said, *"è meglio che sia un miracolo o avrete bisogno di uno"* (it better be a miracle or you will need one). Pasquale laughed and said, *"caro Signore in Cielo mi aiuti"* (my dear Lord in Heaven help me). Pasquale and Raphelia hugged. He put his palm on her cheek and smiled and said *"ti amo."* She gave him a kiss, smiled back, and hugged him again.

Twenty One

Angelo and Emilio met with Mr. Shipman on the third of November. They presented an offer to buy the business. Mr. Shipman was a little surprised that Angelo was making an offer. Angelo explained about his company in Italy and his business background. Mr. Shipman congratulated Angelo on the success of the business in Italy. He told Angelo and Emilio that he would think about the offer and he would get back to them in a week.

Angelo and Pasquale met with the familes to tell them about the offer to buy the Shipman Glove Company. Angelo had not even shared his plan with Rosa. He wanted to make sure that he had a good chance to actually make the purchase before he told her. She was aware of his plan to start a business and was actually very pleased to hear that he was considering buying an existing successful business. Vincenzo and Luciana congratulated Angelo. Maddalena and Antonio wished him the best in his endeavor. Raphelia told Pasquale that this was a miracle.

Angelo talked about the plan and the offer made to Mr. Shipman. He told everyone about Emilio's assistance and his handling the legal matters. Vincenzo asked about the timeframe for the purchase and when the agreement would be finalized. Angelo said that Mr. Shipman was reviewing the offer and that if the offer was agreed to or other negotations were needed, the deal would probably be finalized in December.

Angelo made a comment about coming to America and the success it has brought everyone. He talked about Vincenzo's shoe repair shop and how well the shop was doing. He mentioned Antonio's job skills and how in demand he was for new construction projects. He said the women were all working for glove shops and doing well. He then talked about Pasquale's success at Shipman's. He told everyone that when the deal was finalized and Angelo owned the business, Pasquale would be the shop manager for Angelo.

Pasquale was surprised by Angelo's comment. He always knew that Angelo wanted him to work for him in his company but to be made the manager was more than Pasquale had imagined. Angelo told the group that Pasquale had the best skills of anyone he knew in the business and his expertise would help make the business more successful. Angelo said his brother in Italy handles the business there and his brother in America, Pasquale, would be the person who would handle all of the shop activities while Angelo would responsible to make sure there was a constant flow of orders. Angelo would also handle the overall operations of the business. Angelo mentioned that the business would be more than a glove shop, although that would remain the major part of the business. He said just like the business in Italy, the shop here would expand to make leather garments and other leather goods in time.

The families were very supportive of Angelo's ideas. They also liked his way of thinking about the future. Pasquale mentioned that Mr. Shipman cared deeply about his employees and that Angelo had that same quality. He said together they would make the company the best place to work in Gloversville. Angelo agreed and pledged to make sure all employees were treated with dignity and respect. Angelo told them he would be changing the company name from the Shipman Glove Company to the Guiliani Leather Company. He wanted the business to be known for all its leather products, including a plan to sell whole hides as well as making leather gloves, leather garments, and other leather accessories.

Mr. Shipman had been considering Angelo's initial offer. Angelo had offered five hundred thousand dollars to buy the business. With the financial institution willing to lend six hundred thousand dollars and Angelo having another one hundred thousand in cash, there would be enough cash in hand in case negotiations had to take place. The business in Italy would also provide up to five thousand dollars each month as needed for operating capital for the company in Gloversville until the firm could be fully self supporting.

On November 13, Mr. Shipman notified Angelo and Emilio that he would sell the business for seven hundred and fifty thousand dollars. Angelo was not surprised by the counteroffer but would not agree to that amount. Angelo and Emilio discussed the counteroffer with the lender. The financial institution would not agree to the amount and recommended that negotiations be continued. After three more weeks of negotiations, Mr. Shipman and Angelo agreed to finalize the deal for six hundred and twenty five thousand dollars. The lender agreed to finance the entire purchase leaving Angelo with his one hundred thousand dollars for operating capital.

Mr. Shipman and Angelo completed the deal with a handshake. Mr. Shipman told Angelo that he would immediately begin working with him on the transition. Mr. Shipman said he would introduce Angelo to his accountants, business associates, and clients. Mr. Shipman was confident that the existing Shipman clients would continue to do business with the new company, especially since Angelo had been working there as an employee. Angelo was pleased that Mr. Shipman would work with him and provide a smooth transition in the business exchange.

The lawyers would complete the paperwork for the purchase and sale of the Shipman Glove Company to Guiliani Leather Company. On December 8, Mr. Shipman and Angelo signed the documents completing the transfer of the business. The agreement stipulated that Angelo would begin business operations on the first of January in 1900. A new century, a new business, a new beginning. Emilio, Angelo, and Pasquale met at the lodge after the agreement was signed. They had a glass of wine to celebrate. Pasquale said that the new century would bring prosperity to all as Emilio had predicted. Emilio said Pasquale's *alba nuova* had been made complete. A new dawn, a new age, a new beginning and living the American dream that has become reality.

The three men met with the all of the family members at Maddalena's that evening and shared the good news. During the summer Antonio had constructed a wood-fired brick pizza oven in the yard. Maddalena would make pizza to celebrate the new business. Angelo provided all the information about the purchase of Shipman's. He said over the next few weeks, he and Mr. Shipman would be working together on the business ownership transition.

Emilio described the legal details of operating a business in America. Emilio would become the legal counsel for the business and also a business advisor to Angelo. Vincenzo said his business was a local operation. He asked if there were any restrictions for Angelo in how the business could be operated. Emilio explained that laws in the United States required certain conditions for corporations but the legal paperwork for that had been completed. He said other than tax liabilities, there were no government restrictions on how the business operated. There were no limits on the business for growth and other business opportunities. Emilio also said New York State was one of the first states that had a simplified business registration process. That would help Angelo as the amount of required legal paperwork was significantly less. Corporate law was one of Emilio's specialties. He would be able to guide Angelo to ensure the business complied with all regulations.

During the last three weeks of December Mr. Shipman and Angelo worked together daily on the transition. Together they held a joint meeting with all employees to explain the transition of the business. The day after Christmas Mr. Shipman said his goodbyes to all employees. Although Angelo was scheduled to officially take over on the first of January, Mr. Shipman was ready to turn over the company a few days early as Angelo had a good handle on the operations.

The employees presented Mr. Shipman with an engraved gold pocket watch that they had purchased. The watch was engraved with the words, *Thank you Mr. Shipman for your generosity, caring, and treating us with respect. Your employees.* Pasquale presented the watch on behalf of all the employees. Mr. Shipman, with tears in his eyes said, *"it is not easy leaving you. It is my time to let go. My entire life has been helping people. This business was just a way to make that happen. I love each of you and thank you for making this business what it is today. Tomorrow you have a new owner, but the traditions of the business will continue and with Angelo's leadership the continued success of the business is ensured. God blesss you and your families."*

The employees applauded loudly for Mr. Shipman. They then each said a personal goodbye. The last thing Mr. Shipman did as he left was take down the small Shipman Glove Company sign by the front door and replaced it with a new custom made oval shaped sign that identified the Guilani Leather Company. The sign had the Guiliani name at the top of the oval, a silhouette of a leather hide in the center, and the words Leather Company at the bottom of the oval. Angelo was in tears when he saw the sign. He and Mr. Shipman hugged. Angelo in the Italian tradition kissed Mr. Shipman on both cheeks and said in English, *"God bless you. You are a wonderful gentleman;"* Mr. Shipman replied in Italian saying, *"Grazie paisano. Dio mi ha benedetto e tui ti ha benedettto to pure."* (Thank you brother. God has blessed me and he has blessed you as well).

The New Year turn of the century celebration in Gloversville was almost an all night party. The lodge held what was becoming an annual New Year's eve celebration. Before the party that night, Angelo met with Pasquale and told him that beginning next week Pasquale would be paid fifty-five dollars each week and would receive an annual bonus based on the profitabilty of the company but not less than one thousand dollars. Pasquale did not know what to say. He looked at Angelo and thanked him. They hugged and Angelo grabbed both of Pasquale's hands and said, *"alba nuova."*

With the business closed for New Year's day, Angelo went to the shop to make sure everything was ready for the next day. He planned on greeting each employee as they came to work. He also planned on having a meeting with the employees to provide some information about objectives of the business. Angelo figured that giving the employees an upfront idea of where the business was heading would give them a better sense of security under the new ownership. He then took some time just to walk around the inside of the building and to reflect on his life since coming to America.

The next day Angelo greeted each employee as they came to work. He then held his meeting with them. He introduced Pasquale as the shop manager. Everyone was very pleased that Pasquale would be in charge of the shop. Angelo told the employees that over time the plan for the business was to expand the product line to include producing leather garments and other leather products. He said that combined with the business in Italy the company would be sending products worldwide. He told them that today is a new beginning and this is the new dawn for the Guiliani Leather Company and for each of them. All the employees applauded.

The Italian immigrants in America had been experiencing some continued discrimination recently. There seemed to be a growing resentment against the Italians. More immigrants had also been coming to live and work in Gloversville. There were no outward signs of discrimination in Gloversville but there were some verbal incidents that caused some concern for the immigrants. Many Italians who had been in America for some time began to change either their first names, last names, or both to an American name. Some changed their names to make the name easier to pronounce. Others would make the change as they thought they could make more money using an American name or that it was just appropriate for business. Pasquale decided to make a name change for his first name only. He chose the name Charles. He was not concerned about discrimination or any other issue regarding his nationality. His reason was just to be more American, to blend into the more predominate population. Pasquale's sons also wanted to follow their father's choice. Eduardo became Edward, Francesco became Frank, and Arturo became Arthur. Raphelia would keep her first name. Pasquale told his family that they were not losing their Italian heritage or culture, they were just adapting to the American culture.

Vincenzo and Antonio also decided to Americanize their first names. Vincenzo changed his name to Vincent and Antonio changed his to Anthony. Emilio and Angelo would keep their Italian names. None of the changes were made as legal changes. In most situations they all were still called by their given Italian names by their Italian community. The non-Italians in the community would for the most part call them by their American names. Many other Italian immigrants in Gloversville also changed their names.

It was over a month since Angelo took over the business. Pasquale had settled easily into his role of shop manager. He kept production levels high and maintained an excellent level of quality. Pasquale would take time to show the cutters some techniques that would make the quality of their cuts better. He showed them the ideal stretching method for the hides. He also showed them how to get a better feel of the hide using the palm of their hand to feel any imperfections that were not immediately visible. He would tell the cutters that their hands were their eyes.

Eduardo began working part-time as a glove cutter. He would work a couple of hours after school each day and on Saturday mornings. Maddalena, Rosa, Luciana, and Raphelia all began sewing gloves at home for the company. Angelo was intent on making his business a true family affair. Angelo was fast gaining a reputation of being a good businessman, an excellent owner, and a boss who cared about each and every employee. Angelo would walk the shop to say good morning to each employee. Angelo was the first person at work each day and the last to leave. He wanted to set the example for his employees that he was there for them at anytime. Pasquale would step in and cut gloves with the other cutters if needed. They all appreciated that and knew that Pasquale would help. As the orders grew the demands for increased production required the hiring of more cutters. Pasquale brought two more experienced cutters on board.

Pasquale would have daily meetings with Angelo. In one meeting Pasquale was concerned about running out of space for the cutters. The cutting room tables had become more crowded and hiring more cutters would not be possible without having more room. Angelo had already considered the issue and told Pasquale that first they would rearrange some of the shop areas to allow more space for cutting tables. That rearrangement would also require that some of the women would begin sewing gloves at home instead of at the shop. That would serve to create more space as well as allowing the women to spend more time with their children. Pasquale was appreciative of Angelo's thinking and of his way of solving problems. Pasquale not only felt good about his job, he felt very comfortable with the business and the outlook for its success.

Twenty Two

February was a big month for the DaCorsi family. Pasquale turned forty-nine. Raphelia had a celebration party for Pasquale that was held at the lodge. Typically in Italy, the person having a birthday would buy their cake and would invite others to help celebrate. Pasquale usually did not celebrate his birthday. Raphelia figured she would take control and put the party together. She told Pasquale that the lodge had a function and they were invited to go. When they arrived, Pasquale had no idea that the party was for him. When he walked in, eveyone cheered for him. For a minute he was wondering what all the cheering was about. When he caught on, he was a little embarrased. He looked at Raphelia and she just gave a sheepish grin back.

The boys were told by their mother that there would be a party for Pasquale, but to not tell their father about the function. Everyone shouted," *buon cumpleanno!*" (happy birthday!). Pasquale was flooded with gifts. One gift from Raphelia for Pasquale was a new flat cap. Pasquale had worn his old cap for over ten years. Raphelia told him it was time to *"sbarazzarsi di quella cosa usurati"* (get rid of that worn out thing). There were many homemade food items for Pasquale as gifts, a typical Italian tradition.

Emilio gave Pasquale a bottle of imported Italian wine. Angelo and his family had a small wooden model of the SS Aller made for Pasquale. Angelo told Pasquale that he knew how much Pasquale liked carving items out of wood. He said this was one item that he did not have to carve but one that would have a lasting memory. Maddalena gave her brother new rosary beads made of agate with silk thread and a silver crucifix. Pasquale was humbled by the party and the gifts. He thanked everyone. He told the group that Raphelia had kept the birthday celebration a secret. He thanked her for a wonderful party and for the nearly twenty years as his wife and the love of his life.

Pasquale was continuing his search to buy a home. In early February Pasquale looked at a home that had just been built. It was a bungalow-style, single family home. The home had one bedroom on the first floor and three bedrooms on the second level. There was a nice large parlor area, a separate formal dining room, a bathroom, and a large kitchen with an eating area, and an alcove space off of the kitchen that would work well for Raphelia's sewing machine room. There was plenty of storage and closet space along with a nice attic. The outside of the home had a roof covered front porch that spread across the width of the house. Pasquale took Raphelia to look at the house. She immediately knew this was to be her home. Pasquale decided to make an offer on the home.

The home location is 35 Park Street in Gloversville. The home is in the southeast section of Gloversville off the East Pine Street hill from South Main Street to the Park Street site. The house is about one half mile from the glove shop. The asking price for the house is five thousand three hundred dollars. After making the offer, Pasquale successfully closed the sale at five thousand dollars. On the twenty-first of February Pasquale and Raphelia signed the closing documents. The DaCorsi's were homeowners. They moved in on the twenty-fourth of February. Less than a year and a half after Pasquale had immigrated from Italy, he became a homeowner in America.

Raphelia loved her home. The Park Street area had a number of new homes under construction. Most were being built as two-story flats. The bungalow home that Pasquale and Raphelia bought was one of just a few in that area. Home building in Gloversville was on the rise. With the population continuing to grow, keeping up with housing was a challenge. The glove and leather tanning industries were the major employers in the area. Those companies needed more workers to meet the demand for products and those workers needed housing.

There were some growing labor issues in the industry in Gloversville and across the country. Workers at some companies in Gloversville complained about working conditions and wages. In other parts of the country, labor unions authorized strikes against employers. Strikes had occurred in 1891, 1893, and 1897 (Redmond, 1913). The glove companies in Gloversville were not unionized. This was a result of fairly good wages and having shops that produced over fifty percent of the glove products in America. There was, however, a need for more factories to keep pace with the demand.

The issue of working conditions and wages was only with a few small shops in the area. Also the existence of a single industry that employs over eighty-five percent of the local workforce exerts pressure on companies to pay fair wages and to provide good working conditions.The prosperity of the business community in Gloversville is dependent on the glove and leather industries (Redmond, 1913).

The labor issues in Gloversville were quickly resolved. The industry in Gloversville was approaching ten million dollars in annual revenues, accounting for about fifty-seven percent of the glove products sold in the country (Redmond, 1913). The industry coalition worked successfully to address and resolve the issues. Fortunately, there were no labor issues at Guiliani's. Angelo paid his workers piece rate. The average rate for cutters was seventy cents to ninety-five cents per dozen pairs. The well experienced cutters could cut an average of twenty-two dozen pairs of gloves per week making approximately twenty-one dollars per week. The piece rate at Guiliani's was one of the highest in the area. Cutters in the area still earned about twelve dollars to seventeen dollars each week on average.

Most glove shops in Gloversville had converted to the piece rate system. That also encouraged increased production levels. The quality of the products was still the major driver for sales. Cutters still had to stretch the hides right to maintain high quality levels. Improper stretching could produce inferior products. Pasquale was constantly checking the stretching method of his cutters. If he noticed an issue, he would immediately intervene to correct the situation. That constant and continuous training allowed the Guiliani Leather Company to maintain some of the highest quality products in the industry.

Some glove companies began to move away from table cutting and started using a block cutting process. The table cutting method provided for systematic stretching of portions of the skin and individual glove pattern cutouts. In block cutting, the entire hide was stretched in a single process. Steel patterns would be placed on the hide covering the entire area. The block cutters would use a cylindrical mallet to strike the patterns producing six to eight glove cutouts at one time. This method produced a lower quality product.

The average cost of manufacturing gloves in Gloversville was five dollars and fifty cents per each dozen pairs (Redmond, 1913). This cost was higher than the average in worldwide production. Foreign manufacturers were subjected to a tarriff for exporting products to the United States making the higher costs in Gloversville a non-factor. The Gloversville manufacturers still produced about ninety-five percent of the men's fine leather gloves in America as compared to about six percent of women's fine leather gloves (Redmond, 1913). The profits for men's gloves were higher than women's gloves. Companies in Gloversville knew the market conditions well and were able to capitalize on the most profitable products.

Angelo decided to build an addition to the shop. The space adjustments had been made to accommodate more table cutters. The majority of gloves were now sewn at home by the women. The plan to add a garment manufacturing divison would require more space. Relocating the business to a larger space was a possibility. The negative side of that was a larger space would have to be located in a rented builiding. Angelo owned the building occupied by his company. Constructing an addition would increase the property's value and also increase the value of the business.

Later that summer construction of the addition was underway. The addition would nearly double the size of the building. Pasquale had hired four more cutters as glove sales for the company kept increasing. The company now had seventeen cutters. Adding more women sewing gloves at home brought the total number of employees to fifty-eight. The company had a total of sixteen women working from home including Raphelia, Maddalena, Rosa, and Luciana. Angelo also employed ten people who ironed the finished gloves. That work required the employee to place a finished glove over an upright steel hand pattern that would steam the glove leather smoothing and removing any wrinkles. The company also employed five administrative workers, five in shipping and receiving, and five salespeople.

The summer was eventful for the DaCorsi boys. Francesco completed the eleventh grade. Eduardo achieved high grades in all his classes. He was in the top ten percent of his class. He was also fluent in five languages now. Arturo also did very well in all of his classes. Francesco planned to work full time during the summer. Emilio invited the boys to spend a few days at a newly constructed summer camp at Lake George. Located at the base of the Adirondack Mountains, Lake George was a historical area where battles were fought during the French and Indian War. The boys enjoyed swimming, boating, fishing, and playing games with others at the campgrounds.

The addition to the shop was completed at the end of January in 1901. The garment division of Guiliani Leather was officially in business. Angelo had invested in the machinery and equipment needed for making leather coats. There would be no work done at home for this division. All fabrication and assembly would be done in the shop. Angelo also hired a separate manager to oversee the garment division. This was done so Pasquale could maintain full control over the glove manufacturing division. The glove orders continued to increase. Pasquale added four more cutters at the shop and six home workers to sew gloves.

The garment division start-up began with seven employees. The employees included one pattern maker, two cutters, two machine operators to sew the garments, and two finish workers who also handled the packing and shipping duties. There was a two-month training program for all the garment division employees. The manager of the divison had worked for a leather garment maker in Italy. He also conducted all the training for the employees. Angelo handled all the initial sales for the garment division. He used samples of products made by his company in Italy for sales demonstrations.

The production of leather coats began in March. Angelo had secured sales that provided a two month backlog for the division. Two sales staff were added to the divison in April. Angelo also hired a person to handle all of the marketing for the garment division. The initial product line had four styles of leather coats for men and three for women. Guiliani Leather Company was the only leather garment manufacturer in Gloversville at that time.

There was now a total of seventy-eight employees at the company. Guiliani Leather Company was now one of the largest employers in Gloversville with over seven hundred thousand dollars in sales in 1900. The projection for 1901, including the new garment division, was approximately one million dollars in sales. As Angelo had told Pasquale, there would be a bonus based on profits of the company. In January Angelo gave Pasquale a one thousand five hundred dollar bonus and increased his weekly wages to sixty- five dollars. Angelo also reduced the work hours for employees from fifty-four hours per week to fifty. All employees had Saturday off. The cutters could work on Saturday if they wanted and were paid the standard piece rate for Saturday work. Most of the cutters worked at least two Saturdays per month.

As shop manager, Pasquale promoted one lead cutter a foreman position. That allowed Pasquale to concentrate on managing the overall glove division while maintaining production levels. Pasquale still did all of the training for new glove cutters. After one year of operations with the new company, all of the cutters were making more money. This was also partly due to Pasquale's guidance and training. For piece rate cutters, the more one produced the more they would earn. They would have to maintain high quality. Any glove pairs that could not be sewn were returned for rework. The cutters did not receive any compensation for rework. For the Guiliani cutters, the amount of rework was very small in quantity.

Francesco graduated from high school in June 1901. The family had a graduation party for Francesco at the DaCorsi house. With a large yard the party was held outside. Francesco's fellow workers and the butcher shop owner came to the party. Raphelia always felt good about having parties for her sons. She was proud of her boys and did not hesitate to showcase her sons. High school graduation was a special event. In Italy many young people did not complete secondary education. Raphelia and Pasquale both left school when they were sixteen. That was fairly typical of the times. With the oldest son completing high school, especially in America, made both Raphelia and Pasquale very proud. Raphelia and Pasquale also knew that the younger two boys would follow their older brother in completing their high school education.

As the months progressed the garment division at Guiliani's was performing steady production rates. The orders from wholesalers was increasing. The employees in the garment division were keeping pace with the orders and backlogs were still around two months. Angelo looked at improving the timeframe for shipping finished products. That would require an increase in production. Although more employees would be needed, Angelo knew that faster shipping would result in an increase in orders. Angelo was prepared to add employees as needed.

In September of 1901, the company had added six more employees to the garment division. The total sales for the year for the garment division was over two hundred and seventy thousand dollars. The glove division produced eight hundred and fifty thousand dollars in sales. The overall sales for the year exceeded the forecasted amount by one hundred and twenty thousand dollars. Angelo gave each employee a one hundred dollar bonus. Pasquale received a two thousand dollar bonus and the garment division manager received a seven hundred fifty dollar bonus.

Pasquale was very pleased with his decision to join Angelo and work for him in the business. Pasquale admired Angelo for continuing to care about the well being of the employees. The reputation of the Guiliani Leather Company had many potential workers applying for jobs with the company. The company was able to select the best workers for employment. The glove manufacturing portion of the business was very profitable. The garment divison was showing some profit for the first months of operation.

The DaCorsi family was doing very well in America. Francesco would be turning eighteen in October. He was doing very well working at the butcher shop. Arturo would be entering the ninth grade. Eduardo was becoming a very good glove cutter and had learned the basics of the Chinese language. Raphelia was happy in her new country and had begun to learn some English. Italian was still the predominate language spoken at home although some English would be in a conversation on occasion.

The regular Sunday after church gatherings were still taking place. The families would alternate homes each week. The food was still the grand Italian style meals. Pasquale had begun making his homemade wine again. There was never a lack of wine at the dinners or for any other event. Emilio was becoming like an uncle to the boys. Emilio joined the family for the weekly gatherings and continued to take the boys places on occasion.

There was a grand party for Francesco's eighteenth birthday. The party was held at the at the lodge and was well attended. The celebration was a litte embarrassing for Francesco. He was not very outgoing and all the attention was a little strange to him. He asked his mother why all these people would want to celebrate his birthday. She told him that turning eighteen in Italian tradition was very special. Emilio made that a little clearer for Francesco. Emilio invited Francesco to join him in the front of the room. Emilio gathered the group together and told everyone and Francseco that today he was a man. He told the group that when Francesco was thirteen he came of age with the Sacrament of Confirmation. He then said, *"oggi Francseco passeggiate da fanciullezza all'età adulta"* (today Francesco walks from boyhood to adulthood). Everyone raised their glasses of wine and said, *"saluti Francesco!"*

Gloversville in 1901 also saw the beginnings of a new mode of transportation. The automobile was making its presence known in the city. There had been a few motor vehicles that some people had driven in town a year or so earlier. About fifty vehicles were now in the hands of Gloversville residents. Angelo had also purchased a runabout style automobile for use by the glove division delivery and pickup employee. That person delivered the work to the women working from home and would pick up the finished gloves to return them to the factory. The one cylinder crank start vehicle cost six hundred dollars.

The runabout was a vehicle with a single bench seat. There was no windshield and no doors. The vehicle was an open style that resembled an open wagon in appearance with no top. The vehicle had to be registered in the state of New York. Vehicle operators were not licensed at that time. The transition from a horse-drawn wagon to the motor vehicle for the Guiliani delivery and pick up employee was very challenging. After about a month using the automobile, the employee was adapting to the change. Pasquale did not like automobiles. He said he would never use one. The boys told him in time they would buy an automobile and they would take Pasquale for a ride in it. Pasquale would point to his feet and tell the boys that they worked for him and would take him where he needed to go.

Pasquale was a little hesitant about certain types of progress. He was a traditional table cutter and did not believe that newer forms of glove cutting were good for the industry. He knew that some innovations would be beneficial but he was still set on the methods he had been taught and that he passed on to other cutters. The same was true for other types of progress. He did not feel that having a lot of automobiles would be good for the country. He felt that automobiles would contribute to a faster pace of life. He thought that would be bad and would have a negative impact on family life. He knew that whatever progress took place, he would need to accept change. He had talked to Raphelia about this many times. He told her as long as his wine-making methods did not change, he would be fine.

Twenty Three

On May 26, 1902 seventeen year old Maria Finizio, and her twin brother. Achille, arrived at Ellis Island from Italy. They were accompanied by their sixteen year old cousin, Antonio Beato. They were traveling to Gloversville to meet their father and uncle Francesco Finizio, who had emigrated from Italy to America in 1900. Maria and Achille grew up in the Barra neighborhood of Naples. Barra is close to the foot of Mount Vesuvius, the famous volcano that destroyed Pompeii in 79 A.D. That eruption killed more than sixteen thousand people (Ball, 2005).

Francesco Finizio was a master glove cutter. He had been hired by Pasquale to work at Guiliani's shortly after his arrival in Gloversville. Francesco was seven years younger than Pasquale. Francesco was also known as Ciccio (chee-cho). He had been called Ciccio since he was a boy. Ciccio's glove cutting skills were very close to Pasquale's. Angelo also liked the way Ciccio cut gloves. Ciccio and Eduardo worked across from one another at the same cutting table. Pasquale's sons called their father Papa. Eduardo, mostly as a sign of respect, referred to Ciccio as *Papa due* (father number two). Eduardo was the same age as Ciccio's daughter and son.

On the first Monday in June, Ciccio brought Maria and

Achille to the shop to meet Pasquale, Angelo, and his co-workers.

Ciccio introduced Maria to Eduardo. They exchanged greetings.

Eduardo asked Maria about her voyage. She told him the trip took

fourteen days and was rough at times. She told him she came over

on the SS Neckar. She said there were about five hundred

passengers in third class. Eduardo said that his ship had over one

thousand in third class. Maria told him it must have been very

crowded. Eduardo said it was but he was small and did not take

up much space. Maria laughed. He asked her why her trip took so

long. She said it was a slow ship. Eduardo laughed.

Pasquale invited Ciccio, Raphela (Ciccio's wife), Maria and

Achille for dinner for that Saturday. Raphelia and Raphela talked

about family. Pasquale and Ciccio talked about work. Eduardo

and Maria shared stories about each other. Maria was amazed that

Eduardo was fluent in six languages especially at his age. He told

her he was going to start learning Portugese. She asked why he

wanted to know so many languages. Eduardo told her that

knowing how to speak the languages would provide a better

opportunity in the future for doing business with other

nationalities. He also told her he would help her learn English.

She liked the offer. The boys all became quick friends with

Antonio and Achille. In Italy, Achille was known as Chilli. He mentioned that to the boys and they immediately began calling him Chilli.

Eduardo graduated from high school in June. There was a party for Eduardo similar to Francesco's a couple of years ago. Eduardo received gifts from everyone who attended. A special guest, Mr. Shipman, also came to the party. Mr. Shipman gave Eduardo a book of Chinese characters and writing techniques and a gold pen to write with. Mr. Shipman had found out that Eduardo had learned the Chinese language. Eduardo was in awe of the gift from Mr. Shipman. He thanked Mr. Shipman for the wonderful gift and told him he would treasure the gift forever.

Pasquale told Eduardo that he would now begin working full time at Guiliani's. Eduardo's glove cutting skills were improving. Only a few cutter apprentices achieve the master cutter rating. Pasquale was teaching Eduardo every techinque he had used to become a master cutter. Eduardo was working as an apprentice and now could look at completing his apprenticeship working full time. Eduardo liked cutting gloves but he also had his sights set on other goals and opportunities for his future.

Eduardo even in his early learning process of glove cutting was always looking for ways to improve the method of table cutting. He began to sketch ideas and kept a file and record of those ideas. Eduardo would question why and how certain cutting processes were done that way. He would experiment with his ideas using butcher paper that Francesco provided to him for cutouts and templates. Eduardo would cut the butcher paper to replicate the shape of a hide to test his ideas. Pasquale encouraged Eduardo to continue to experiment with his innovative concepts.

Pasquale and Ciccio had become close friends by this time. In one conversation Pasquale asked Ciccio about his mother and father. Ciccio told Pasquale that his mother died in 1878 when he was twenty years old. He said his father, Luigi, came to Gloversville in 1880 at the age of fifty. His father is seventy-two years old and still cuts gloves at a small shop in Gloversville. Ciccio's father taught him how to cut gloves. Pasquale shared that his good friend, Luigi Amato, had taught him how to cut gloves. He also told Ciccio that Luigi had passed away about a year ago. Ciccio said he was sorry for that. Ciccio also told Pasquale that he when his father came to America, the glove business was doing very well. It took Ciccio a while to be convinced to come to America. Ciccio did not want to leave his home in Italy. Ciccio's father finally convinced him to come to Gloversville. Ciccio's father, Luigi, had people write letters to Ciccio telling him about Gloversville. Luigi could not read or write in Italian or in English.

Over the next few months, the families became very close. Raphelia taught Maria how to sew gloves. Maria was now working for a large glove shop in Gloversville. Maddalena's husband, Antonio, was able to get a job for Chilli as a masonry apprentice. Young Antonio Beato, who had been an apprentice barber in Italy, was hired as an apprentice by a local Italian barber in Gloversville. Under the watchful eye of Raphelia and Raphela, Eduardo and Maria had been allowed to see each other socially. Over the next year that relationship began to take on a more romantic involvement. Eduardo was continuing to learn the Portugese language.

By the end of 1903, Guiliani's had a total of eighty-five employees. The garment division had revenues in excess of five hundred thousand dollars. The glove division had its best year with over one million dollars in sales. The growth of the company required additional management staff. Angelo hired a sales manager, an operations manager, and an administrative manager. Pasquale continued to oversee the glove division. Ciccio was made a foreman of the glove cutting division. Eduardo had completed his apprenticeship program. Eduardo also continued to explore his numerous ideas on improving the manufacturing process of glove making.

In 1903 Maddalena's husband, Antonio, started his own masonry business. The construction in the area was still thriving. Antonio had secured a number of jobs that would keep his company busy for the entire year. Antonio hired four masons and two full time laborers to work for him. Chilli was one of the masons working for Antonio. Young Arturo was also working part-time as a laborer for Antonio. Arturo is in the eleventh grade and is planning to attend business college when he graduates from high school.

Angelo's son, Giovanni, is in the seventh grade and Leonardo has started school. Guiliani Leather Company has been in business four years. Angelo was the youngest leather company owner in the area when he bought the Shipman Glove Company. At the age of forty-one, he remains one of the youngest leather company business owners in the area. Maddalena was no longer sewing gloves and is now working at Guiliani's shop overseeing the packing and shipping department.

Vincenzo and Luciana's daughter, Maria, married Giuseppe Alberti in July 1903. Maria gave birth to a son in October 1904. Maria and her husband named their son, Gaetano Vincenzo. The baby was baptized when he was seven weeks old. Eduardo DaCorsi and Maria Finizio were chosen as the child's godparents. As godparents, Eduardo and Maria play a significant role, and in some respects, have more responsibility than blood relatives. They will serve as substitute parents to guide, protect, and raise the child in the proper religious ways according to the Italian and Roman Catholic traditions. In Southern Italy, godparents are known as *comare* and *compare*. This was a great honor for Eduardo and Maria. Both now just twenty-one years old and asked to take on this responsibility shows a high level of trust, confidence, and respect the family has for them. Eduardo and Maria accepted the responsibility and pledged to uphold their duties as godparents during the baptismal service.

A large celebration was held at Vincenzo and Luciana's home after the baptism. Gaetano's gifts were abundant. Family members, friends, neighbors, people from church, the officiating priest, and others such as Emilio, all attended the party and paid their respects to the child and parents. The food included antipasti, lasagna, roasted lamb, pasta, and a *dolce alla Neapolitana*, a traditional Italian layer cake with a pastry cream filling and covered with slivered almonds. Another wonderful gathering in true Italian tradition.

Eduardo and Maria had been in a relationship for about six months when they were asked to be the godparents for Gaetano. The couple would be chaperoned by either Raphela or Raphelia when they were together. Eduardo and Maria would see each other two or three times a week. Pasquale and Ciccio talked about the relationship and how well Eduardo and Maria got along. Eduardo and Maria had similar upbringings in Italy. They lived within a mile of each other in Italy but did not know each other. Their fathers were both glove cutters in Italy. There were many similarities between the two families. Eduardo and Maria liked the Italian traditions, even though they both had become adapted to some American ways.

Raphelia and Raphela felt that Eduardo and Maria would get married. Eduardo had not approached Maria's family on this as of yet. Eduardo had made comments that he wanted to have some financial security before he got married. He was able to save some money working at Guiliani's. Both Francesco and Eduardo contributed to the family finances while living at home. Francesco was now twenty-three. He was still working at the butcher shop but had been talking about having his own business. Francesco had no plans at this time to marry.

Over the next twelve months, Eduardo and Maria discussed marriage. It was difficult to have private conversations as there was always a chaperone present. They did however, have some time alone going on walks in the neighborhood or they would meet after work and Eduardo would walk Maria home. Maria told Eduardo he needed to ask her family for her to marry him. He was a little nervous about asking but he promised Maria that he would.

On Christmas eve in December 1905 at the annual family event that now included Maria's family, Eduardo asked Raphela and Ciccio if he could marry their daughter. Eduardo had already talked to Pasquale and Raphelia and had their approval to make the request. Maria's family said that they approved Eduardo marrying Maria. Eduardo then took Maria's hand in his and asked her to marry him. She said, *"so il mio amore lo sposerò"* (yes my love

I will marry you). Pasquale asked everyone raise their glass of wine to congratulate the couple. The evening ended with everyone attending midnight Mass. Eduardo and Maria were allowed to sit together. They held hands during the entire Mass.

When Eduardo arrived at work on Tuesday following Christmas day all of his co-workers congratulated him. Pasquale and Ciccio told everyone at work about the engagement. Maria did not tell her co-workers but some of them knew about the marriage proposal and brought some Italian pastries to work to congratulate her and to celebrate her engagement. Maria was a little embarrassed but thankful for what her co-workers did for her. Eduardo had told his father that he wanted to make sure that before he and Maria got married that he had financial stability. He said that would include buying a home and having that as a place to live when they got married. Pasquale told Eduardo that could take some time to accomplish that. Eduardo agreed and said that he and Maria had discussed this. Maria was in agreement as well and knew that the engagement could last a couple of years.

While much of the attention was on Maria and Eduardo, Arturo began attending business college in Gloversville for bookkeeping in September 1905. The cirriculum included courses in banking, accounting, and business law. Pasquale paid the tuition for Arturo to attend the school. Arturo had decided that he wanted to be a banker. The Gloversville Business College began

265

operating in 1891. In its fifteenth year of providing higher education, the school had students attending from many other states. The school offered both day and evening classes. The school also provided room and board for those students who needed that accomodation (Stewart, L, & Shiel, J.2008).

On the twenty-ninth of September, Ciccio's father, Luigi, passed away. Luigi was seventy-seven years old. Services for Luigi were held at Out Lady of Mount Carmel. The funeral was mainly attended by family members. Luigi was still working at the glove shop when he died. Luigi left work on Friday evening and had complained about not feeling well. On Sunday after church, Luigi went back home and shortly after arriving home, he collapsed and died.

Arturo finished his coursework at Gloversville Business College in October 1907. He turned nineteen in April. He immediately secured a job as a bank teller assistant at the City National Bank and Trust Company. That bank began operations in Gloversville in 1852. Arturo was placed in a six-month training program. In addition to the assistant teller duties, Arturo would also learn the bookeeping system at the bank. Pasquale was very proud of his youngest son for his eduational accomplishments. Arturo chose not to become a glove cutter. Since childhood, with his passion for mathematics, Arturo wanted to work in a profession that required math in the job. Pasquale supported his son and enouraged his continued learning of math and similar skills.

Eduardo had completed his goal of learning the Portugese language and was now also fully fluent in Chinese. He was now fluent in seven languages. Mostly self taught, Eduardo could read and write in Italian, English, Spanish, German, French, Chinese, and Portugese. In later years these languages would prove to be very beneficial for Eduardo. There were occassions when Emilio would request assistance from Eduardo for translating needs for clients. In one situation, a Chinese client, who spoke some English, needed help with legal documents that Emilio had prepared. Eduardo was able to explain the documents and the details for the client. Eduardo was becoming known in the community for his multi-language abilities.

Maria and Eduardo had also set the date for their wedding. They were married at Our Lady of Mount Carmel Church on Sunday, the fifth day of January in 1908. Maria had worked with her mother to prepare for the wedding. Her gown was made by her mother with help from Raphelia. Maria completed all the arrangements with the church. Maria Alberti was her matron of honor. Eduardo asked his older brother Francesco to be his best man. Francesco was very pleased that his brother wanted him as the best man.

Francesco had also moved out of the house and purchased a home of his own. Francesco bought a single family home on Forest Street just a few blocks from Pasquale and Raphelia's house. He also has been working with Emilio to prepare business documents for starting his own business. Although Francesco has been a butcher for many years, he saw an opportunity in Gloversville to open a fruit and vegetable market. Fruits and vegetables were available from grocers and one small specialty market in the area but much of that produce came from outside of the area. Francesco wanted to sell fruit and vegetables produced by local farmers. With his innovation for cooling meat, he felt he could do a simliar process for fruit and vegetables.

Eduardo and Maria had been looking for a home to buy as well. There was a newly completed two story flat directly across the street from Pasquale and Raphelia's home on Park Street. The home had a large front bedroom, a nice living room, a formal dining room, two other bedrooms located off of the living room, a bathroom, and a large kitchen at the rear corner of the house off of the dining room. The upper flat was similar in layout. The home also had an enclosed front porch. Being close to Pasquale and Raphelia was something both Eduardo and Maria wanted. In December, Eduardo and Maria made an offer to buy the home. The offer was accepted. They planned to move into their new home at 36 Park Street after the wedding.

Twenty Four

It was the wedding day for Maria and Eduardo. It was a cold, snowy, blustery day in Gloversville. Not a perfect day for a wedding but it was a day when weather conditions did not matter. All snow had been removed earlier in the day for Mass and church staff continued to shovel and sweep the walks and stairs to create a clear path for the wedding guests. In the true Italian tradition, the interior of the church was decorated with white, red, and yellow flowers. A ribbon adorned the doors at the entry to the church. The church was filled with relatives and guests.

Eduardo and Francesco were at the altar along with Arturo and Chilli. The three brothers and Chilli were dressed in new Italian suits handmade by a local tailor. Preceding Maria down the aisle was Maria Alberti, her sister Angela Leoni, and Elizabetta Adalora and Margurite Donatelli, co-workers and very close friends of Maria Finizio. The bridesmaids and matron of honor wore light green gowns. Green is a symbol of good luck for Italian weddings. As the organist played Mozart's Marcia Nuziale from *La Nozze di Figaro* (the marriage of Figaro), Maria in her exquisite white gown accented with lace, walked down the aisle arm in arm with her father. As they approached the altar, Ciccio gave his daughter a kiss. He looked into her eyes with tears in his eyes and his right hand over his chest and said, *"mia figlia il nio amore siete nel mio cuore per sempre"* (my daughter my love you are in my heart forever). Ciccio took Maria's hand and placed it in Eduardo's hand.

Maria and Eduardo smiled as they looked at each other. The priest began the ceremony. Pasquale and Raphelia held hands during the entire ceremony. Both had tears in their eyes. Ciccio and Raphela also shed tears as they watched their daughter take her wedding vows. Francesco handed the rings to the priest who blessed the rings. When the vows were completed and the rings placed on the fingers of the bride and groom, Eduardo lifted Maria's veil for their first kiss as husband and wife.

Both Maria and Eduardo had broad smiles as they walked back down the aisle arm in arm after the ceremony. Because of the weather conditions, the bride and groom were congratulated in the vestibule of the church. The snow had stopped but it was still a cold afternoon. A wedding reception was waiting for the couple at the *Alba Nuova* lodge. The guests were on their way to the reception while some pictures were being taken of the bride and groom. Following the pictures, Eduardo and Maria took a horse-drawn, covered carriage from the church to the lodge.

The reception party was hosted by Emilio. Musicians were hired for entertainment and to provide music for dancing. A grand Italian feast had been prepared. The guests filled Maria's purse with envelopes containing monetary gifts. Eduardo and Maria handed the guests doily wrapped sugar coated almonds known as *confetti*. Francesco offered the first toast to the bride and groom. That was followed by toasts from Pasquale, Ciccio, Angelo, Vincenzo, and Antonio.

The day was filled with happiness and joy. The long engagement was over. As the evening was ending, the bride and groom were escorted to their new home on Park Street. As they walked through the door of their home with their parents behind them, Eduardo and Maria were shocked to see a complete set of living room and dining room furniture. Maria and Eduardo had purchased bedroom and kitchen furniture and had planned to complete the furnishings after the wedding. Pasquale, Raphelia, Cicccio, and Raphela together bought their children the new furniture. Eduardo and Maria thanked their parents and gave each one kisses and hugs.

Eduardo and Maria settled in their home. They both had been very busy. Work demands required that each work many extra hours. Guiliani's was doing more business than ever anticipated for both the glove division and the garment division. Maria had transitioned from working at the large factory to sewing gloves at home for Guiliani's. In April Maria announced that she was pregnant. The families were extremely happy about the upcoming birth. Pasquale could not believe that he was about to become a grandfather. Raphelia and Raphela were already making plans to welcome their first grandchild.

Francesco located a spot for his fruit and vegetable store. He opened the DaCorsi Fruit and Vegetable Market in June. Francesco constructed a cooler based on his meat cooler design at the store. He could keep some fruits and vegetables for a longer period of time without the fruit becoming over ripe or the vegetables rotting. Francesco immediately had many customers who shopped at the market. Featuring local produce was the reason why customers shopped at the market. Francesco also stocked the store with plenty of Italian products. In addition to produce, Francesco sold Italian cheese, salami, and other varieties of cured meat

Arturo had been promoted to a teller position at the bank in July. He was also doing much of the bookeeping for the bank. Many of the glove shops in the area did their banking at City National. Employees of the shops also set up accounts at the bank. Arturo helped many of the Italian employees with their accounts. The bank manager relied on Arturo to serve the Italian community customers. Arturo convinced many Italian customers to open savings accounts. He explained the importance of having that type of account. Most Italian familes lived on what they earned.

The glove cutters in some shops were not making quotas due to the quality of hides they had to cut. Poor quality hides caused cutters to produce less. The shops also charged the cutters for damages to the gloves that did not meet quality standards, regardless of the poor quality of hides. This resulted in a loss of income for the cutters. Many cutters were now earning between ten and fifteen dollars per week. When the quality of the skins was better in the past, the cutters earned more and there were less rejects. Shop owners told the cutters they had to use as much of the skin as they could to get as many cuts as they could. In the past the cutters had the discretion to trim the hides to get the best quality possible. It seemed now that cutters were expected to produce quality gloves from the entire hide without trimming the inferior parts. Cutters had complained but there was no resolution to the issues.

On Saturday, the ninth day of January 1909, Maria gave birth to a son. Eduardo and Maria named their son Charles. The traditional Italian naming of the first grandchild was to name the child after the paternal grandfather. As Pasquale had taken the American name Charles, Eduardo and Maria felt that using the American name was appropriate, especially since Italian's still faced issues at times with their given Italian names.

Many births still took place in the home. Maria had decided to go to the hospital as recommended by her doctor for the birth. Maria was taken to Nathan Littauer Hospital in Gloversville around four in the morning. Charles was born eleven hours later. Most of the family was at the hospital in time for the birth. Shortly after Charles was born Pasquale, Ciccio, and Eduardo handed out cigars. Even the doctor got a cigar from Pasquale. Maria would remain in the hospital for three days before being released with the baby to go home.

That Monday after the birth Pasquale, Ciccio, and Eduardo returned to work with cigars in hand. Everyone at Guiliani's received a cigar. Eduardo was allowed to leave work early to be with his family. After work Pasquale and Ciccio visited Maria and Charles. When they arrived Raphelia and Raphela were there. Maria was also visited by Angelo and Rosa that afternoon. Vincenzo and Luciana came by that evening as did Francesco and Arturo. Maddalena and Antonio arrived shortly before Eduardo. Maddalena brought Charles a *camicini della fortuna*. This is a white silk shirt meant to bring good luck to the newborn. Emilio stopped by to congratulate the parents and to see Charles. Emilio told Eduardo and Maria that Charles would grow up to be a strong man.

The following Tuesday, three days after the birth, Maria and Charles were released from the hospital. Angelo and Rosa met the family at the hospital and took them home in the Guiliani's new automobile. Angelo also had one of the shop vehicles there to take Pasquale, Raphelia, Ciccio, and Raphela to Eduardo's home. Angelo had recently purchased a new vehicle. He bought an American Austin Touring Automobile. The vehicle had rear seats, a covered top, capacity for seven passengers, and a six cylinder ninety horsepower engine. Angelo traveled to Michigan to buy the vehicle. The price of the automobile was five thousand dollars (Southby's, 2016).

Eduardo and Maria could not believe they were being driven home in such a luxury vehicle. Eduardo had been looking at Ford Model T's to purchase. Pasquale still had no interest in owning an automobile. He told Eduardo he was *pazzo* for considering buying an automobile. Eduardo told his father that this is progress and the automobile would become a common means of travel. Pasquale would just flip his hand in the air and walk away.

Maria was relieved to be home with the baby. Eduardo had prepared the bedroom for Charles although for the first few weeks the baby would sleep in a bassinet in Eduardo's and Maria's bedroom. Eduardo was a little sleep deprived for the first weeks that Charles was home. He would get up in the middle of the night with Maria when Charles woke up for feedings.

One week after Charles was brought home, Gloversville was crippled by an ice storm. The city was virtually shut down for days. It was almost impossible for people to get to work. Most stores could not open. Neighbors assisted each other and shared food. Francesco also brought fruits, vegetables, and salami and cheese to Eduardo, Maria, Pasquale, and Raphelia. Eduardo and Pasquale did go to the shop to work but many employees could not make it to work. The ice storm was finally coming to an end as temperatures climbed. The storm lasted four days.

After the baptism of Charles two months following his birth, Maria and Eduardo placed the baby in his bedroom at night. Charles was beginning to sleep almost through some nights which was a welcome relief for Eduardo. The routine of getting up with the baby two times every night or more was over. Maria was pleasantly surprised when Charles began sleeping many of the nights at only two months of age. With Raphelia and Pasquale living across the street, there was always a lending hand whenever needed, day or night.

Maria had returned to sewing gloves at home again. She would work when the baby was sleeping and then for a couple of hours in the evening when Eduardo would take care of his son. There were regular and frequent visits from the grandparents. On some Sundays after church, the family meal would be at Eduardo's and Maria's. Raphelia, Maddalena, and Raphela would do the cooking. Maria welcomed this from the family as it gave her a little break. The family would also take care of Charles when he was awake.

Charles was about seven months old when he began to crawl. Eduardo thought this was amazing watching his son navigate the house. Pasquale said that Charles reminded him of Eduardo when he was a baby. Eduardo also had an inquisitive manner and would look at everything in sight. Charles would stop and look at something and seemed amazed by what he saw. Maria had a cut glass vase that would reflect sunlight and create a rainbow effect in the living room. Charles would stop and stare at the movement and the colors.

When Charles turned one, he had been walking for a couple of weeks. He could also say mama and papa. He was also a big boy for his age. Eduardo told Maria that Emilio's comment about Charles growing up to be strong was happening. Eduardo had rented the upper flat to a young Italian couple six months ago. The couple had been expecting their first child and had their child one day after Charles turned one. Maria helped the new mother after the baby was born. The young couple was appreciative of Maria's help. Most of their family lived in New York City. Maria was happy to assist.

In April of 1909, Maria was pregnant with her second child. There was also a marriage that month. Maria's twin brother Chilli, was married. Chilli and his bride Teresa were married at Our Lady of Mount Carmel Church. The same priest that performed Maria's and Eduardo's wedding married Chilli and

Teresa. Their reception was held outdoors at Meyers Park located on Burr Hill off of Beaver Street. The park was about one quarter mile from Eduardo's and Maria's house.

In early May, everyone had learned that Mr. Shipman had passed away. He had been in ill health over the past year. He was eighty-one when he passed away. His funeral service was attended by over three hundred people. In his retirement, Mr. Shipman had continued to donate money to various causes and continued to help people in need. Pasquale and Angelo were especially saddened by the death of Mr. Shipman. Angelo commented that it was Mr. Shipman who made Angelo so successful. Purchasing his glove shop was the business end of the deal.

Angelo said he owed his gratitude to Mr. Shipman for showing him how to treat the people who work for you and that they are the ones who make a person a success. Pasquale found not only a job at Shipman's but became very close to the man who believed in him and who assisted him and his family. Both men, along with many others, eulogized Mr. Shipman at the funeral. Following the services, Angelo had a memorial plaque made and installed it at the entry to the factory. He wanted all his employees to know that the business now owned by Angelo was started by Mr. Shipman. Pasquale thanked Angelo for what he did.

Eduardo had now developed a concept for a glove cutting method that could change the industry. He worked closely on the design with Ciccio and with Pietro Cinelli, another co-worker. Pasquale encouraged the group to keep working on the development of the concept. Eduardo's idea was to create a glove pattern that was of a single piece of material including the thumb portion. The thumb part had always been a separate piece of leather that was cut out and then individually attached to the glove in the sewing process. The new method created a cut flap that formed the thumb section and that would be stitched as part of the single piece of the leather cutout pattern.

While the testing and development continued, Eduardo and his partners met with Emilio to discuss applying for a patent. Emilio informed the men that obtaining a patent takes a long time and that they would have to prove that this was a new process. He suggested that they continued to develop the process, see if would Angelo agree to make gloves from this method to test the concept and determine if the design would work. They took Emilio's advice and continued with the development. When they tested the product themselves multiple times, they would approach Angelo. Raphelia helped the men and agreed to sew the test samples as the development process progressed. Her input was extremely important and valuable. If she could not sew the cutout and make a quality glove, then the design and process would fail. Pasquale told Angelo what the men were attempting to do and Angelo encouraged them to continue to work the design and test the method.

Eduardo, Ciccio, and Pietro were committed to making this work. They spent many hours at Eduardo's home working on the concept. Pasquale would join them on occasion to offer suggestions. Eduardo had made more than one hundred separate designs over the past few years. None satisfied him as being truly innovative. This design, however, was one that he knew could work. The main issue was the quality of glove it would produce. Keeping the high quality of table cutting while improving the process and having a method that could speed the production of glove making was the challenge. The industry would not accept a method that would not accomplish those two things.

They would also meet weekly with Emilio to show him where they were in the process and to get his feedback. Eduardo felt he was on the verge of having such a major impact on the industry that his process could be adapted for use worldwide. He would focus on Gloversville for now but he would keep his vision for the bigger picture as the motivation to keep going. Maria also encouraged Eduardo to keep his dream alive. Eduardo needed the expertise of Ciccio and Pietro, both master table cutters, to help perfect the concept. Pasquale assisted his son by reviewing the method as the design work continued with the group. Pasquale was there every step of the way for his son. He was very proud of what Eduardo had done so far and he knew that Eduardo would succeed with his design and concept.

Eduardo was confident about his concept. He had worked long and hard on his invention. The process that he developed could change the glove industry. There were not many innovations in the glove manufacturing business. Sewing machines definitely made a huge impact on production rates and quality improvements. Block cutting was not widely accepted by table cutters. Eduardo's process would change the sewing method by eliminating the attaching of a thumb section separately. Table cutters would not need to cut thumb pieces separately. Eduardo's innovation could be a welcome advance in an ages old industry.

Twenty Five

Maria gave birth to her second child, a son, on the seventeenth of January 1910. Eduardo and Maria named their son, Frank. Naming the second male child after the maternal grandfather was also an Italian tradition. Instead of naming the child Francesco, after Maria's father, Pasquale and Maria decided to use the American name of Frank for their son. The child would be called Ciccio after his grandfather. Maria's father had also considered taking the American name Frank. He did so shortly after the birth of his grandson. More and more Italian immigrants had been changing their given names to American names. Maria had also been using the name Mary recently.

With one-year old Charles and the new baby, Maria decided to take some time off from sewing gloves. Eduardo was making enough as an experienced glove cutter to keep the family financial situation stable. There was never a lack of assistance from the grandparents as well. When Maria and Eduardo were visited by Ciccio and Raphela or by Pasquale and Raphelia, they always brought food to give to Eduardo and Maria. The same occurred when Eduardo and Maria visited them. They were always given food to take home. In the Italian way, parents, grandparents, and other relatives such as aunts and uncles would always give food to their children, grandchildren, and to their nieces and nephews. Eduardo and Maria had so much food that they did not need to purchase much food for themselves.

For the most part, Pasquale still practiced Italian traditions, including sharing food with relatives. Over the past ten years or so, Pasquale also continued to hold true to his simple life style. He did not like some of the modern inventions. He did not like automobiles. He was not impressed with airplanes. He definitely did not approve of block cutting hides for leather gloves, and he did not want a telephone in his home. His sons, after some constant talking about the situation, did finally convince Pasquale to have telephone service installed in his house.

All three of his sons had telephones, Maddalena had a telephone, as did Vincenzo and Luciana, and of course Angelo. The shop had been equipped with telephones a few years ago. When the telephone was installed in Pasquale's home, Eduardo called him. Pasquale would not answer the phone when it rang. Raphelia answered the phone. She gave the phone to Pasquale. He just held it in in his hand. Raphelia looked at Pasquale as she mimicked placing her hand by her ear like she was holding a telephone said, *"mettere il telefono all'orecchio e la bocca e dire ciao"* (put the telephone by your ear and mouth and say hello). Pasquale shrugged his shoulders while holding his hands open with the palm side up. He took the phone in a manner that Raphelia demonstrated and said, *"ciao."* He shrugged his shoulders again and then heard Eduardo talking. Pasquale quickly handed the telephone back to Raphelia who then talked to Eduardo.

When Raphelia hung the phone up, Pasquale walked to Eduardo's house and asked him, *"perchè mi chiami in quell telefono quando io sono dall'altra parte della strada?"* (Why do you call me on that telephone when I am across the street?). Eduardo just laughed. He then demonstrated to Pasquale how the use the telephone. Pasquale told Eduardo, *"solo perché hai mostrato me non significa che ip ho intenzione di usarlo"* (just because you showed me does not mean I am going to use it). Eduardo told Pasquale he was *"testardo"* (stubborn) and will get used to using the telephone. Pasquale again shrugged his shoulders. He then flipped his hand in the air saying, *"mannaggia"* (a polite sort of the word damn), *"tutte queste cose moderne mi fanno impazzire"* (all these modern things make me crazy). Eduardo told his father that he was already a little crazy before the modern inventions.

Pasquale shrugged his shoulders again while waving his upward pointed hands back and forth at the wrist with thumb and fingers bunched together with all the tips of the fingers and thumb touching in what is known as a finger purse. This Italian gesture is asking the other person, *"ma che vuoi?"* (What do you mean?), suggesting that they could not be serious. Pasquale then looked at Eduardo and said, *"addio, vado a casa ora"* (goodbye, I go home now). Eduardo responded, *"OK, io chiamerò più tardi"* (OK, I will call you later). Pasquale just looked at Eduardo, shrugged his shoulders, said *"mannaggia"* and left.

In early April, many of the glove shops and leather tannery owners in Gloversville began looking closely at working conditions. Concerns had been raised by glove shop and tannery workers as a result of a recent deadly factory fire in New York City. On Saturday, the twenty-fifth of March in 1911, the Triangle Shirtwaist Factory in Manhattan caught fire. The factory was located on the eighth, ninth, and tenth floor of the Asch Building, which were the three top floors. The fire resulted in the deaths of one hundred forty-six people. Most of those who died were young Jewish and Italian women who were employed as garment workers. As the workday was ending, a small fire was noticed in a scrap bin. The fire quickly grew in intensity. Attempts to put the fire out by employees failed.

The company employed about five hundred people. Many of the employees were young girls and young women between thirteen years of age to their mid-twenties. Working conditions were poor. Employees worked six days a week, twelve hours a day. The rapidly spreading fire could not be controlled. The only firefighting equipment was small buckets filled with water and non-working fire hoses. Almost everything in the factory was flammable. The workers on the tenth floor made it to the roof of the high rise structure. Those employees made it to safety by moving to the rooftops of adjacent buildings.

Many of the workers on the eighth and ninth floor tried to reach exits but were trapped in the building. The doors to the one staircase and exit leading to the street had been locked as a practice directed by the factory owners to prevent theft. A second staircase had a door that only opened inward. Apparently with no keys readily available for the locked doors at the time, employees rushed toward the windows to try and escape the flames. Only one of four elevators in the building was fully operational. That elevator was being used by some employees in an attempt to reach the ground floor. The elevator was filled beyond capacity. The fire quickly spread to all of the elevators. The one fire escape on the building had collapsed as a result of having too many people trying to escape using that structure. Firefighters arrived at the building shortly after the fire started. Their ladders, however, reached only the sixth floor.

Many of the workers on the ninth floor stepped onto the window ledges to escape the fire. With no hope of being rescued, those workers began either jumping or falling to their deaths. Others were trapped in the factory and burned to death. The fire was extinguished by the firefighters within thirty minutes after their arrival. Twenty-five people of the one hundred and forty-six that perished were on the fire escape when it buckled and collapsed. With the factory doors locked and no provision for the safety of the workers, there was no way to escape the flames (Rosenberg, 2015).

Many of the glove shops and leather tanneries in Gloversville were multi-story, wood-framed buildings. Factory owners looked at how they could improve conditions and address concerns raised by their workers. Two factory fires had also occurred in nearby Broadalbin that also concerned the factory workers in Gloversville. One fire in Broadalbin in 1905 destroyed a four-story, wooden-building where a knitting factory was located, resulting in the loss of one hundred forty jobs. The other fire occurred in 1910. That fire leveled a box factory and attached home. There were no deaths in either of those fires (Cornell, G & Shiel, J., 1999).

Although there was little that could be done to change or modify the wooden structures in Gloversville, many owners of the glove shops and leather tanneries improved conditions by providing additional escape routes and adding more firefighting equipment. They also made sure that factory doors were accessible and not locked during business hours. Angelo installed additional fire escapes in his building, rearranged work areas to make aisles wider, provided for the removal of scrap material and flammable items, and installed chemical foam fire extinguishers throughout the factory. Pasquale and the other managers conducted frequent checks in their departments to make sure potential fire hazards were identified and removed. The devastation of the Manhattan fire brought a higher level of action for the factories in Gloversville. Employee safety became of primary importance.

In July 1911, Maria again announced that she was pregnant. Charles was two and one half and Frank was almost one and a half. This was also a special year for Pasquale. He turned sixty this year. Pasquale's hair was now snowy white. His hands still showed the lines and creases from years of cutting gloves. Although Pasquale was the glove shop manager at Guiliani's, he would still cut gloves when orders were behind or when other cutters needed assistance. The workers were still amazed at Pasquale's glove cutting skills. Even at age sixty, he had not lost his touch and was still one of the fastest cutters in the area.

An extreme spell of cold weather hit Gloversville and the surrounding region in November 1911. Snowfall began before the Thanksgiving holiday. The harsh weather impacted local businesses. It was very difficult for people to get to work. Some of the glove shops operated on a modified schedule. Temperatures plunged to sub-zero levels for days. Snow was continuing to fall during this period. This unexpected freeze also caused power outages. Guiliani's lost electric power for nearly three days.

With power restored, businesses for the most part returned to regular schedules. Glove shops began to ship products as close to schedule as possible. The snow continued to fall over the next two weeks. Thanksgiving Day was met with another round of extremely heavy snowfall. The next few days would also have businesses either closed or on another modified schedule. For the remainder of November and through December temperatures hovered in the teens to below zero. Between the end of December and into late January, temperatures again were in the sub-zero range. The extreme weather would continue into March 1912. The winter of 1912 was one of the coldest in modern history.

While the deep freeze hit the region very hard, Eduardo and his partners continued testing their new glove product. Testing was completed in January. With Emilio's help, the design and detail for the product was submitted to the United States Patent Office for approval on the seventh day of February in 1912. After years of research, design, planning, and testing, Eduardo was extremely pleased that his idea had finally been accepted and recognized as an innovation in the glove cutting industry. Both Ciccio and Pietro had been assigned one-third of the patent submission by Eduardo for their participation in the process. Emilio told the men that approval of the patent could take one year or more. Eduardo felt that it had taken this long to reach the point for the patent application, another year or so would be worth the wait to receive the actual patent.

Francesco's market was doing very well. He had added new products and was keeping produce available throughout the winter months with products from local farmers who were using greenhouses to grow their produce. Francesco had a total of four employees at the market. He was also doing some home deliveries of products. The store was also set up in a self-serve arrangement to allow shoppers to select and pick the products rather than placing orders where the store clerks would select the products. Customers liked this and used the market as their main source of buying fruits and vegetables.

Arturo had been promoted to lead bookkeeper at the bank. He was also in charge of opening new accounts for both commercial customers and individual personal account customers. Arturo still convinced many customers to save money. Many Italian clients trusted Arturo's advice and although they had limited finances, they would set up savings accounts. Francesco had also set up his accounts with the bank. Arturo had also become quite adept at buying and selling stock. He had been making investments since he began working at the bank. He had built a decent portfolio of stocks and watched the market closely. He taught many bank customers how to buy and sell stock.

Arturo also discussed investing opportunities with his brothers. Francesco had made some investments in the stock market. Eduardo was just starting to look at making investments. Arturo also mentioned life insurance to Eduardo. With a young family and another child on the way, Eduardo was interested in purchasing a policy. Eduardo met with an agent from a well-known insurance company that began selling insurance in the 1840s. Eduardo bought a whole life policy from the company.

The agent also talked to Eduardo about becoming an insurance salesman. Eduardo told the agent he worked as a glove cutter. As the discussion continued, the agent learned that Eduardo was fluent in seven languages. The agent told Eduardo with that skill he could serve a wide population in the region as a salesman. The agent offered to teach Eduardo the insurance business. Eduardo was interested and agreed to meet the agent at his office to get further information.

A few weeks later, Eduardo met the agent, manager and broker of the local office of the insurance company. The manager provided information to Eduardo on insurance laws, agent licensing, and the general sales process. He gave Eduardo books on various insurance subjects. He also provided sample forms on all available insurance policies. Eduardo took all the material home and began studying for his agent license. Eduardo would also have to take an examination as required by state law to receive a license to be an insurance sales agent.

Eduardo was in no hurry to become an insurance agent. He liked being a glove cutter but he was always looking at opportunities. Nine months had passed and there was no news on the patent. Guiliani's had begun to use Eduardo's glove pattern technique on one of its glove products. Angelo decided to test the market on a limited basis to see how the product was accepted by the public. Angelo set up a profit sharing of the sales of the product for Eduardo, Ciccio, and Pietro. They received two percent each of the net profit from each pair of gloves sold. Although it was not much money, the profit sharing provided some additional income.

Eduardo figured that when the product received a patent and if glove shops adopted the process, the three men could realize substantial compensation from authorizing the use of the patent. Emilio had guided the three men on how to allow use of the patent and what they should charge for the use. Emilio had prepared sample contracts that provided existing glove manufacturers use of the patent under a licensing agreement. That arrangement would provide royalties for Eduardo, Ciccio, and Pietro.

If the royalties provided income that could support the family, Eduardo decided he would then obtain his license to become an insurance agent. Eduardo had discussed this with both Maria and Pasquale. Eduardo also assured his wife and his father that he would not stop cutting gloves until he was sure any royalties were substantial enough to continue to provide income to support the family. Eduardo was very optimistic and confident that his invention would be patented. There were not many innovations in the glove industry. Improvements such as his single piece glove cutout could change the industry. Eduardo also knew that he would have to demonstrate his invention to glove shop owners. He was prepared to do so and he had already prepared a presentation for marketing his invention.

Although Pasquale had spent his life in glove shops, he encouraged Eduardo to look seriously at the insurance agent work. Pasquale did not want to see his son spending his entire life tied to the glove shop. He knew that Eduardo had a great mind and could do very well in the insurance business. Pasquale was actually pleased that Francesco and Arturo did not become glove cutters. He did not share that with anyone including Raphelia. He was proud of all three of his sons. They were all successful. Having a son who was an inventor, a son who was a banker, and a son who was a business owner was beyond what Pasquale had thought when he emigrated to America. Pasquale was so happy he made the decision to come to America and to bring his family to the new world. He knew that America would provide opportunities.

Pasquale reflected on the last fourteen years since he came to Gloversville. Coming to an unknown land, not knowing or speaking the language, unsure of getting and holding a job, and starting over at age forty-seven was extremely stressful for Pasquale. He was determined to succeed. He wanted the best for his family. Bringing his family to be with him and uprooting them from the only culture they had known was something that concerned him every day while he was in Gloversville and they were in Italy. The success he and his family did have these past few years was overwhelming at times for Pasquale. He thanked God every day for what He had done for the family. He saw and lived every day as an *alba nuova*.

These years have been good for Pasquale as well. His income was very good. His job was very satisfying. He loved working with and for Angelo. He had become an officer in the lodge. The lodge had grown to almost two hundred members. In addition to Sunday Mass, Pasquale attended Mass a couple of times during the week. He was serving on committees at church. He and Raphelia had become grandparents. He now uses a telephone and has become more tolerant with progress. Maddalena was still doing very well. The relationship Pasquale had with his sister was better than ever. They remain very close and see each other almost daily. Raphelia and Maddalena are like sisters. They did everything together.

Pasquale was a happy man. It was hard to believe, however, that his oldest son was almost thirty years old or that he had two grandchildren with another on the way. He and Raphelia had been married for thirty-two years. Pasquale adored his wife. They still prayed together. They still joked with each other. They would also take care of Charles and Frank and loved having their grandsons with them. They also enjoyed their evening meals together. Pasquale still worked long hours and Raphelia still worked at home making gloves. Having a few hours to themselves a few nights a week was special, relaxing, and comforting.

Pasquale still enjoyed the family Sunday gatherings. The meals were always great. The large after church get together still included Angelo and his family, Vincenzo and Luciana and their family, Maddalena and Antonio, the entire DaCorsi group, and on occasion, Emilio would still join them. Sunday's were the most enjoyable and relaxing day for Pasquale. To him family was everything.

The past fourteen years had many memories and thoughts of good times, good friends, and good accomplishments. Pasquale really liked Gloversville. The city was such a friendly place. The city had grown in population to nearly twenty-one thousand.

More Italian immigrants had come to Gloversville, many of them glove workers. Park Street had nearly every lot filled with a home. His sons had all bought homes. Maddalena and Antonio also had bought the home they had been living in. They purchased the house a few years ago when the owner decided to sell. Although they had been looking to buy another home that they had looked at many times, they felt it was best to purchase the home they lived in. Not only could they rent the upper flat they always considered the house as their home.

Pasquale was content. His life had been so rewarding since he emigrated. His family was with him. He had great friends. Everything was in order and he was feeling good about his life in the new world. He was in a good place. His home was Gloversville. He was a proud Italian-American. He was an Italian immigrant who found his new life in America and fulfilled his dream of his *alba nuova*.

Twenty Six

Maria and Eduardo welcomed son, Robert, into the world on the second day of April 1912. With a growing family, Eduardo had become more intent on making sure he took care of the needs of his wife and sons. One item Eduardo figured would be good for the family was to purchase an automobile. After several months of actually considering buying a vehicle and looking extensively at various automobiles, Eduardo decided to buy a Model T Ford Touring car. He purchased the vehicle in May 1912. The vehicle accommodated five passengers. The vehicle cost was just under seven hundred dollars. Eduardo had saved enough money to pay cash for the vehicle.

Angelo had taught Eduardo how to drive a few months ago. Eduardo had been driving the company vehicles and had helped with some of the pick-up and delivery of gloves to the women who assembled gloves at home. Eduardo felt that having his own vehicle would allow the family to have an easier time with taking the children places. Angelo would take Eduardo and Maria on rides around the area. Eduardo enjoyed traveling outside the Gloversville area looking at the farms and other scenery. Maria enjoyed that as well.

When Eduardo brought the new car home, Maria wanted to go for a ride right away. Pasquale came over to Eduardo's house to see the car. He looked at it, shrugged his shoulders and said in broken English, "ittsa OK." Raphelia thought it was wonderful that Eduardo and Maria had a car. Eduardo took Maria, the children, and Raphelia for a ride. Pasquale declined the offer to go along. Eduardo drove them down the Pine Street hill to South Main Street and along South Main into the City of Johnstown. On the way back to Gloversville, Eduardo took them up a country road off of Briggs Street in Johnstown past the farms and then on another country road going back toward Gloversville (now Route 29A) returning to the Pine Street location.

When they got back to the house on Park Street, Pasquale asked where they had gone. Eduardo explained the route and told Pasquale that it was a nice drive. Pasquale looked at his son and again in broken English said, "attsa nice." People in the neighborhood came to look at the automobile. Only a few people on Park Street owned a vehicle. Francesco and Arturo also came over to see the new car. Maria had her mother and father over later that day to see it as well. Ciccio was very excited that Eduardo had purchased the car. Ciccio told Maria that he may buy an automobile. She told her father that Eduardo could teach him how to drive.

Although it took some time, Eduardo convinced his father to ride to work in the car each day. Pasquale had become accustomed to walking everywhere or taking the trolley. He did agree, after a while, that driving to work every day was better than walking. Pasquale still walked a lot and would only ride in the car to work and to church. More and more people in Gloversville had vehicles. There were a lot of Model T Fords and other Ford models, some had Maxwells, Oldsmobile's, and Buicks, and there were even a few Cadillacs. Angelo still had his American Austin, the only one of its kind in Gloversville. By this time there were over one million automobiles registered in the United States (U.S. Census, 2000).

Robert was nine months old when Maria learned she was pregnant with her fourth child. Eduardo and Maria were both thirty years old. Eduardo began thinking more about his patent and the potential of selling insurance. The financial security of his growing family was his primary focus. Emilio had heard from the U.S. Patent office that the approval process was progressing. Emilio anticipated an approval by the end of the year. In preparation of the pending approval of the patent, Emilio finalized the documents for licensing agreements. There were royalty stipulations within the agreements. The royalties were based on the gross sales of products that used the patent. Emilio wanted a graduated royalty schedule so Eduardo, Ciccio, and Pietro could maximize their earnings.

Eduardo was getting a little anxious about his patent application. He asked Emilio every week if there had been any news on the patent. Emilio kept telling Eduardo to be patient and without a doubt in Emilio's mind, the patent would be approved. The time just seemed to drag on for Eduardo. Then on Thursday, the eleventh of December 1913, Emilio asked Eduardo, Ciccio, and Pietro to come to his office. Emilio told the men he had news on the patent. Eduardo was visibly nervous. Emilio took out an envelope from his desk and held up a document from the U.S. Patent Office awarding *Patent 1,080,813 Glove* to Edward DaCorsi Gloversville, New York, and assignor of one-third to Frank Finizio, and one-third to Pietro Cinelli, Gloversville, N.Y., under *serial number 675,934*. The accompanying documents detailed the patent.

The patent documents described the design of the glove:

A glove comprising of front and back formed of a single piece of material folded along the line of the outer edge of the first finger and along the line of the outer edge of the little finger to form front flaps, a wrist-opening and an enclosed thumb-opening, said front flaps being secured together by two short seams, one extending from the wrist-opening to the inner side of the thumb-opening and the other extending from the crotch between the first and second fingers to the base of the thumb-opening at a slight angle to the side-line of the first finger; and a thumb-piece formed of a single piece of material folded for a portion of its length along its longitudinal middle line with its edges stitched together to form a thumb-pocket and having an angular projection extending a substantial distance beyond the pocket forming portion of the thumb-piece, said thumb-piece being secured within the thumb-opening, one of said front flaps of the body extending continuously along the front side of the first finger past the crotch of the thumb and terminating in a quirk for the thumb.

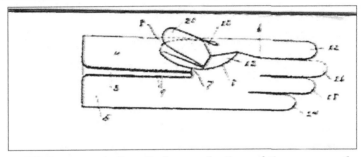

With patent in hand, the marketing of the new method to cut and sew gloves would begin. With Angelo's help, completed samples, sales information, and demonstrations for both the cutting process and sewing process were made available. Angelo invited glove shop owners in the area to his shop to see the demonstrations. Eduardo, Ciccio, Pietro, Pasquale, Angelo, and Maddalena would do the actual demonstrations. Emilio was present at the demonstrations to help close the deal with glove shop owners.

In the first month of the demonstrations and with Angelo providing information on sales and customer acceptance and satisfaction, seven glove shop owners signed agreements to use the process. Royalties based on the wholesale price of gross sales volumes would be between ten cents and twenty cents per pair of gloves sold. The greater the sales, the lower the royalty with the lower royalty set aside for sales volumes of five thousand pairs of gloves per month or more and the highest amount for one thousand pairs of gloves per month or less. Amounts between one thousand pairs and less than five thousand were at a fixed royalty of thirty cents per pair of gloves. All agreements were for a period of ten years with a seven year renewal term. The life of the patent was seventeen years.

The benefit for the manufacturers was increased production rates. Angelo had indicated to the other shop owners that his production rates improved by more than eighteen percent using this process versus the standard multi-piece glove cutout and sewing method. One of the glove shops signing the agreement was the largest manufacturer in the region. They estimated their annual sales volume for a selected product using the method to be a minimum of one hundred thousand pairs of gloves per year after the first year introductory period.

Over the next six months, royalty checks began arriving. Emilio handled all the legal aspects of the royalties. Arturo set up separate accounts for the royalty income. Eduardo, Ciccio, and Pietro agreed that distributions would be made to each of them at seventy-five percent of the total amount which would be transferred into their personal accounts forty-five days after receiving the royalty. The remaining twenty-five percent would remain in the royalty account. The purpose was to provide for the future security of the individual families. Emilio had prepared contract agreements between the three men for the distribution of the royalties and for the residuals of the royalties.

With a sense of some financial security now, Eduardo would pursue his insurance agent license. He would continue to cut gloves as well as did Ciccio and Pietro. Eduardo also gave his father ten percent of his royalties. Pasquale was very emotional when Eduardo told him about his intent to share the royalties. Pasquale never imagined that he would receive anything. He asked Eduardo why he was doing this. Eduardo simply said, *"tu sei mio padre e mi ha insegnato tutto quello she so e perchè ti amo"* (you are my father and you taught me everything I know and because I love you).

Just before the announcement of the award of the patent Maria gave birth to another son. Edward Junior was born on the ninth of December 1913. There were four boys now: Charles, five years old, Frank, three years old, Robert, was one year and eight-months old, and baby boy Edward. With the family growing,

Eduardo wanted to make sure his family was well taken care of in future years. He set up a family trust taking fifty percent of his royalty distribution and placing that into the trust account. Eduardo was always preparing for the future. He continued to work on other inventions. He was also using his language skills serving as an interpreter.

There was a slight setback at this time. Approximately one thousand, five hundred glove cutters in the area went on strike. Although that was only about ten percent of the workforce, the industry was severely impacted. The issue was wages and working conditions. Angelo's shop was not affected by the strike. The majority of strikers worked for the larger companies. The largest company that had signed an agreement with Eduardo and his partners had workers on strike. The company still produced products but at a much lower volume. The new process also affected the overall amount of all gross sales. The strike would last a little over two months. The manufacturers prevailed but the workers were granted some concessions including minimal wage increases (Zahvi, 1999).

Most of the shops with agreements with Eduardo and his partners did not have workers go out in strike. The royalties were impacted, however, especially due to the lower than projected volumes of the large manufacturer. The impact was not that severe to Eduardo and the others as 1914 was a start-up year for the new glove pattern and cutting method. The projections made by Eduardo were actually less than what was produced by the manufacturers. Eduardo predicted about two hundred and fifty thousand pairs of gloves would be sold using the new process.

Eduardo would spend the balance of the year each evening preparing for his insurance agent test. Maria was sewing gloves just a few hours a week now. The majority of her time was spent caring for her children. As 1914 ended, the family celebrated their great accomplishments. It had been about a year since the royalty agreements had been signed. That first year a total of fifteen glove shops had executed a royalty contract. The total gross volume for that first year from all royalty manufacturers combined was over three hundred thousand pairs of gloves.

The beginning of 1915 also brought more royalty agreements. Five more glove shops began using the process. The industry was adapting well to the improved method. Emilio had another ten shops he was working with on completing agreements. By mid-year those agreements would be finalized. Eduardo and his partners were very pleased with how well the process had been accepted. Although there were well over one hundred shops in the area, the three men were happy with their market share. Eduardo, Ciccio, and Pietro set a goal of having twenty-five shops under contract in the first two years. With fifteen under agreement in the first year and five more added recently, they were well ahead of their goal.

Eduardo successfully passed his insurance agent examination and became an insurance agent in May. He left the glove shop but continued to work on marketing his glove manufacturing method to shops in the region. As an insurance agent, Eduardo quickly built a client network. With his multi-lingual skills he served many different ethnicities in the area. There was a German speaking group of residents in Gloversville. Eduardo also served Chinese immigrants in the area.

Eduardo firmly believed that every family deserved to have a life insurance policy, regardless of their financial condition. He would always structure a policy where even small payments would provide a policy that would be beneficial for the family. Eduardo always offered a whole life policy that would also allow a build-up of money for the family similar to a savings account. With his guidance, families were convinced to buy insurance policies. Eduardo would also continue to follow up with all his clients on a regular basis. He knew by staying in touch with the families, he could provide help when needed for any situation.

He was also well recognized for assisting and helping other people in the community. He was more than the local life insurance agent. If Eduardo came across a family who had been struggling, he would find ways to help the family. Eduardo would talk with many people to see what could be done to help families. Sometimes it was buying food for the family. Other times there would be some short-term financial assistance. Whatever the situation, Eduardo always tried to find a solution.

Eduardo was becoming well known in the area for his accomplishments. He had been recognized by the lodge for outstanding contributions to the glove industry. Pasquale proudly gave Eduardo a medal from the lodge for his award. Arturo and Francesco were also recognized by the lodge. Emilio told Pasquale that all three of the boys, as sons of an Italian immigrant and as Italian immigrants, had made a great success in America. Emilio, in addressing the lodge at the award ceremony, said that the successes of the DaCorsi boys were due to a caring, guiding, and loving father, Pasquale. He went on to say that Pasquale had always believed that a new beginning was there for everyone who desired it and worked hard for it. Emilio said that is exactly what Eduardo, Francesco, and Arturo had done in Gloversville.

Twenty Seven

In June 1915, Maria became an aunt. Her brother, Chilli and his wife Teresa became parents. Teresa gave birth to daughter, Alma. Chilli and Teresa lived at 69 Park Street in Gloversville. They purchased the home six months before Alma was born. They lived about three blocks from Maria and Eduardo. Teresa was five years younger than Chilli. She came to Gloversville from Italy in 1899. She was ten years old when she immigrated with her parents.

Also in June, the *Alba Nuova Lodge* joined the ranks of the Order of the Sons of Italy in America. The lodge became Alba Nuova Lodge #387. The Order of the Sons of Italy in America was founded in New York City in 1905 by Dr. Vincenzo Sellaro along with five other Italian immigrants. The organization provided assistance to Italian immigrants for gaining citizenship in the Unites States and offered English classes at no charge. The support for Italian immigrants also included health and death benefits. The organization offered other assistance such as life insurance and scholarships for member's families in need (Order of Sons of Italy in America, 2016).

Earlier in the year, Chilli left his job as a mason with Antonio and became a glove cutter. Construction involving masonry work in the area had been slowing down. Chilli had periods of no work and with a child on the way; he needed a full time job. Antonio understood and supported Chilli's decision. Ciccio had taught his son how to cut gloves in Italy when Chilli was fifteen years old. Pasquale gave Chilli a job at Guiliani's. It took a while for Chilli to get up to speed cutting gloves but with Ciccio and Pasquale guiding, him Chilli quickly regained his skill of the trade. The steady work at Guiliani's provided the income Chilli needed to support his family. Chilli's father, Ciccio, also helped Chilli and Teresa with household expenses.

The royalties from the patent were doing well. Eduardo, Ciccio, and Pietro now had twenty-six glove shops under contract. About one-fourth of the shops with the royalty agreement were small operations. Those shops combined averaged less than one thousand pairs of gloves sold per month using the patent. There were also three large shops using the patent. The monthly sales volume from those manufacturers combined was over seventeen thousand pairs of gloves per month. The remaining sixteen shops under contract were medium-size shops. They each averaged approximately three thousand pairs of gloves sold per month. The total annual sales volume from all manufacturers was over eight hundred thousand pairs.

Arturo became the manager of the bookkeeping department at the bank in October 1915. At age twenty-seven, he was the youngest manager in the bank. Arturo also continued to work with the immigrant community to service their financial and banking needs. More than eighty percent of new clients established savings accounts under Arturo's guidance. With the establishment of the 1913 Federal Reserve Act, the banking system in the country became a national system. Prior to the enactment of the Act in December 1913, banking was a local or state controlled system or was attempted to be a national system. All previous national systems did not last. The Federal Reserve System, although controversial with some of the Acts regulations, seemed to be a process that would finally establish a solid national bank system.

The City National Bank had issued currency under the bank name. The Federal Reserve Act now controlled the issuance of currency. The new currency was the Federal Reserve Note which was introduced into the banking system over a two-year period. Many immigrants were concerned with and confused by the new currency. Arturo assured account holders that the new currency was a replacement for the local currency.

Over the next eighteen months, the DaCorsi families continued to do well. Francesco had again expanded his fruit and vegetable market. New grocery stores had opened in the area requiring Francesco to lower his costs to remain competitive. The patent was still producing reliable royalties. Pasquale, who was now almost sixty-five, began working five days per week. Eduardo had become one of the top selling insurance agents in the region. The glove shops in the area were now producing military gloves to supply soldiers as the United States had entered World War I. These were tense times as well with the war. The United States had declared war against Germany in April 1917. The war declaration was due to Germany's continued submarine attacks against passenger ships in the North Atlantic and Mediterranean along with Germany encouraging Mexico to join Germany in an allegiance against the United States (Office of the Historian).

This was also a time for celebration. Chilli and Teresa had their second child. Marie Finizio was born in June 1917. This was also about the time that Maria once again announced her pregnancy with her fifth child. The Guiliani's also became grandparents this year. Twenty-four year old Giovanni and his wife welcomed a baby boy. Giovanni had been working for his father at the glove shop for the past five years. Leonardo was attending college at the Rensselaer Polytechnic Institute in Troy. Leonardo was pursuing a degree in mechanical engineering.

On the eighth of February 1918, Maria and Eduardo welcomed their fifth son, Leon Mario, into the world. Nine-year old Charles was extremely happy that he had another brother.

With a house full of young boys, there was never a dull moment in the home. Seven-year old Frank was the mischievous one. He always seemed to be causing trouble or being in trouble. Eduardo was the disciplinarian. When young Ciccio would misbehave, all Eduardo had to do was start taking his belt off of his trousers. Eduardo never used the belt. Just knowing that the belt was coming off was enough for young Ciccio and on occasion for the other boys to immediately begin behaving.

On the ninth of August 1919, Arthur, the sixth son of Maria and Eduardo, was born. Arthur was a large baby weighing over ten pounds at birth. The DaCorsi house was full. The older boys, Charles, Frank, and Robert shared a bedroom. Edward, Leon and Arthur were in the bedroom closest to Eduardo's and Maria's bedroom. The bedrooms were all large and accommodated the beds for the boys. Evening times proved to be a little chaotic on occasion. The boys had different bedtimes. Charles went to bed at nine. Bedtime for Frank and Robert was eight-thirty. Edward went to bed at eight. Leon at eighteen months still had an early bedtime and would usually go to sleep around eight. Maria and Eduardo would be exhausted from the evening bedtime ritual. Even though bedtimes were set, there were times when it took a while for the boys to calm down before they went to sleep. Usually with one or sometimes two trips from Eduardo to the boys' rooms would be enough for the boys to get the message. After the boys were asleep, Maria and Eduardo would go to bed.

The next few years saw the population in Gloversville grow to more than twenty-two thousand. The glove and leather industries were still doing well. The majority of the population was employed directly in those industries or associated industries. A recession hit the country in 1920 and lasted for about eighteen months. Much of the war time manufacturing was gone or the factories across the country were rebuilding for new production processes. The federal government implemented tax cuts to stimulate the economy. By 1922 the economy had begun to recover. Mass production stimulated consumer purchases. Installment buying was gaining popularity. Items such as automobiles and major appliances were now in more households contributing to a vibrant economy (Sullivan, 2003).

The year 1922 also brought the seventh and last child born to Eduardo and Maria. Claude Archielles DaCorsi was born in October. This was also the year of Pasquale's seventy-first birthday. Eduardo had also purchased a new automobile. The 1912 Ford Model T had finally broken down beyond repair. Eduardo, Francesco, and Arturo retired the vehicle in a rather strange way. With the help of thirteen-year-old Charles and eleven-year-old Frank, they all dug a large hole in the back yard at Eduardo's house. It took them two weeks to dig the hole. When the hole was what they figured to be the right size including width, length, and depth, they proceeded to push the broken down Model T into the hole. They buried the car! Maria called them all *pazzo*. Pasquale said in broken English, "whatta ya do?" Eduardo in his humorous way told his father that the car had died so they gave it a proper burial. Pasquale, pointing with his index finger against his temple responded, *"siete tutti pazzi e bisogno di aiuto con le vostre teste"* (you are all crazy and you need help with your heads). Charles then told his grandfather, "It's OK Nonno we got a new car." Pasquale smiled and pinched Charles on the cheek saying, *"sei un bravo ragazzo"* (you are a good boy).

Eduardo bought a 1922 REO seven passenger automobile. The car was blue with black leather seats. The vehicle cost was two thousand three hundred dollars. Maria and Eduardo also bought all new furniture for the house. This was also the year that Maddalena and Antonio both retired. Maddalena had been sewing gloves since she was a young girl. Now seventy-four she was ready for some relaxation. Antonio sold his masonry business and spent most of his time tending his large garden. Pasquale had been in America for over twenty-four years now. He also was ready to slow down a little. He decided to return to cutting gloves for Angelo part-time. Pasquale recommended that Giovanni take over the glove division manager job at Guiliani's. He had been in training under Pasquale and Angelo. Pasquale told Angelo that

Giovanni was ready to take on the role. Angelo agreed and young Giovanni became the manager.

Pasquale now worked three days a week at the shop. He was not as fast as he used to be but he was still an excellent table cutter. Raphelia also retired from the glove shop. She enjoyed staying home and working on projects around the house as well as doing crocheting. Raphelia and Maddalena would meet a few times a week to work on their crocheting and doily making. They gave doilies away to neighbors, friends, workers at glove shops, and they gave them to Eduardo for his insurance clients as a thank you for buying insurance policies.

A celebration for Pasquale's seventy-first birthday was held at the lodge. As usual there was a huge Italian feast. The lodge room was packed with well-wishers. The highlight of the party was a presentation to Pasquale from Angelo. For all the years of faithful service to the glove shop, and for being a friend of nearly forty years, Angelo gave Pasquale a gold pocket watch. The two men hugged for what seemed like an eternity. Both men were in tears. The people at the party applauded loudly. Raphelia and Rosa hugged the men as well. Pasquale's sons and grandsons all gave Pasquale a kiss.

Pasquale addressed the group at the party thanking them for all their friendship over the years. He especially thanked Emilio and told the group about the first time he and Emilio met.

Emilio had also recently retired from practicing law but was still helping people in Gloversville when needed for no charge. Pasquale told everyone how much he enjoyed Gloversville and how good the community had been to him. They all raised their glasses of wine to Pasquale in a salute to him and his family. Pasquale blew out the candles on the cake with help from his grandsons. He then cut the massive cake that Emilio had bought for the birthday party.

Pasquale was still a strong man who continued to do plenty of walking. He was slightly hunched over from all the years of table cutting gloves. His hands still showed the toils of the job with lines, callouses, and crooked fingers. His snowy white hair was also becoming prevalent on Eduardo whose hair started turning white about two years ago. Francesco had some streaks of grey while Arturo still had dark brown hair. Eduardo also looked like his father. Francesco had more of his mother's features. Arturo also had a close resemblance to Pasquale. One trait Eduardo and Arturo had were dimples on their cheeks. Pasquale had told them that the dimples were a DaCorsi characteristic that went back as far as he could remember. Some of Eduardo's boys had the DaCorsi dimples.

After the birthday party, Pasquale and Raphelia returned home. They sat at the kitchen table sharing a glass of wine. They talked about the nice birthday party and of their forty-three years of being married. They both agreed that the past twenty-three years together in Gloversville had provided a good life. They also agreed about the good decision to come to America. They rebuilt their lives in America. The hopes of a new beginning for immigrants definitely came true for the DaCorsi family.

Pasquale told Raphelia that when he left Italy he was confident that he would quickly find a job cutting gloves. He told her that it was the good training he had received from Luigi that made the difference for him. He said that is what Mr. Shipman saw in him to give him a chance. He was a little emotional talking about Luigi and Mr. Shipman. These were two men he greatly appreciated and admired for what they did for him. He also said that it was a blessing when Mr. Shipman sold the business to Angelo. That kept the business alive, gave Angelo his own glove shop in America, and the company has employed more people than either he or Angelo imagined.

Raphelia was also happy about her many years of sewing gloves. She was one of the best in the area as well. She specialized in P.K sewing. That process lapped the seams of the glove so when sewn together the raw edges would be hidden. The quality of the gloves was much better with that type of seam. The majority of gloves she made with that process were women's cape with an embroidered finish. That type of glove was one of the top selling products in the industry. Raphelia had been working for

Louis G. Meyer and Sons for the past two years. That company was one of the largest glove shops in the area. Raphelia and Pasquale wondered how many gloves they had made over their careers. They figured between the two of them the amount had to be well over one hundred thousand dozen pairs of gloves. Pasquale told Raphelia that is why his hands are so deformed. They both laughed when Raphelia told Pasquale he should just wear gloves all the time and no one would notice his hands.

The glove industry in Gloversville was world recognized. Some shops shipped products to South America, France, and Canada. Many of the shops in Gloversville had also opened retail stores in locations across the United States. There were retail outlets in New York City, Boston, Detroit, Chicago, and as far away as San Francisco. Some of the local glove shops had been purchased by large corporations. Some of those shops employed hundreds of workers. Pasquale was proud to have been associated with the industry for all these years. He was also very pleased that Guiliani's remained a family-owned business.

Pasquale and Raphelia ended their day staring into each other's eyes while holding hands. Pasquale and Raphelia were just as much in love now as they were when they married each other. A day did not go by without Pasquale saying *"ti amo"* to Raphelia to which she always replied, *"anch'io ti amo"* (I love you too). They had put their wedding picture on a wall in their bedroom when they bought the house. The picture had not been moved in all these years. It was a reminder to both of them of one of the happiest days of their lives. Forty-three years of marriage, three sons, and seven grandsons. The DaCorsi lineage was destined to grow for many more generations.

Twenty Eight

Pasquale retired from glove cutting and from Guiliani's on the sixth day of March in 1925. He was seventy-four when he decided it was time to give up his long and enjoyable work as a glove cutter. Angelo, who was now sixty-three gave his long-time friend and associate a framed pair of gloves that were the last pair cut by Pasquale. All the employees were there at the time of the presentation. The employees had all signed their names on the mounted framed glove display. Pasquale's entire family also attended. Emilio also joined his friend. Pasquale was emotionally moved and thanked everyone for being so kind to him for all these years. Angelo hugged Pasquale and said, *"amici preoccupa sempre per l'eternità"* (friends forever brothers for eternity).

Life after full retirement was enjoyable for Pasquale and Raphelia. They would work in their garden together. Pasquale would take walks every day. He began to work on wood carvings again. He actually had purchased chisels and other wood carving tools. He loved to carve replicas of small animals. He saw a squirrel in the yard one morning and decided to carve squirrels. He would give his carvings away to friends, relatives, former co-workers, and to neighbors.

Pasquale also continued to make his wine. He would bring his wine to the lodge meetings for everyone to enjoy. He always gave bottles of wine to lodge members. The lodge now had over three hundred members. The lodge had outgrown the original location. Emilio purchased a building a little further down on South Main Street. That building had a space large enough for about seven hundred people. The facility also had a large kitchen so all cooking could be done at the building. The space was used for lodge meetings, banquets, dinner parties, dances, wedding receptions, and other events. The building was also rented out to other groups for many different functions.

The lodge was also one of the most notable groups providing donations in the area. One of the key projects for *Alba Nuova* was to purchase lined leather gloves for children. The lodge would host a party around the Christmas holiday and give children a pair of gloves. The group also provided dinners one night each week for free at the lodge for people who needed assistance. The lodge donated money to the community chest especially to help veterans of the war. The lodge also provided one hundred dollar scholarships each year to five students attending college. The scholarships were presented to immigrants or those whose parents were immigrants.

On Sunday, the fifth of July in 1925, forty-two year old Francesco married thirty-one year old Maria Dinapoli. This was

Francesco's first marriage. Young Maria was a widow. Her husband died of apoplexy (stroke) in 1920. He was only thirty-nine years old at the time of his death. Francesco met Maria at his fruit and vegetable store. Maria would shop at the store two or three days a week. They began dating in May 1924. Maria did not have any relatives in America. She came to the country with her parents when she was seven years old. Both her parents had passed away. Her mother died in 1922. Her father had passed away in 1918. Francesco told his brothers he was going to ask Maria to be his wife. They were very happy for him as was Pasquale and Raphelia.

The wedding was held at Our Lady of Mount Carmel Church. Father Dominic Ottaviano officiated over the ceremony. Eduardo was the best man for his brother. The wedding ceremony was a simple affair. All the relatives attended the wedding as well as friends of both Francesco and Maria. A reception was held at the church hall after the ceremony. Maria and Francesco did not want an elaborate reception.

Francesco had sold the Forest Street house last year just as he was beginning to date Maria and purchased a home at 75 Fifth Avenue in Gloversville. The home was a two story flat with two bedrooms for each flat. There was also a large kitchen, dining room, and living room for each flat. The exterior siding was cedar shakes. Francesco lived in the lower flat and he rented out the upper flat. Francesco had also taken up a new hobby. He was a photographer. Francesco had purchased a Kodak® Autographic camera. This was a roll film camera that had a knurled screw for focusing. The camera cost seventy-four dollars (History, 1999). Francesco took most of the pictures for the wedding except for the bride and groom pictures. Arturo took those pictures for his brother.

In August, Pasquale and Raphelia sold their home on Park Street and purchased a single family home located at 50 West Fulton Street. While they both loved their home on Park Street both wanted a home that was a little easier to care for. The West Fulton Street home was smaller in size. It was a two bedroom home with a nice front porch. The yard was also smaller than the one on Park Street. Pasquale had a small spot for his gardening. He had reduced the amount of vegetables for his garden at Park Street the past year. He grew so much produce in his garden; he gave most of it away. At the West Fulton Street home he would grow a few tomatoes, some peppers, eggplant, and zucchini and just enough for he and Raphelia. The back yard had a gazebo-type structure that was perfect for sitting outside in the nice weather and for taking a break from gardening.

For retirement, his new home was perfect. It was close to downtown and convenient for shopping. Although West Fulton was a busy street, the home was set back far enough that there was no real issue with road noise or other types of disturbances. The basement was dry and would work well for Pasquale's wine making. Raphelia also liked the large windows that brought in a lot of sunshine on nice days. The cottage-style house was very comfortable. There was even a driveway so when Eduardo came to visit, he had a place to park his vehicle.

Grandson Charles was now sixteen. He had begun to learn how to cut gloves. Angelo let Charles work a couple hours a day at the shop learning the process of table cutting. Charles had also become an amateur boxer. The Gloversville YMCA, built in 1913, had a boxing program for youth in the area. Charles joined the YMCA in 1924 and began taking boxing lessons. Charles was a fan of Jack Dempsey, World Heavyweight Champion from 1919 to 1926. Charles was a big boy. He was six feet tall and weighed one hundred eighty pounds. That weight put him in the heavyweight classification.

Charles had participated in six boxing matches over the last year. He won five of the six matches and lost by one point in one of the matches. Each match was three rounds with three minutes for each round. Amateur boxing was very popular in Gloversville. The matches usually had about one hundred or more people attending. Matches were arranged by the instructors. The matches took place on Saturday afternoons at the YMCA.

Charles was also a football fan. He liked the New York Giants professional football team. On Sunday, the eighth of November, Charles traveled to New York City with the boxing group to attend a Giants football game. The game was played at the Polo Grounds in New York City. The Giants faced the Cleveland Bulldogs who had won one game and lost three games so far in the early season. The Giants defeated the Bulldogs 19 to 0 (Pro Football, 2000). Charles had a great time at the game and also for his first time in New York City. The group would spend two days in New York City.

Since many of the boxers were from families who had emigrated to America the coaches took the boys to Ellis Island the next day to see the site where many of their relatives had entered the country. Charles was very interested in seeing the site where his parents had arrived in America. Charles knew that his grandfather and grandmother had arrived at Battery Park instead of Ellis Island. Charles was also thrilled at seeing the Statue of Liberty. He had seen the statue that Pasquale had carved. He was really surprised how well Pasquale's statue resembled the actual Statue of Liberty.

When Charles arrived home, he told his parents and grandparents all about Ellis Island and the Statue of Liberty. Pasquale told Charles about the voyage to America and about arriving at Battery Park. He also shared how the immigration processing was conducted when the immigrants arrived. Charles loved hearing the stories of his parents and grandparents. Being Italian-American was something Charles was very proud of. He enjoyed the large family gatherings for dinners. He was especially proud of the glove cutting skills his family had and that the trade was being passed down to the grandchildren.

Maria did not like to watch Charles box in his matches. Eduardo and his brothers attended the boxing events. Pasquale attended a few of the matches. Raphelia would visit Maria on the day of the matches. Even when Charles would come back home, Maria would examine him to see if he was alright. Charles would tell his mother, *"non sto male. L'ho fatto bene. Ho battuto l'altro ragazzo"* (I am not hurt. I did well. I beat the other guy). Maria would just look at Eduardo, put her hands together like in prayer and shake them back and forth saying, *"Madonna mia."* Eduardo would shrug his shoulders just like his father would do.

Charles, who was now called Charlie by his friends, continued his amateur boxing and in 1926 he won nine out of ten matches. In late 1926, Charles and three other fellow boxers traveled back to New York City with their coaches to participate in a four-day amateur boxing tournament. The boxers would each participate in a minimum of two matches. They could box in a total of four matches, one each day, if they continued to win the bouts. Charles won three days in a row. His fourth match was a close contest. Charles lost the match but did well against a much more experienced opponent who had over six years of boxing experience. All the boys did well finishing in the top five in their weight divisions.

In January 1927, Raphelia began to have some serious health issues. She had been feeling ill for a few months. The doctor had diagnosed Raphelia with heart disease a couple of years earlier. She had been undergoing treatment and the doctor prescribed medications for her condition. It was hard for Raphelia to get around. Eduardo would come to the house and drive her and Pasquale to her doctor appointments. Her doctor would also visit her at home each week to check on her.

In mid-April Raphelia was admitted to the hospital. Doctors conducted a series of tests and had her placed on intravenous medications. She remained in the hospital over two weeks. Her health worsened. On Wednesday morning on the twenty-seventh day of April in 1927, Raphelia passed away. Pasquale and her sons were at her bedside when she died. Pasquale wept uncontrollably when Raphelia gave her last breath. The love of his life was gone. He held Raphelia's hand and said, *"ti amo il mio della mia vita"* (I love you the love of my life). Pasquale did not want to leave her. Francesco held his father and helped him to his feet. Pasquale gave his wife a kiss on the forehead as they left the hospital room.

Francesco and his wife Maria stayed with Pasquale in his home. Family and friends came to see Pasquale and offer their condolences. Angelo came by and spent an entire day with his dear friend. Maddalena and Antonio also spent most days and evenings with Pasquale. Eduardo made the funeral arrangements for his mother. The family had previously purchased six vaults in the mausoleum at Ferndale Cemetery.

Raphelia's funeral was held on the fourth of May. The service began at the DaCorsi home followed by a funeral Mass at the church. There were over four hundred people attending the service. The support for the family was remarkable. The church was filled with flower arrangements. Pasquale was so grateful for all of the people who came to the funeral. His heart was broken. He wept during the service. His sons and family were beside him during the entire time. His sons sat on one side with their wives and his grandchildren while his sister Maddalena sat on his other side with her husband. Maddalena had her left arm wrapped around Pasquale's right arm the entire time during the service. The funeral was beautifully conducted.

The article in the evening newspaper read,

"The funeral of Mrs. Raphelia M. DaCorsi was held at nine yesterday morning at the home, 50 West Fulton Street, and at Our Lady of Mount Carmel church at nine thirty. The service was very largely attended. Flowers were from friends, relatives, directors of the Trust

Company of Fulton County, Metropolitan Life Insurance, Louis B. Meyer and Sons, and the Alba Nuova Lodge. The pall bearers were John Papa, Achilles Finizio, James Greco, Mario Papa, Philip Catanzaro, and Alfred Evangelista. A requiem high Mass was conducted by the Reverend Father Dominic J. Ottaviano."

There was a large reception that began at noon at the lodge following the internment ceremony. Emilio had made all the arrangements for the reception. The lodge facility was filled with people still paying their respects to Pasquale. Although deeply saddened, Pasquale thanked each person individually for coming to the service and to the reception. This was the saddest day of Pasquale's life. He had lost his love, his best friend, and the mother of his children.

The family would take turns staying with Pasquale at the home over the next few weeks. It was a very slow process for Pasquale. He missed his Raphelia so very much. He would read their letters at night. He would also say the Rosary for his wife each night. The years of their lives together seemed so short. Pasquale wondered where all the years went. There was such a rich relationship between the two of them. Each night as he laid his head on his pillow Pasquale would shed tears and say goodnight to his beloved Raphelia.

Twenty Nine

The year following Raphelia's death was a difficult one for Pasquale. He had his daily routines but he was just going the motions. Pasquale is still overcome with grief. His sons were by his side every day. Eduardo took Pasquale to the cemetery once a week. Pasquale stood next to the crypt and talked to Raphelia. He told her some of the things that are happening in Gloversville. He talked about the grandchildren. He told her that he is eating and even cooks sometimes.

Pasquale sold the house on West Fulton Street. Eduardo had purchased the house at 35 Park Street, Pasquale's and Raphelia's former home. Eduardo moved his father back into the house at 35 Park Street. Pasquale liked being back on Park Street as he was across the street from Eduardo again and he was back in the house with the best memories of Raphelia. Pasquale was also more relaxed at the Park Street house. He still grieved for his wife but he was doing better.

As more time passed, Pasquale's sadness lessens but he still misses his Raphelia every day. Pasquale spends a lot of time at the lodge. He plays cards every day with a group of friends including Emilio. He attends all of the functions at the lodge and helps with the set-up of the hall. He has also become the official greeter at the door. He welcomes members and guests to the meetings and other functions. Emilio also visits Pasquale at the house a couple of times each week.

Angelo also has Pasquale come to the shop once a week. Angelo meets with Pasquale and asks him for suggestions on issues and other things happening in the business. Pasquale enjoys his time with Angelo and with the employees at Guiliani's. Many of Pasquale's co-workers have retired. Pasquale is happy to see the new younger workers and also to see that table cutting is still the primary method for cutting gloves at the shop.

Pasquale and Maddalena meet at his house for lunch each week. Antonio and Pasquale sit on the porch together and watch people walk by. They talk about the good times over the years. Antonio helps Pasquale with the garden as well. They both enjoy working in their gardens. Vincenzo, who is also retired now, and Luciana also visit every week. The big Sunday gatherings have become much smaller now. Usually the family goes to Eduardo's for the Sunday meal. The day is still something Pasquale looks forward to. He likes being around his grandsons especially since they are getting older. Pasquale spends a lot of time talking to six-year-old Claude. He tells Claude about the time on the ship coming to America. Claude likes to sit on his grandfather's lap when Pasquale talks to him.

Throughout the remainder of 1928 and into early 1929 Pasquale was doing much better. He still went to the cemetery every week. He was still keeping very busy. Eduardo and Maria had purchased a camp home at Caroga Lake. They would take Pasquale and their sons to the camp on weekends during the summer. The boys enjoyed the lake and the amusement park. Pasquale liked to watch the boys at the park, riding the carousel, and going to the penny arcade. He also liked watching the younger grandsons having fun on the various amusement rides like the Ferris wheel. The family would have dinner at Sherman's Restaurant on Saturday nights. The Sherman family opened the amusement park in 1920. Caroga Lake is about ten miles northwest of Gloversville.

The grandsons also spent a lot of time swimming in Caroga Lake. Claude was an excellent swimmer. Even his older brothers could not keep up with him. Many people would rent wooden paddle boats at Sherman's. Sunday afternoons the lake was packed with paddle boat enthusiasts. Eduardo would take Maria and Pasquale for rides on the paddle boat. Pasquale one time said that the paddle boat was quite a bit smaller than his ship that he came to America on, and not as bumpy.

October 1929 was a devastating time. The crash of the stock market would lead to a spiraling decline in the economy over the next few years. Although the market rebounded, it was a

ALBA NUOVA

temporary recovery. The country would fall into the greatest economic decline in history. The crash of '29 would bring nearly ten years of depression across the nation. The DaCorsi's had some investments in the stock market. Most of their assets however were in cash. Arturo guided the family with financial management advice and counseling. He also watched the stock market carefully and made recommendations to the family on a regular basis including the period just before the crash. As a result most of the family stocks were sold before the crash. Some stocks made a profit, some were sold at a loss, and others would just break even. The overall result was that the DaCorsi's would have some financial stability during the entire period of the depression years.

Arturo married in June 1931. He had been engaged to Anna DelNegro for about one year. Anna taught school in Gloversville. Arturo is nine-years older than Anna. They met when Anna came to the bank to open an account. The couple married in a small ceremony held at Our Lady of Mount Carmel. The reception for family and friends was held at Anna's parent's home. Anna's mother and father emigrated from Italy in 1895. Anna was the oldest child. She has four younger brothers.

In late September 1931, eighty-year-old Pasquale was again honored by the members of the *Alba Nuova Lodge*. Pasquale received a plaque for his outstanding years of service to the lodge and to the community. Pasquale's dear friend, Emilio, presented the plaque. Pasquale's family was there for the ceremony. As always Pasquale was very humble in accepting the recognition.

Pasquale now used a cane to help him walk. He was also still slightly hunched over from all the years of table cutting gloves. His sons would take turns visiting him each day. Both Francesco's wife, Maria, and Eduardo's wife, Maria, would help Pasquale with preparing meals. Pasquale and Emilio visited each other on a regular basis. Pasquale had actually become used to riding in automobiles. Eduardo had purchased a new car last year. This time forty-five-year-old Eduardo bought a little more conservative model, a 1930 Oldsmobile, four-door sedan. Francesco and Arturo both drove a 1928 Model A Ford.

With the nation now in the Great Depression, the DaCorsi family continued to seek out those in Gloversville who needed help. Eduardo was providing financial assistance to some of his insurance clients. Arturo, now a manager at the bank, would help his clients with managing their savings accounts and with other financial needs. Francesco was assisting his loyal customers who shopped at the store. If people could not afford to buy food at his, Francesco would offer credit and, in some situations, he would give food to his customers. Francesco's wife, Maria, had been working at the store for the past three years. She would take food baskets to families in the area. Maria also made minestrone soup four days a week. Francesco and Maria would give bowls of soup to people who came by the store but did not have money to buy food.

On Saturday, the twenty-third of January 1932, at the annual lodge membership banquet, Pasquale was asked by Emilio to address the group. Pasquale told Emilio that he would *"aprire il mio cuore si membri"* (open my heart to the members). This was Pasquale's way of saying how much he cared for his fellow lodge members. He was helped to the front of the room by Eduardo and his grandson, Charles. Pasquale stood before the group and said, *"Sono venuto in America per cercare un nuovo inizio, la mia alba nuova. Ho vissuto la mia vita come Dio mi avrebbe voluto. Sono orgoglioso di essere un Italiano - Americano. Sono diventato un cittadino naturalizzato. Io miei figli sono diventati cittadini naturalizzati. Io amo l'America anche se ho sempre manca la mia amata Italia. Io sono un uomo umile. La mia vita è stata piena di amici meravigliosi, una bella famiglia, e la mia amata Raphelia che mi manca a caro prezzo ogni giorno. Il mio paese è l'America. La mia casa è Gloversville. La mia patria è l'Italia. Sono Pasquale DaCorsi una persona benedetta, una persona riconoscente, una persona piena di amore forma ciascuno di voi, e una persona che realizzato il mio sogna di alba nuova."* (I came to America to seek a new beginning, my new dawn. I lived my life as God would have wanted me to. I am proud to be an Italian-American. I became a naturalized citizen. My children became naturalized citizens. I love America although I always miss my beloved Italy. I am a humble man. My life has been filled with wonderful friends, a beautiful family, and my beloved Raphelia whom I miss dearly every day. My country is America. My home is Gloversville. My homeland is Italy. I am Pasquale DaCorsi a person blessed, a person grateful, a person filled with love for each of you, and a person who has accomplished my dream of the new dawn.").

The members gave Pasquale a standing ovation. They stood in his honor and applauded for five minutes. Emilio gave his friend a hug and the traditional kiss on both cheeks. Pasquale and most everyone else were in tears. Pasquale's family joined him at the front of the room. Maddalena hugged her brother. Pasquale's sons and grandsons all gave him a kiss. Everyone in the room raised a glass of wine in honor of Pasquale.

On Sunday morning the entire DaCorsi family accompanied Pasquale to Mass. Our Lady of Mount Carmel Church, under the leadership of Father Ottaviano, had constructed a new church building located at 149 South Main Street. The new church was completed in 1930. As Pasquale entered the church, he walked to the kneeling area at the main altar and with help from his sons, he knelt down. Pasquale looked at the large crucifix that was next to the altar. He made the sign of the cross, held his open hands up shoulder high with arms bent at the elbow in a tribute to his God and said, *"mio Signore, mio Dio, alzo le mani in lode di te. Apro il mio cuore a voi. Prego la costar pietà di me. Prego la tua benedizione su di me. Vivo ogni giorno per voi. La mia vita è stata fatta piena come avete previsto. Il mio Signor, e mio Dio, mi guardi alla tua presenze oggi e sempre, Amen"* (my Lord, My God, I raise my hands in praise of you. I open my heart to you. I pray your blessing on me. I live each day for you. My life has been made full as you have provided. My Lord, my God, keep me in your presence today and forever, Amen).

After church there was a family gathering at Eduardo's and Maria's home. Maddalena and Antonio were there as was Angelo and Rosa with their children, and Luciana and Vincenzo. Ciccio and Teresa and their daughters and Francesco and Maria along with Arturo and Anna were also at the gathering. The traditional large family meal was served. Both of the Maria's and Anna prepared the meal. Pasquale especially enjoyed the day. With the entire family being there along with Angelo and his family brought back memories for Pasquale of the days in Italy and the early days in Gloversville when everyone would spend the entire day together. After the meal was served, the men sat on the front porch and smoked cigars and had a glass of wine. Pasquale had not smoked a cigar in years. The evening ended following another serving of food. It was getting late and Pasquale was a little tired. Arturo and Anna walked Pasquale home. As they escorted Pasquale into the house, Pasquale gave his son and Anna a kiss and thanked them for a wonderful day.

Over the next couple of months Pasquale was having a little harder time using his cane to walk. He legs seemed to have weakened. He was not getting out of the house much except to sit in his lounge chair in the yard at times. His sons would come to see him every day. They took turns staying with their father until he went to bed at night. Eduardo's wife, Maria, would help Pasquale during the day. Pasquale's grandsons also visited quite often.

The morning of the twenty-sixth of April Eduardo walked across the street to help his father get ready for a doctor appointment. Each of the sons had a key to Pasquale's house. When Eduardo opened the front door, he did not hear his father. Eduardo went into the bedroom and saw his father was still in bed. He called his name but Pasquale did not respond. As Eduardo checked his father, he realized that Pasquale had passed away. Although Pasquale did not use it much, his sons had a telephone installed in the home. Eduardo called his brothers and his wife immediately. They all came to the home right away. The brothers all hugged. The tears flowed as they looked at their father.

Pasquale had died peacefully in his sleep. The coroner was called and pronounced the death of Pasquale. The family had his body removed by a funeral director. The paperwork that was completed by the coroner for Pasquale had the name as Charles DaCorsi on the death certificate. The sons kept the name Charles on the paperwork. With all his years in Gloversville, the boys felt it was proper to use the American name that most people now knew Pasquale by. Only his family, lodge members, and close friends called him Pasquale. In the general community, he was Charles.

The funeral for Charles was held on Friday the twenty-ninth day of April. The services were held at Our Lady of Mount Carmel Church after a brief ceremony at the house. The church was filled to capacity. The Reverend Dominic Ottaviano conducted the funeral Mass. Friends of Charles from the *Alba Nuova Lodge* served as pall bearers. They were James Lauria, John Corrado, Frank Sgambato, Frank DeMarco, Patsy Russo, and Michael Lombardo. The caravan procession down South Main Street to the cemetery was nearly one half mile long. The Gloversville Police Department motorcycle officers led the procession. Pasquale (Charles) was laid to rest next to his beloved Raphelia in the mausoleum at Ferndale Cemetery.

Pasquale was eighty-one years of age with thirty-four of those years spent in America and in Gloversville. The legacy that Pasquale DaCorsi left behind is one of a man who loved his wife, loved his family, loved his work, and was dedicated to making life better for all. He raised three sons who all had great success and long careers. A banker, an insurance agent, and a store owner, these are the sons of Pasquale. These things were only made possible by a decision of a nineteenth-century Italian immigrant who had a vision and a dream of coming to America for a new beginning, a better life for his wife and children, and his dream of *alba nuova*.

The DaCorsi name lives on. The descendants of Pasquale DaCorsi include three sons, seven grandsons, twenty-three great grandchildren, and over seventy-five great-great grandchildren. The DaCorsi name will continue for many generations. The legacy of that *alba nuova* will live on as well. Although Pasquale's grandsons have all passed away, and some of the great-grandchildren have passed away as well, the story of that Italian immigrant continues to be passed down to each generation.

Eduardo's sons all told their children of the stories of Pasquale and his brothers. Francesco passed away in January 1942. Arturo died in March 1973. My father, Leon DaCorsi, after a thirteen-year battle with leukemia passed away in 1972 at the age of fifty-four. Claude, the youngest brother gave the ultimate sacrifice. He gave his life in World War II. He died in the Canal Zone. Claude was twenty-one years old. Charles, the oldest brother passed away in 1962. Frank died in 1969. Frank and his wife, Eleanor, lost their youngest daughter to polio in 1955.

Catherine Ann DaCorsi was eight years old when she died. Robert, who lived in California where the family had moved in 1936 for a couple of years, died in 1972, a few months before my father passed away. While the family was in California, my father Leon, graduated from John Marshall High School, Class of 1937. Edward Junior, who also stayed in California, passed away in 1985. Arthur, the last surviving brother died in 1995.

The richness of culture and heritage is prevalent in all of the DaCorsi's today. Great-great grandchildren know of Pasquale. The DaCorsi heritage and Italian traditions continue. The warmth, the compassion, the love, and keeping the Italian heritage alive in each family member provides that connection to that nineteenth century Italian immigrant known as Pasquale DaCorsi. This is a new beginning. This is a new dawn. Each DaCorsi family member whether in past times, today, or tomorrow has experienced or will experience their own *alba nuova.*

# ACKNOWLEDGMENTS

I wish to offer my thanks and gratitude to those who provided support, proofreading, research, and encouragement in creating this book.

Thank you to the City of Gloversville, Historian James Morrison, City Clerk Susan Semione, and especially to Deputy Clerk Cindy Ostrander for conducting outstanding and valuable research on my family. You provided information that contributed to the context of this book. Your findings of the family birth and death dates have allowed the family tree to be more complete.

Thank you Dr. Largo Wales for the encouragement, proofreading, and the positive comments.

Thank you to my brother L.J. DaCorsi who shares my enthusiasm for our family history.

Thank you to my sister Dawn Marie Hayes. We did not grow up together but we have grown close to one another. Our lives are entwined forever.

To my cousin, Mary (DaCorsi) Graham-hayes. Thank you for the research and your knowledge of our family history.

Thank you to the Order of the Sons of Italy in America. As a thirteen year member of the organization I am proud to be part of an organization that my great grandfather was a member of. Thank you to the members of the Auburn (Washington) Lodge #1955 for sharing our Italian heritage with our community.

Thank you Pattee Baggett for the editing and proofreading. For everything you have done I am forever grateful.

To my children, Claude Jr., Shannon, and Michael. Keep your dreams alive. Life is but a moment in time. Make each day your *Alba Nuova*.

Downtown Gloversville
Circa 1900

https://www.facebook.com/fpgloversville/photos/a.629123977130330.1073741866.511628085546587/678562985519762/?type=3&theater

Fonda, Johnstown & Gloversville Railroad Depot, 102 West Fulton Street, Gloversville (1896)

http://frontpagegloversville.squarespace.com/pictoral-history/fonda- johnstown- gloversville-railroad

F. J. & G. R. R. DEPOT.

Nathan Littauer Hospital 1905
http://frontpagegloversville.squarespace.com/pictoral-history/the-beginnings/18858412

Claude E. DaCorsi, Sr.

Former Gloversville Business School

https://www.google.com/search?q=historic+photos+main+street+gloversville+new+york&biw=1600&bih=791&tbm=isch&tbo=u&source=univ&sa=X&ved=0ahUKEwj8ytOfpOfMAhVh54MKHS-aDjkQsAQIJA#imgrc=DV5mMVgP3bPv0M%3A

The City National Bank

https://www.google.com/search?q=historic+photos+main+street+gloversville+new+york&biw=1600&bih=791&tbm=isch&tbo=u&source=univ&sa=X&ved=0ahUKEwj8ytOfpOfMAhVh54MKHS-aDjkQsAQIJA#imgrc=DV5mMVgP3bPv0M%3A

Claude E. DaCorsi, Sr.

https://www.facebook.com/fpgloversville/photos/a.629123977130330.1073741866.511628085546587/661167663925961/?type=3&theater

the vehicle, said frame being provided with curtains, clamp members carried by and interior to the side members of the frame and adjustable to move one toward the other to grip the body of the vehicle, side curtains carried by the clamp members and participating in the movements of adjustment toward and from the body of the vehicle, and means for connecting the frame to the vehicle top when the latter is extended, the frame being also provided with a member extending transversely thereof between its sides and adjustable lengthwise of the sides of the frame, and positioned to engage the upper edges of the sides of the vehicle.

3. A storm front attachment for vehicles having tops, comprising a substantially rigid frame of a length substantially equal to the full height of the storm front and of a width greater than the width of the body of the vehicle and also provided with curtains, clamp members on opposite sides of the frame each hinged at the upper end to a respective side member of the frame near the upper end thereof at the inner side of the side member and at the lower ends said clamp members being constructed to engage the outer faces of the respective sides of the body of the vehicle to which the storm front is applied, a side curtain carried by each hinged clamp member and participating in the movements thereof, connecting members carried by the frame at the end thereof remote from that to be attached to the vehicle body, and means for attachment thereof to the top of the vehicle.

4. In a storm front for vehicles, a frame comprising side members and top and bottom members, longitudinally slotted toothed plates carried by the frame near one end thereof, a clamp screw carried by each plate near one end thereof, a rod extending through the slotted plates and between the side members of the frame, clamp blocks and nuts carried by the rod to engage the toothed plates of the frame, and a bar interior to each side member of the frame and hinged thereto near the end of the frame remote from the clamp screws, each bar being provided with a slotted passage for the rod and with an engaging member at the end remote from the hinge to contact with the vehicle body and at said end being located in the path of the clamp screw on the adjacent side member.

5. In a storm front for vehicles, a frame comprising side members and top and bottom members, longitudinally slotted toothed plates carried by the frame near one end thereof, a clamp screw carried by each plate near one end thereof, a rod extending through the slotted plates and between the side members of the frame, clamp blocks and nuts carried by the rod to engage the toothed plates of the frame, and a bar interior to each side member of the frame and hinged thereto near the end of the frame remote from the clamp screws, each bar being provided with a slotted passage for the rod and with an engaging member at the end remote from the hinge to contact with the vehicle body, each of said hinge bars being provided with a spring roller and a side curtain attached thereto and also at the slotted end being located in the path of the clamp screw on the adjacent side member.

[Claims 6 to 18 not printed in the Gazette.]

1,080,813. GLOVE. EDWARD DACORSI, Gloversville, N. Y., assignor of one-third to Peter Cinelli and one-third to Frank Finizio, Gloversville, N. Y. Filed Feb. 7, 1912. Serial No. 675,934. (Cl. 2—9.)

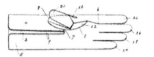

A glove comprising front and back formed of a single piece of material folded along the line of the outer edge of the first finger and along the line of the outer edge of the little finger to form front flaps, a wrist-opening and an inclosed thumb-opening, said front flaps being secured together by two short seams, one extending from the wrist-opening to the inner side of the thumb-opening and the other extending from the crotch between the first and second fingers to the base of the thumb-opening at a slight angle to the inner side-line of the first finger; and a thumb-piece formed of a single piece of material folded for a portion of its length along its longitudinal middle line with its edges stitched together to form a thumb-pocket and having an angular projection extending a substantial distance beyond the pocket-forming portion of the thumb-piece, said thumb-piece being secured within the thumb-opening, one of said front flaps of the body extending continuously along the front side of the first finger past the crotch of the thumb and terminating in a quirk for the thumb.

1,080,814. RIM FOR MOUNTING PNEUMATIC TIRES. EDWARD FREDERICK DREGER, Oakland, and FRANK ELVIN PFISTER, Piedmont, Cal. Filed Mar. 2, 1912. Serial No. 681,053. (Cl. 152—22.)

1. In combination with an outer casing having a series of simultaneously inflatable tube sections therein, of a rim for mounting the same, said rim being divided longitudinally into sections, means for clamping said sections together, one of said rim sections being provided with a plurality of circumferentially disposed openings communicating with the interior of said outer casing for the insertion of the tube sections therein, a valve controlled closure for each of said tube sections, said rim section being further provided with an annular bore therein communicating with each of said valve controlled closures, an inflating valve common to all of said inflatable tube sections, and means for retaining said valve controlled closures in said tube sections.

2. In combination with an outer casing having a series of simultaneously inflatable circumferentially disposed inflatable tube sections therein, of a rim for mounting the same, said rim being provided with a plurality of circumferentially disposed openings therein communicating with the interior of said outer casing for the insertion of the tube sections therein, said rim being further provided with an annular bore arranged circumferentially thereof and communicating with each of said openings, a disk adapted to be seated in each of said openings and close the open end of said tubes, a valve controlled channel in said disk and communicating with said annular bore and said inflatable tube sections, an inflating valve extended from one of said disks and communicating with each of said inflatable sections through said annular bore and means for retaining said disk in said openings.

3. In combination with an outer casing having a series of simultaneously inflatable circumferentially disposed tube sections therein, of a rim for mounting the same, said rim being provided with a plurality of circumferentially disposed openings therein communicating with the interior of said outer casing for the insertion of said tube sections therein, one of said tubes being seated within

https://www.google.com/search?q=pictures+of+a+glove+cutter+gloversville+new+york&biw=1280&bih=586&tbm=isch&tbo=u&source=univ&sa=X&ved=0ahUKEwiNrdT5wt_LAhVP92MKHQZUAD8QsAQIGw

Table Cutters

ALBA NUOVA

https://www.facebook.com/fpgloversville/photos/a.629123977130330.1073741866.511628085546587/700177270025000/?type=3&theater

GLOVERSVILLE

The Home of
FINE GLOVES
and
LEATHER PRODUCTS

Gloversville Produces 75% of All Fine Gloves Manufactured in the U. S. A.

The Following List Shows a Diversity of Industrial and Commercial Products Made in Gloversville

Leather Gloves	Chemicals
Fabric Gloves	Silk and Hosiery
Pocketbooks	Boxes
Leather Novelties	Baskets
Mittens	Foundry Products
Fur Gloves and Fur Linings	Machinery
Leather Finishing and Dyeing	Concrete and Plastic Building Materials
Knit Goods	
Glove Fasteners and Button Stays	Beverages and Ice Cream
Hides and Tallow	Hair Processing
Shoe Leather	

For Further Information Regarding the Industries of Gloversville,
Write or Call the

Chamber of Commerce

21 BLEECKER STREET   Phone 5-5419   GLOVERSVILLE, N. Y.

Claude E. DaCorsi, Sr.

https://www.facebook.com/photo.php?fbid=1082291191809622.10&set=gm

Glove Shop – Sewing Gloves

My father

John Marshall High School Class of 1937

Los Angeles, California

Leon M. DaCorsi

Claude E. DaCorsi, Sr.

http://holyspirit12078.org/media/1/20120727-Ador-Persp-433x651.jpg

Our Lady of Mount Carmel Church

ALBA NUOVA

http://fultonhistory.com/Newspaper%2011/Gloversville%20NY%20Morning%20Herald/Gloversville%20NY%20Morning%20Herald%201927%20Grayscale/Gloversville%20NY%20Morning%20Herald%201927%20Grayscale%20-%201482.pdf

THE MORNING HERALD, SATURDAY, APRIL 30, 1927.

Funerals

Mrs. Raphella M .DaCorsi

The funeral of Mrs. Raphella M. DaCorsi was held at 9 o'clock yesterday morning at the home, 50 West Fulton street, and at Our Lady of Mt. Carmel church at 9:30 o'clock. It was largely attended. Flowers were from friends, relatives, directors of the Trust Company of Fulton County, offices and employes of the Trust Company of Fulton County, Louis Meyers & Sons, Metropolitan Life Insurance Company, and Alba Nuova Lodge, 387.

Claude E. DaCorsi, Sr.

2011/Gloversville%20NY%20Morning%20Herald/Gloversville%20NY%20Morning%20Herald%201932%20Grayscale

visit in this city for some time.

FUNERALS

Charles ı Corsi

Funeral services for Charles Da Corsi were held yesterday morning at 9 at the home, 35 Park street and at 9:30 at Our Lady of Mt. Carmel church. A high mass of requiem was celebrated by Rev. D. J. Ottaviano, pastor of the church. The bearers were James Lauria, John Corrado, Frank Sgambato, Frank De Marco, Patsy Russo, Michael Lombardo, members of the Alba Nuova lodge. The remains were placed in the mausoleum in the Fern Dale cemetery.

Flowers were received from relatives, friends, neighbors, Ackel Brothers, Metropolitan Life Insurance company, Gloversville District; t h e Alba Nuova lodge, Twenty-Five year employes at Louis Meyers & Sons, the Exchange club the Trust Company of Fulton County and Louis Meyers & Sons and employes.

Mrs. Mary DaCorsi

Funeral services for Mrs. Mary DaCorsi were held at 9:30 Saturday morning at the home, 36 Park street, and at 10 in Our Lady of Mt. Carmel church. A solemn high mass of requiem was celebrated by the Rev. Edward C. Crowley. The Rev. Henry Burke of the Church of the Immaculate Conception in Johnstown was deacon and the Rev. Peter Winkelmann of the St. Francis de Sales church was sub-deacon.

Floral tributes were from relatives, friends, neighbors, employes of the Bigelow-Sanford machine shop, girls at Gates & Mills annex, employes of Gloversville and Johnstown A & P stores, Red Men Teroga Tribe, neighbors on the third shift of the G. E. and the Art welding department of the G. E.

The bearers were Alfred Evangelista, Orville and Adelbert Hurd, John Papa, Phylis Mangiale and Richard Stock. The body was placed in the mausoleum at Fern Dale cemetery.

http://fultonhistory.com/Newspaper%2011/Gloversville%20NY%20Morning%20Herald/Gloversville%20NY%20Morning%20Herald%201943%20Grayscale/Gloversville%20NY%20Morning%20Herald%201943%20Grayscale%20-%200541.pdf

THURSDAY, FEBRUARY 25, 1943.

Claude E. DaCorsi, Sr.

FRIDAY, JULY 29, 1949

Edward Da Corsi

A prayer service was held this morning at 9 at the Clarence Brown funeral home, 301 North Main street for Edward Da Corsi and a solemn high mass of requiem celebrated at Our Lady of Mount Carmel church at 9:30. The celebrant was the Rev. Harold McKeon; deacon, the Rev. D. J. Ottaviano and the sub-deacon, the Rev. Joseph D'Agostino.

Flowers and mass cards were from relatives, friends, neighbors, Red Men raising staff and degree team, employes of Borman Sportswear, Wo-Wi-Tan Council, Holy Name society of Our Lady of Mount Carmel church, Rockovitz & Son, Gloversville Aerie of Eagles, Vincent Sanges & Sons, Teroga Tribe of Red Men, Mohawk Council degree team, Triangle Employes social Club, Santella & Salluzzo, dressing department of Triangle Finishing Corp., Ossan Glove and Novelty Co., employes of Mohican, Ackel Brothers.

The bearers were Harry Amaduri, Louis Cuomo, Dominic Vertucci, Frank Basileo, John DiGiacomo, and Robert Bearce.

The body was placed in the mausoleum in Fern Dale cemetery.

http://fultonhistory.com/Newspaper%2011/Gloversville%20NY%20Morning%20Herald/Gloversville%20NY%20Morning%20Herald%201949%20Grayscale/Gloversville%20NY%20Morning%20Herald%201949%20Grayscale%20-%202771.pdf

PFC. DA CORSI DIED, MAY 26, IN CANAL ZONE

Private First Class, Claude A. Da Corsi 21, of the United States Army, son of Edward Da Corsi of 36 Park street, died May 26, somewhere in the Panama Canal Zone. This information was received in a telegram from the Adjutant General's office which did not give any details as to the cause of death.

Text of Telegram

The telegram reads: "The Secretary of War desires that I tender his deepest sympathy to you in the loss of your son, Private Claude A. DaCorsi. The report has just been received he died May 26 in Latin America. Letter to follow."

The family received a letter from Private Da Corsi on May 13. He set forth in it he was in good health. He was stationed somewhere in the Canal Zone. He had been attached to a Coast Artillery outfit.

Home Some Time Ago

Private Da Corsi came home some time ago on an emergency furlough following the death of his mother. He received an extension of his furlough at that time through the Gloversville Red Cross Chapter.

He was inducted into the service on October 8, 1942. Following his basic training he was sent to the Canal Zone, where he has been stationed some time. He was born and had always resided in Gloversville and had a large number of friends.

The survivors, besides his father, are six brothers, Charles and Frank of this city, Robert, Edward and Arthur of Johnstown and Leon of Amsterdam.

WEDNESDAY, JUNE 2, 1943.

http://fultonhistory.com/Newspaper%2011/Gloversville%20NY%20Morning%20Herald/Gloversville%20NY%20Morning%20Herald%201943%20Grayscale/Gloversville%20NY%20Morning%20Herald%201943%20Grayscale%20-%201460.pdf

RECIPES

Spaghetti con Olio d'oliva è Aglio

Spaghetti with Olive Oil and Garlic

Ingredients:

1 lb dry spaghetti
½ cup extra virgin olive oil
6 large cloves of garlic (slivered thin)
1 tbsp garlic powder
¾ cup grated Parmesan cheese
Red pepper flakes (optional to taste)
¼ cup Fresh Italian Parsley (optional)

Directions:
Cook pasta (al dente) per package instructions
Heat olive oil in a large sauté pan (medium heat)
Add slivered garlic and cook until translucent (do not brown)
Add optional red pepper flakes (if desired)
Add ¾ cup pasta water to the olive oil and garlic sauce
Drain pasta (do not rinse)
Add pasta to the sauce
Add the Parmesan cheese
Add optional parsley (if desired)
Toss the pasta and olive oil/garlic sauce
Add garlic powder and toss again
Cook mixture on low heat for about five minutes more

Let pasta rest of couple of minutes before serving

Add more Parmesan cheese to taste if desired

Nonni's Biscotti

Ingredients:

½ cup butter
1 cup sugar
1 tsp Anise Extract
1 tsp Almond Extract
2 ½ tsp baking powder
3 eggs
3 ¼ cups flour

Directions:
Heat oven to 375°

In a large mixing bowl cream together butter, sugar, anise extract, almond extract, and baking powder

Beat in eggs (one at a time)
Gradually add and mix in the flour

Form into a dough and knead for two minutes

Flatten dough into a 12" long by 3" wide and ¾" thick shape

Bake dough on a cookie sheet lined with parchment paper for 20-25 minutes. Remove from oven and cool for 20 minutes.

Cut biscotti from the widthwise dough shape ¾" to 1" wide

Reset oven to 325°

Place cut edge of each biscotti on cookie sheet and bake about 4-5 minutes per side

Cool and serve – makes about 3 dozen

Bibliography

Ball, J. (2005). Mount Vesuvius Italy. Retrieved March 16, 2016, from
http://geology.com/volcanoes/vesuvius/
Mount Vesuvius: Eruption History

Bateman-House, A., & Fairchild, A. (2008, April). Medical Examination
of Immigrants at Ellis Island. Retrieved May 10, 2016, from
http://journalofethics.ama-assn.org/2008/04/mhst1-0804.html
AMA Journal of Ethics Illuminating the Art of Medicine History of
Medicine Volume 10 Number 4: 235-241

Bogue, D. (2007, June 23). Tales Similar to Cinderella. Retrieved March
21, 2016, from
http://www.surlalunefairytales.com/cinderella/stories/ceneren.html
Translated by John Edward Taylor

Bryer, Lucy & May, Christine (2009). New York State Department of
Parks, Recreation and Historic District Preservation. *Downtown
Gloversville Historic District*, nomination document, 1985, National
Park Service, National Register of Historic Places, Washington, D.C.
Retrieved April 15, 2016 from
http://www.livingplaces.com/NY/Fulton_County/Gloversville_City/
Downtown_Gloversville_Historic_District.html

Centennial Classroom (n.d.). Facts of Life in Greater New York.
Retrieved January 10, 2016, from
http://home.nyc.gov/html/nyc100/html/classroom/hist_info/nycfacts.
html

Church of the Holy Spirit. (2012). Retrieved April 12, 2016, from
http://www.holyspirit12078.org/parish-life/about
About Our Parish - A Brief History

Cornell, G., & Shiel, J. (1999). Fire - Friend or Foe? Retrieved May 8, 2016,
from http://www.fulton.nygenweb.net/history/BRfire.html

Editors of the Encyclopedia Britannica. (2014, July 17). Risorgimento Italian History. Retrieved March 24, 2016, from http://www.britannica.com/event/Risorgimento

Falco, E. (2012, July 10). When Italian Immigrants were 'the other' Retrieved March 3, 2016, from http://www.cnn.com/2012/07/10/opinion/falco-italian-immigrants/

Giambattista Basile Italian Author. Retrieved March 10, 2016, from www.britannica.com/biography/Giambattista-Basile

Heritage History Academy. (n.d.). Wars of Italian Unification. Retrieved January 17, 2016, from http://www.heritage-history.com/index.php?c=academy&s=war-dir&f=wars_italianunity

Historic Gloversville. The City of Gloversville. (n.d.). Retrieved February 21, 2016, from http://www.cityofgloversville.com/index.php/2015/06/02/1568/

History of KODAK Cameras (1999). Kodak Technical Data. Retrieved May 15, 2016 from http://www.kodak.com/global/en/consumer/products/techInfo/aa13/aa13.shtml

Italian Christmas Traditions – The legend of la Befana. (n.d.). Retrieved from http://monteverdituscany.com/italian-christmas-traditions-the-legend-of-la-befana/

Leather. (n.d). Retrieved April 18, 2016, from http://www.britannica.com/topic/leather The Editors of the Encyclopedia Britannica

Maggi, L. (2014, December 1). Italian immigrants: 175 years of New Orleans history. Retrieved March 3, 2016, from http://www.nola.com/175years/index.ssf/2012/01/italian_immigrants_the_times-p.html

Menear, P., & Shiel, J. (2000). History of Gloversville. Retrieved January 9, 2016, from http://fulton.nygenweb.net/history/glovshistoryE.html

Mohawk River Basin. Mohawk/Cayadutta Creek Watershed
(0202000410). Cayadutta Creek, Lower, and minor Tribs.
Cayadutta Creek, Upper, and minor Tribs. Retrieved March 18,
2016 from
http://www.dec.ny.gov/docs/water_pdf/wimohawkcayadutta.pdf

Molnar, A. (2010, December 15). From Europe to America: Immigration
Through Family Tales - History of Italian Immigration. Retrieved
February 28, 2016, from
https://www.mtholyoke.edu/~molna22a/classweb/politics/Italianhist
ory.html

Morrison, J. F. (2008, May 13). Gloversville's Community Page. Retrieved
April 1, 2106, from
http://fulton.nygenweb.net/towns/fulngloves.html
James F. Morrison, Historian, City of Gloversville

Morrison, J., & Shiel, J. (2008, May 13). Anthony's and Purdy's Business
Directory for Gloversville 1890. Retrieved February 9, 2016, from
http://fulton.nygenweb.net/people/Ghand1890B.html

Office of the Historian (n.d.). U.S. Entry into World War I, 1917.
Retrieved May 5, 2016 from
https://history.state.gov/milestones/1914-1920/wwi

Order of Sons of Italy in America (2016). OSIA History. Retrieved July 3,
2016 from https://www.osia.org/about/history.php

Parks, R. R. (2009, April 27). An Eastern Regional Railroad of the 1930's -
1940's Fonda Johnstown & Gloversville Railroad. Retrieved
February 4, 2016, from http://www.r2parks.net/FJ&G.html

Pro Football (2000). 1925 New York Giants. Retrieved May 25, 2016 from
http://www.pro-football-reference.com/teams/nyg/1925.htm

ALBA NUOVA

Redmond, D. W. (1913). *The Leather Glove Industry in the United States.*
New York: Columbia University.
doi:https://books.google.com/books?id=_AwsAAAAYAAJ&pg=PA3
3&lpg=PA33&dq=labor problems in the glove industry in
1900&source=bl&ots=LTIk8ZGcji&sig=lolNN66it1U4yfuKDYnAXgQ
igBI&hl=en&sa=X&ved=0ahUKEwiyxKee7o_NAhUD1mMKHb1tAG
kQ6AEIHTAA#v=onepage&q=labor problems in the glove industry
in 1900&f=fal

Rosenberg, J. (2015, October 18). Triangle Shirtwaist Factory Fire.
Retrieved May 8, 2016, from
http://history1900s.about.com/od/1910s/p/trianglefire.htm

Snowden, F. M. (2002). *Naples in the Time of Cholera 1884 - 1911.* New
York, NY: Cambridge University Press

Solem, B. (2004). Machinery of the Atlantic Steamships. Retrieved March
15, 2016, from
http://www.norwayheritage.com/articles/templates/ships.asp?articlei
d=87&zoneid=5

Southby's. (2016). Retrieved May 16, 2016, from
http://www.rmsothebys.com/am13/amelia-island/lots/1909-austin-
model-60-touring/1056754

Stewart, L., & Shiel, J. (2008, May 13). Gloversville Business School.
Retrieved February 4, 2016, from
http://fulton.nygenweb.net/schools/glovbussch.html

Sullivan, N. (2003). American Economy in the 1920's: Consumerism,
Stock Market, and Economic Shift. Chapter 5. Lesson 2. Retrieved
May 12, 2016 from http://study.com/academy/lesson/american-
economy-in-the-1920s-consumerism-stock-market-economic-
shift.html

Summary of Immigration Laws, 1875-1918. (n.d.). Retrieved March 14,
2016, from
http://people.sunyulster.edu/voughth/immlaws1875_1918.htm

Tanning Leather Manufacturing. (2016, April 4). Retrieved April 18, 2016, from http://www.britannica.com/technology/tanning The Editors of the Encyclopedia Britannica

The Immigrant Journey. (2008). Retrieved March 10, 2016, from http://www.ohranger.com/ellis-island/immigration-journey

The Keys to Success Have Always Been Here. (n.d.). Retrieved April 15, 2016, from http://www.fccrg.org/county-assets/the-keys-to-success-have-always-been-here/ Fulton County Center for Regional Growth

The Library of Congress (n.d.). Immigration - A City of Villages. Retrieved February 15, 2016, from http://www.loc.gov/teachers/classroommaterials/presentationsandac tivities/presentations/immigration/italian5.html

The Library of Congress. (n.d.). Immigration - L'Isola dell Lagrime. Retrieved February 15, 2016, from https://www.loc.gov/teachers/classroommaterials/presentationsanda ctivities/presentations/immigration/italian4.html

The Library of Congress. (n.d.). Immigration - The Great Arrival. Retrieved February 15, 2016, from https://www.loc.gov/teachers/classroommaterials/presentationsanda ctivities/presentations/immigration/italian3.html

The Museum of History Presents From the Pale to the Golden Land. (2008). Retrieved January 5, 2016, from http://www.museumoffamilyhistory.com/mfh-ellisisland-06.htm The Museum of History The Ellis Island Fire of 1897 as reported by the New York Daily Tribune

The Statue of Liberty - Ellis Island Foundation, Inc. (n.d.). Retrieved June 7, 2010, from http://www.libertyellisfoundation.org/passenger-details/czoxMjoiNjAzMDE0MDMwMTc2Ijs=/czo4OiJtYW5pZmVzd CI7

The Statue of Liberty - Ellis Island Foundation, Inc. (n.d.). Retrieved March 1, 2016, from http://www.libertyellisfoundation/the-new-colossus

The Theater and its History. (n.d.). Retrieved February 15, 2016, from http://www.teatrosancarlo.it/en/pages/historical-highlights.html

U.S. Census (2000). Motor Vehicle Registrations. Retrieved May 9, 2016 from http://www.allcountries.org/uscensus/1027_motor_vehicle_registrati ons.html

Yannucci, L. (n.d.). Mama Lisa's World International Music & Culture Funiculì, Funiculà. Retrieved March 25, 2016, from http://www.mamalisa.com/?t=es&p=2351&c=120

Zahvi, G. (1999). The Glove Cutters' Strike of 1914: New York State Board of Mediation and Arbitration Hearings, October 5-14, 1914. Retrieved March 20, 2016 fromhttp://www.albany.edu/history/glovers/GloveCuttersStrike.htm l

About the Author

Claude E. DaCorsi Sr. was born and raised in Gloversville, New York. He is a second generation Italian-American. His formative years were shaped by the Italian culture and heritage passed down by his paternal and maternal family members. As a teenager and young man he worked in the leather tannery business. His experiences included learning the leather tanning and finishing process from the raw hides to the finished product.

Claude's mother, grandmothers, great grandmothers, aunts, and some cousins were employed by glove shops sewing gloves from the cutout glove patterns into retail ready products. Many of Claude's other relatives including grandfathers, great grandfathers, great uncles and uncles were glove cutters or leather tannery workers.

Claude is the past-president of the Burien, Washington Piccola Italia Sons of Italy Lodge and is a current member of the Auburn Sons of Italy Lodge #1955, in Auburn, Washington.

Claude resides in Auburn (Seattle), Washington. He has been married to his wife Mary for forty-two years, Together Claude and Mary raised three children. They have ten grandchildren.

Claude has a master of public administration degree from Seattle University.

Made in the USA
Middletown, DE
16 January 2022